Son Trap

Janet Fisher

authorHOUSE

AuthorHouse™ UK Ltd.
500 Avebury Boulevard
Central Milton Keynes, MK9 2BE
www.authorhouse.co.uk
Phone: 08001974150

This book is a work of fiction. People, places, events, and situations are the product of the author's imagination. Any resemblance to actual persons, living or dead, or historical events, is purely coincidental.

© 2007 Janet Fisher. All rights reserved.

No part of this book may be reproduced, stored in a retrieval system, or transmitted by any means without the written permission of the author.

First published by AuthorHouse 12/19/2007

ISBN: 978-1-4343-5879-0 (sc)

Printed in the United States of America
Bloomington, Indiana

This book is printed on acid-free paper.

PART ONE

THE PRESENT — EDWARD

Edward turned the climate control button to a more comfortable level. The road ahead was far from busy and he slowed, enjoying the scenery on either side. He looked out onto the most extraordinary rock formations resembling limestone columns that stuck straight into the air and the light as it fell across them was amazing. A perfect setting for some sci-fi movie location he thought. It was great to be able to drive around like this without feeling caged or shouting with frustration at careless drivers as he crawled along the busy streets. Living here made him appreciate so many different things. He even had time now to go and watch a film if he wanted or better still visit the theatre. He'd always enjoyed them both before but when he lived in England he never managed to find time to go and see either. Now he could concentrate on the things he'd grown to enjoy like walking, going to the odd exhibition and even his garden. Who would have imagined he would have found an interest there? In the past he had never really realised how much of his time was taken up with work. His career had obliterated so much of himself. As a student he had been a keen activist but gradually he had compromised as the years past and, he supposed, mellowed. Now in his sixties he was content to voice his opinions from within the home, discussing with friends over a good meal the state of the world and how best to put it right. He was disillusioned by most politicians and had given up supporting any party for the past few years. Today he was returning from a business meeting but his journey was not overly long. The radio was on. He had tuned into a channel by mistake and although the presenter was a frantic young man his selection of music was interesting spanning several decades. Most young people in the media gave him a headache but this one had refrained from choosing the kind of music Edward loathed. He was disturbed for a moment by a passing motorcyclist who wove in a large arc, the wind blowing his open jacket at an angle, waving cheerfully. Edward spontaneously raised one hand from the wheel. The noise from the cyclist engine obliterated the radio for a moment and as it returned a shooting sensation of panic raced through him and his heartbeat drummed in his ears. It was that damnable tune "I Can See Clearly" and every time he heard it he was transported to that extraordinary day ten years ago. Was it ten years? Good god it must be. Peter and Kate's wedding. He still felt hot and uncomfortable even with the intervening years. He had re run the day so many times wondering how they could not have seen what was coming. He should have been more perceptive that morning and sensed something was wrong. Polly had been very irritable, hurrying him along, refusing to take any part in the choice of his shirt and tie. Normally she'd have selected for him, particularly as it was a special occasion. He should have had his suspicions when she made odd aspersions in the taxi about his recent activities. But would it have made any difference? Could he really have thought life could continue as it was then? He'd had no time to talk to her once they reached the venue as Douglas had approached her so suddenly and what with other guests milling around he 'd hardly spoken to her again. He had absolutely no idea of what she was plotting or her intentions.

He now had two years left before retirement. The memory of those days and the stress of his working life then made him appreciate his working hours now. He'd travelled around a good deal of the time, airports, hotels and meetings day after day. Sometimes he forgot where he was and constantly battled with jet lag. Thank heavens it was over. He was still asked to fly out to other cities in Australia, heading up the odd meeting, but now he could do so much on his computer .His Life was so different from those days and he certainly had no feelings of regret, quite the contrary. Everything had radically changed and he was delighted. Having made his decision he'd never looked back. Hardly been back, in fact, apart from the odd visits to his parents and sadly, their funerals. The break had been messy for a while but now felt he could reflect on his past life in an objective way. Polly had, in reality; made it easy for him although at the time the word easy wouldn't have sprung to mind.

Edward's thoughts drew him back to the early days of their marriage. It had been good for many years but in a rather insidious way their own ambitions took them in different directions and when they did meet, they met as virtual strangers. He found it more and more difficult to be the man she both wanted and expected him to be. Perhaps if they'd had a family it might have been different. He knew how unhappy being childless made her but had no idea it was festering in such a manner waiting to erupt in the way it finally did. She was very miserable, he supposed, but at that time he was too tired and, he hated to accept this of himself, disinterested to discover any reason for it. They ceased to talk. He hadn't realised how much she loved him throughout that time. That did come as a surprise. His emotional life had reached a kind of plateau as far as Polly was concerned. He found it difficult to think of himself as a brutal kind of man either mentally or physically yet in retrospect he was forced to concede he probably was. Their relationship was just a part of his life. They did things together; even slept together almost to the end, and all the while he was able to do this without feeling. What an extraordinary thing to admit. Now, as the song said, "Gone are the dark clouds that had me down". They really had but was he happy now? He smiled, tapping his fingers on the steering wheel. Oh yes, he was happy now.

The outskirts of the city were within sight. Edward reached the next set of traffic lights and turned left heading out across the surrounding landscape towards the small township that was now his home. The people there were chiefly commuting to Perth each day but it was far enough away from the speed of city life to make it an attractive area for young families and old alike. His house stood in several acres of ground. Over the years he had become more and more involved in landscaping. Most weekends heading out to the local nursery to buy yet more plants. He had never been interested in gardening in England, yet the reward he felt reclaiming a rocky area or nurturing a sickly plant was considerable. He caught sight of the house and as ever enjoyed a small thrill of ownership. It was an attractive piece of real estate. There were two cars in the drive, one was theirs and the other he was not sure he recognised. He drove to park his own as close to the smallest as possible. Ridiculous given the space he had for garaging but it amused him to park closely and see them together. Edward turned off the engine and reached for his briefcase and laptop.

The sun was shining on the upper window cases sending thick bars of light way out into the atmosphere. The climate here was a steady twenty-eight degrees and the sun a constant companion. He loved to be so warm all the time. The house was beautifully cool in contrast.

Old age creeping in no doubt, that he should care so much about the climate and its regularity.

As Edward closed the car door he heard the sound of conversation coming from the back. Although the house was some way out, people thought nothing of distance in this country, happy to drive sixty miles to buy a good bottle of wine. He placed his hand on the door handle, opened the door sufficiently wide enough to allow him to transfer his case and computer inside, closed it and made his way toward the rear of the house. Harvey, the Yorkshire terrier, came rushing round to greet him throwing himself at his legs, barking a welcome. Edward ran his hands through the wiry hair. He had hated dogs, yet now, this little creature meant so much to him. With Harvey at his heels he walked through the side gate, trying to decipher above the noise of Harvey, who the visitor might be. He turned the corner and there they were. They had obviously been sitting on the shaded terrace sometime as the remains of lunch still littered the table.

"Edward!" He walked towards them in greeting and leant forward to kiss the face beneath a large and very floppy hat. She was looking so beautiful, her skin soft and clear, her eyes sparkling with amusement and affection. How he loved her. He recognised the face of her companion. It was a work colleague who had befriended them when first they settled here. Walking round to where she sat, he bent to kiss both cheeks. "Hallo Ginny. Good to see you. I'll come and join you both as soon as I change out of this suit. There's a very good bottle of wine inside just waiting to be drunk. Are you both up for it?" They nodded enthusiastically. "I'll bring it out." Edward let his hands rest on her shoulders as he spoke, then straightening up made his way to the back door. His eyes adjusted to the shadows of the room and the drop in temperature refreshed him immediately. Why they had chosen to be outside, albeit under the shaded blinds, he could not imagine, but it would be dark soon and they would then all come in.

As he climbed the stairs he thought once more of Polly. He heard, via mutual friends, about her occasionally. He meant to write or telephone but rather weakly let other things intervene making the length of silence too long to then break. Early in their marriage she had insisted he telephoned every day whenever he went away. He had wanted to initially but in the latter years her insistence became something of a chore and out of his control. He could never think, "I will phone Polly" but "I must phone Polly". Well now, there was little or no contact and in a manner of speaking the guilt remained. Their divorce had been very ugly. She had been so angry, felt so betrayed and poor Douglas had no idea he was being used. Edward sighed. There had been no intention of hurting anybody. The old adage "what the eye does not see, the heart does not grieve over", and he supposed he and Judith had foolishly believed it so. In retrospect he could see things were beginning to gather pace. Polly behaved strangely questioning him about his movements. She had accumulated the evidence and presented it, ironically, like a gift on that fateful day. After that nothing could ever remain the same. Her actions had affected so many people, rippling out, encasing them all in hurt, or wounded pride. And then the break followed swiftly for Polly refused to return to their home. All contact after that was via the solicitor. He made every effort to see her, to try to talk flying insects and things through but she was adamant they should not meet. It took at least three, maybe four years, before she allowed any contact and that was only because it was her mother's funeral and Edward wanted to let her know how sorry he was. He had been extremely fond of her mother. Telephoning Polly, as he did when he heard the news, caught her unawares and in a vulnerable state. She had not put the telephone down and after that it became easier to speak to each other. Time itself is truly the only healer. Emotions are allowed to settle and as new ones form a covering layer so the old sink deeper and deeper only surfacing as they had today, when a tune, or a smell, or a taste, manages to creep below the layer shaking old memories to the fore. His past life with Polly did count for something and there were memories they shared which were good. He believed he had loved her and yet thinking about his years spent with her evoked no sense of loss. They had both been given a second life. His coming to Australia might not have happened. Now the thought of not being here, of not having what he had was unacceptable.

He looked at his tanned reflection in the mirror and brushed back his hair. He was still in reasonable shape and although his hair had now lost its original colour he had been told by several people his appearance denied his age. Ageing was a strange process, one felt eternally young but knew there must come a time when the body begins to break down. He hated the idea of being an old man. This thought prompted Edward to pull his shoulders back and position his head firmly between his shoulders. He drew his eyes away from the mirror and looked outside at the view. He was lucky to be here in what he considered to be an exciting and new country. Ten years ago he had been given the chance to alter his life and to take the other path. It had halted the rigid flow of years allowing him to breathe again and be himself. It was time now for that drink. Judith and Ginny would be waiting

THE PRESENT — JUDITH

That evening Edward and Judith sat together in the conservatory. It had been so designed to allow them clear views of the stars and surrounding land. They were safe from any small flying insects and could relax. Several years ago they had purchased a telescope to look at the moon and stars on just such a night as this. There was something slightly eerie about looking through the lens and seeing the powdery surface of the moon broken by craters and mountains. The silence could be felt all those thousands of miles away. The dog sat at Edward's heels, half asleep, moving itself now and then to find a more comfortable position. Its damp nose twitched sensing the scent of something or the other. Perhaps it was the smell of the evening meal served earlier hovering in his nostrils and he blew through his nose as though to clear the airways. Edward bent to scratch his head and Harvey luxuriated in the contact. Judith raised her eyes from her book "He needs a bath" Edward continued to scratch "His fur is getting far too thick in places." She waited for a response but Edward continued to scratch. "Saturday tomorrow" she continued, "Nothing is planned. What would you like to do?"

Edward's hands were still for a moment as he thought. "I wouldn't mind going to the cinema, I'm not sure what's on but I can look it up. There's a very good film from Argentina showing somewhere. We could go out for a meal either before or after. How does that sound?" The blue of his shirt contrasted with the pale upholstery as he settled himself deeper into the chair he occupied. His reading glasses lay across the current book selected only yesterday from the bookstore. His legs crossed and from one foot his leather loafer hung, dangling from this toes. A glass of whiskey, half drunk, rested upon a ceramic coaster. There was an ambient atmosphere in the room, the lighting sending soft shadows around the contours of his body. As Judith looked up she was reminded of a portrait painting she had once seen in the National Gallery. It still surprised her sometimes to see him sharing her space.

"Good, I like the idea of eating out" Judith enjoyed cooking but it was still pleasurable to choose something she would not be likely to prepare for just the two of them. Over the past three years Edward had begun to take an interest in cooking and was becoming very proficient. They had gradually taken on their chores, sharing their responsibilities as she had with Ralph, although now she did the big shop and Edward took control of the bills. She felt comfortable here but it had taken a while to accept it as home. Her house in England had been so much a part of her. Every room, creak, views from the windows, all so familiar. At times, late at night when she could not sleep, she would take herself mentally around that house, starting at the front door, stopping to remember each picture, each placement of ornaments or furniture. She could never forget it but she had discovered to her surprise she could now live without it. A family unknown to her lived there now and she sometimes wondered what changes they may have made. She hoped they had not totally destroyed the garden but was comforted to know there were young children in the house again. It was a house for children. A small but discernable lump rose in her throat. The thought of children could stimulate her emotions in a very unpredictable manner. Occasionally when she was out shopping or certain families came to her consulting rooms she experienced a rush of jealousy as she watched the children communicate with their mother in that familiar way she had known. The feel of their bodies, the way they exuded energy and gave one as an adult another chance to look at the world. It had been a wonderful experience watching her three sons grow and develop into adults.

"I was reminded of Polly today" Edward said, breaking the silence.

Judith could still not hear her name without a jolt. She knew Edward telephoned her occasionally and made a point of not being within earshot. Polly and Edward had made a kind of peace but Judith was still plagued with both guilt, for being the perpetrator of Polly's action, and rage for the method Polly had used to reap her revenge. Judith had always felt it a cruel act to involve Douglas, her middle son. It had all gone so horribly wrong. It had not occurred to her all those years ago when she had been so drawn to the painting of "Judith and Holofernes" that the warning she had read into it would be realised by Polly. She had not cut off her head but she had sliced right through her family. Thank God Polly had not succeeded in permanently destroying Judith's relationship with Douglas but she acknowledged, with great sorrow, it was and never would be quite the same. It had taken a long time and a lot of hard work to slowly rebuild their family ties. That horrendous moment when Polly had disclosed the truth of Edward and her infidelity, Judith had been unable to bear the look that spread across Douglas' face. Even now, when she thought about it, the same magnitude of misery possessed her. Douglas had been unable and unwilling to speak to her for almost a year. She had left messages on his telephone and written numerous letters attempting to explain her actions but they were always ignored. Nobody, it seemed, could forgive her or understand that her infidelity was as much a source of pain and suffering for her as it later became for all of them. She had always loved her husband Ralph. She had loved them all and tried her best to be a good mother. She had been forced to reveal her affair with Edward by Polly who had made it seem sordid and deceitful. It was naïve of her but she had never considered her relationship with Edward as " an affair". Of course she knew the risks involved. Perhaps that played a part. That day at the conference she had believed herself to be so far from the reach of prying eyes that she had willingly gone to Edward's room believing nobody would be harmed. She thought of herself back then and how different life was.

Living through those early years after the break had left them all distraught and weary. She had been very ill when she and Edward first arrived in Australia. The doctors had diagnosed suppressed emotional stress, releasing itself through physical means. The sun had been an anathema to her when clouds of misery shrouded her innermost feelings. Edward had been understanding and patient listening to her constant request for reassurance. Her love for him grew even stronger and with his help she reached a point when she could accept that it was up to her to reshape her life. She owed it to Edward who remained positive and loving. Poor Edward, he must have occasionally wondered if they had done the right thing. Whenever she challenged him he was adamant it was what he had always hoped for but had never dared believe could happen. On *that day*, she remembered sitting mute as Ralph took control. It had been impossible to speak. She did not know her lines and watched the enactment of the scenes from the wings. There, but unable to participate in the lead role Polly had assigned to her. She did not know of any words that were appropriate and made no attempt to dispute the accusations. She had been guilty and found out. Afterwards they were placed in an agonising position knowing they must carry out their roles as parents of the groom. Every one was waiting for them. Her red eyes were interpreted as emotional tears for the newly married couple. Ralph had led her away and behaved magnificently dealing with everything as though nothing had happened. The panic of Kate and Peter's day being ruined, the possibility that his youngest son, Hugh, would hear of it from other people and to protect Douglas from his pain were all held uppermost in his mind. Then, of course he had to prevent his own emotions from erupting as he looked at Judith and was reminded of her betrayal. He had taken control and made sure the day continued as planned and that nobody knew the horrors Polly had wrought. They had to mix with people, smiling, catching up with past events, and even dancing together at one point when Hugh dragged them both onto the floor demanding they show everyone how to jive. Ralph had managed to dance with such energy as though the motion and the beat of the instruments could shake away the dreadful things that were to come. They had avoided any eye contact, not really difficult given the steps and afterwards Hugh had come up to hug them both. He was drunk which at the time Judith saw as something of a bonus as he was unaware of the tension between them. Later when they finally told him of their decision to separate, he was incredulous. Recalling the initial agony of that moment still sent splinters of pain through her. He had pleaded with them to reconsider, citing the past by summoning up happy family events. He told them then he had seen Douglas and Polly kiss at the wedding and of how it had spoilt the day for him. He had not been present when Polly confronted Ralph, Edward, Douglas and herself .Had he done so the kiss would have paled into insignificance along side the magnitude of divorce. He was still young, still needing a family home and the break up shattered his sense of security. He wandered round the house, refusing to go out, repeatedly asking them to drop the idea of separation. They had cried together and he often shouted at her accusing her of destroying his life. They talked and talked, she and Hugh, Ralph and Hugh, she and Ralph, often into the early hours of the morning. Initially, and understandably, Ralph was full of rage. She with little defence other than her continued love for him. Hugh became fiercely protective of Ralph, spending time with him; listening to him until eventually they were all forced to accepted things could not continue as they were. Judith must decide. It was when this point was reached Edward had told her of his intention to take the post in Australia. He wanted her to go with him and begin a new life. She had to choose. Her past life seemed to be retreating leaving her alone and unprotected, frozen with indecision. Should she to try to rebuild her relationship with Ralph? Could he ever relate to her in the same way? Could she accept she would never see Edward again? She was in no man's land unable to leave the relative safety of indecision to take a stand. One night, as she and Ralph were sitting together deep in their own tortured thoughts, he had suddenly got up from his chair and crossed the room to where she was seated. He squatted down, taking both her hands in his and told her he had come to realize he could no longer ignore the fact that his feelings for her had changed. It was impossible not to be affected. His life had been dramatically altered and there was no going back. Polly had rocked his foundations and thrown up many thoughts and emotions. There was pain, anger and even hatred, all fanning a strong desire to hurt them both and his mind was forever chasing solutions that were never resolved leaving him impotent, but, over the past few days, his thoughts had begun to clear. A decision had emerged like the moth from its chrysalis and he now felt confident enough to tell her. Had he discovered years ago when the boys were small he might have reached a different conclusion but he had begun to think of life as a single man again and the idea was not daunting, as he might have believed, but challenging? If, as she said, she loved both, Edward and himself, he would now step down. . He would not share. He realised how important it was for him to be first in her affections and if he was not then he must live without her. His love, he explained, had altered. Assessing his feelings over these last few days had enabled him to see things in a different light. Perhaps this turmoil, coming as it had, at this time in their lives, could provide them with new opportunities and a chance to change. Neither of them wanted to lose the affection of their children and if he, Ralph, could be seen to support her it might just be possible to salvage some of the respect and trust Judith had lost. She fully realized the enormity of what he was suggesting and had, somewhat audaciously, resented the fact he could envisage life without her. He had relied upon her for everything. It was, she knew, unacceptable but she could not ignore a sharp pain of rejection when she realised it was Ralph who had made her choose and that it would be impossible to return to their past life. He had given her licence to begin again. She still loved him and perhaps he had made it possible for them to move on before her love distilled itself to little more than steam ready to be blown away by the years. In contrast her love for Edward had been allowed to grow and mature. All those years having to restart and catch up each time they met, unable to do the simplest things because of the preciousness of time. Now, after nearly ten years together, there were still many aspects of his life to be discovered and shared. He had changed but only in the sense he was now free to relax and openly enjoy their domesticity. She supposed of them all he had perhaps suffered least. Polly had freed him from a relationship, which, for his part was spent. He had no children to consider neither did he have the kind of home he recognised as his roots.

"I suppose I should phone her. It's been months since we last spoke". He did not know why he felt compelled to tell Judith he had been thinking of Polly yet had he not done so he would have felt uncomfortable as though he were colluding in a kind of secrecy he did not want.

Judith returned to the moment. "What was it reminded you?" she asked.

"A tune" He was reluctant to dredge up the wedding and fell silent.

What was he thinking Judith mused? When he thought of Polly, did he think of earlier days? There must be many memories tied to her. Moments that she would never know. He said he felt nothing more for her than that of a friend, but inevitably there were still all those years during their early marriage when they were very happy together. Judith chided herself for her jealousy. She had no right when she herself thought frequently of Ralph. That day when she had gone to the airport with Edward, Ralph had taken Hugh away with him on the trip she was to have shared with him had events taken a different turn. Leaving everybody had been such a terrible wrench and enormously upsetting, especially leaving Hugh, so vulnerable, on the threshold of manhood yet still a child needing the support of both parents. She had left not knowing when she would see him again. Douglas had not come to the airport and had returned to Spain with Patrick. Prior to his departure he had spoken to his mother and that meeting had been the most painful of all, Judith being the catalyst for Polly's action. They agreed to a kind of truce, to make no contact for a while which she had found impossible. Initially, Judith had been terrified he would totally reject her. That she would leave for Australia carrying his hatred and loss of respect. But she had salvaged a degree of hope to which she clung like a drowning sailor. She was, however, forced to admit their relationship had been almost destroyed. Peter had contacted Ralph on their return having heard from Douglas what had taken place. Had Ralph not spoken of her without total condemnation, she might still, to this day, be making overtures for peace. The grieving which in part had to be stifled for Edward's sake, took many months, years even, for whom could she ask to console her when she herself was responsible? But, and she drew in a large breath, expelling it slowly with the accompanying relief, gradually Hugh had decided he wanted to see Australia in his gap year and had come to stay with them. It had been so wonderful, especially since, by the end of his stay, Edward and he seemed to be getting on well together. Now Hugh came at least once a year, sent countless e-mails and talked on the phone. She had, she supposed, managed to win him back. Peter too had very slowly come round. Judith's grand daughters were now five and three. With their birth had come the opportunity for her to play a role once more in family life. She felt she had served her sentence. Now she managed to return to England at reasonably good intervals. Edward preferred to stay home when she went on family trips but was always delighted to see them when they came to stay. He still felt something of an interloper unable to accept that behind their words of greeting there might be many of condemnation. He was after all, responsible for the break up of their family. Nobody had been spared. They were all forced to confront and embrace the idea of change. At present he felt safer on his own territory. If they were here it was of their choosing. His guilt assuaged.

Judith, in her mind, pictured the scales of condemnation mentioned in the Bible and the chilling words "You have been weighed in the balance and found wanting". Was she still wanting? Did her losses outweigh the gains? At times one tray might sink or rise throwing everything out of balance but mostly they quivered holding the weight of emotion equally on either side. Here in Australia she had adopted a different personality. Leaving England freed her from many constraints and she could abandon those traits she had previously found restricting. She was far more confident here in this different environment, her clothes less conservative, less inclined to refuse invitations to parties. She felt bolder, unwilling to accept things she would have allowed to pass without comment in England. There was a tangible vibrancy about the country that had rubbed off. Being with Edward allowed her to be this other person. It was as though she had been recharged by her own second rocket booster and was being propelled forward into the future. A future that, years ago, would have been totally unimaginable. Her one deep sin was the dark and potent secret she had kept all these years from those who were most involved. She knew she would carry it to her grave and when judgement came would be found wanting. Judith wrestled with the lock to these thoughts, it was onerous to carry their weight and occasionally she allowed the words an exeat. *She could not be certain who had fathered Hugh.* The sentence came with a rush rising into the air to bounce against the wind like drying sheets. She knew in these modern times it would be possible for Ralph and Edward to have a D.N.A test but now after all these years there seemed little point in causing yet another huge emotional upset to so many people. Sometimes when she looked at Hugh she would think she detected mannerisms peculiar to Ralph and then she would notice a turn of his head or facial expression that could have been Edwards. The knot of anxiety began to form in her stomach and she pulled the words back into their confines and locked the door. Perhaps she had guarded her secret so closely because in Hugh she had the combination of her two loves. The uncertainty of his paternity linked them both and, like the tomb of the unknown warrior, left room for speculation.

Judith was brought back to the present by the pressure of the dog's wet nose against her calf. She looked at her watch and saw it was time for his walk. Edward had fallen asleep in his chair and she was loath to wake him. Her day had been rather lazily spent and he had been working. It was probably her turn anyway.

The dog followed closely on her heels as she slipped quietly out of the room. She drew on her walking shoes and pulled her old soft cardigan from the peg. The nights could be chilly here and her arms needed protecting. Harvey stood, his nose pressed against the door waiting for her to release him into the soft black darkness. She opened the door and stood for a while, as she always did, to look at the sky. The stars were amazing. When she lived in London they were half hidden by the orange glow of the city but here they stood out like diamond buttons on a dark black dress. The moon was almost full and brought into view the surrounding trees, their branches highlighted by an eerie light turning them into tendrils that stretched into space.

Harvey began to walk swiftly knowing the familiar route they would take. The road was wide and empty but she felt no fear. The neighbourhood was safe and friendly. She carried with her the thoughts of her life in England and regretted ever allowing herself to reminisce. She was now enveloped in the aura of her past as though waking from a dream but in this case her recollections were immediate and clear. Thinking of Ralph had resurrected many feelings. She could never dispel the wounding harsh glance he had thrown her. The same Ralph who had looked at her with love and affection only minutes previously. And after the discovery she could not longer meet his gaze without seeing that look. Why had she not been able to settle for the life she had? Why did she take such risks? Edward had such power over her then. Now that power had diluted somewhat but she still felt that same rush of emotion when he came into view. She could not have left him then or now.

Judith was nearing the open space and watched Harvey cock his ear and stand for a few seconds rigid and quiet. What had he heard? She stopped too and listened. There was an animal somewhere; she could hear the rustle of the grass as it made its way. Harvey sprung forward for the chase barking as he ran. She had no need to worry about disturbing the neighbours. Unlike in England when a dog's bark at night would disturb many. Judith glanced once more at the sky and remembered it would be daylight there now. Her family would all be busy doing things. The time difference of the clock made it difficult for her, severing them by sleep. For all their hours of activity she was lying dormant and mute unable to participate in their day.

Later that night, tired yet unable to sleep she could not rid herself from her past. Ten years ago, almost eleven now. Her mind began shifting actions and feelings in a kaleidoscopic fashion bringing certain scenes sharply into view and matching them with strong emotions. She knew sleep was impossible and turned to lie on her back her eyes wide open. Edward's breathing was regular signifying deep sleep. She looked across at him; he still looked youthful even though small lines left furrows here and there. He was a handsome man. She hoped she would spend the rest of her life with him. His eyelids flickered slightly and she wondered who inhabited his dreams. Did Polly frequently make a nocturnal appearance? Was she loving or cruel? How was it she managed to realise her plan on Peter's wedding day? Edward and she were guilty of course but Polly could have revealed she knew months before without ever involving Douglas. She had used him to inflict maximum pain and make revenge sweet. Why had Edward not been alerted to Polly's suspicions before their fateful meeting in

Florence? How different things were back then when she had agreed to represent the consultancy and take that early plane.

PART TWO

JUDITH — THE PAST

She had reacted negatively when she was asked to go to Florence. She knew what it would involve. Conferences were always rather tedious and she would be trapped in rooms listening to monotone lecturers and surrounded by colleagues lulled into early sleep. To be confined to the hotel and its immediate surroundings for the next few days would be sacrilegious and she made the decision to make an inconspicuous exit at some stage. She had no idea her plans would be altered on arrival by an unexpected message. The information it contained had excited her and wishing to be alone she hurried towards the door. Her mood was changing by the minute and she found a new lightness of step as she left her professional duties behind and manoeuvred her way through the groups of new arrivals. She kept her head down averting her eyes. This was not a good time to recognise any of her professional acquaintances. Edward's message was double-edged striking a ring of joy in her heart and a peal of guilt in her mind. Her conscience was stirred. Now might be the only time she had to do something she had promised herself she would do for several years. She walked swiftly in the direction of the Pitti Palace and climbed toward the Boboli gardens. Her pace slackened as she selected a bench on which to sit allowing her thoughts to gather like a wave on the open sea and waited for the break against her consciousness to spread in bubbling ripples across her mind. She searched amongst the flotsam and jetsam trying to select something pertinent. She knew she was hoping for a solution that would whitewash her guilt and make what she knew was soon going to happen acceptable. She was also aware that she needed to either put a stop to the deceitful manner in which she lived or take an enormous leap and leave Ralph. She could do neither of these things. She was too weak. No acceptable solution would present itself, she would have to leave the frothing water to turn to scum and take her mind elsewhere.

Glancing at her watch she rose and entered through the doors of the Galleria Palatina. The walls were heavy with works of art their frames elaborately carved and covered by gold leaf. As she gazed at the paintings she allowed her tongue to roll around such names as Andrea del Sarto, Tintoretto and Perugino, before making her way to a smaller room, which held the painting by Cristofano Allori of "Judith and Holofernes." The familiar painting she had studied so often as a colour plate in her book at home was there before her. She stood in awe of its beauty and the terrifying depiction it portrayed. It was a story that had haunted her since the first time she had seen it as a child. The story of Judith and Holofernes. That this woman, her namesake, whose serene and beautiful appearance denied her actions, could have taken a sword and cut off the head of her sleeping enemy both appalled and fascinated her. Circumstances had driven her to act in a most uncharacteristic way and this behaviour filled Judith with a feeling of unaccountable trepidation. Might we all have this hidden capacity? What must it take to alter a person and summon such emotion? She could not dispel the belief that somewhere in this extraordinarily beautiful painting and the story it depicted, there was a warning. Unsuspecting Holofernes had no idea this woman would end his life that night He had been a mighty warrior ready to fight the following day and there was his head, held in those delicate hands, being lowered into a bag, his power gone, his life over. She continued to stare at the graceful and indifferent face looking down at her and was unable to free herself from the conviction that in this look there was a message. Somehow she believed that if she could hold the gaze of this woman she could protect herself and stood before the painting unaware of the passage of time.

The visit had been a kind of pilgrimage for Judith and as she made her way out of the Pitti Palace she stood to look down at the river Arno and the pastel softness of the rooftops. She was glad she had come, grateful to have the opportunity to look at the genuine image and share with the artist his brush strokes of sentiment.

The guilt of truanting began to worry her and she remembered she was here at some expense as a representative for her partners. They were probably working hard at this very minute and thinking rather enviously of her. Her actions so far had been selfish and she knew she should join her colleagues to collect information for the written reports that would be expected on her return.

Back at the hotel Judith gathered her handbag and document holder, bursting with handouts and advertising matter, and checking the door card in her pocket, took one final look into the long mirror. The woman reflected there was suitably presentable. Hair well cut, framing an open face, the fitted suit lending an air of importance and respectability. Pulling back the set of her shoulders she ran her tongue along her teeth and smiled to ensure the absence of unsightly lipstick stains and stood for a moment savouring the privacy of her room and the mixed feeling of excitement she experienced each time she thought of their meeting later that day. For the present she would adopt the personality of her profession and mingle with other Educational Psychologists who knew the jargon and what her work entailed. She was thankful she had come alone and could act independently and inconspicuously. Many had arrived in groups and would be joined together for their stay.

The conference hall was heavily panelled and somewhat ornate. A large overhead projector hanging from the ceiling challenged the chandeliers of a bygone age. The speaker, a man highly regarded amongst Educational Psychologists, spoke enthusiastically about assessment procedures, standardization and reporting as other members of the conference sat quietly taking notes.

As he spoke she became involved, deliberately forcing her mind to attend. A feeling of agitation began to rise within her as she found herself disagreeing with part of the content and she felt compelled to put forward a question in the hope of opening a general discussion. She knew judgements would be made on its pertinence and others would assess her appearance as she raised her hand and brought herself to his attention but the tack he was taking concerned her. He answered looking into her eyes in a rather disconcerting way. For that brief moment she could have been the only person in the room as he defended his position bravely but did not, in her opinion, justify his point very convincingly. Several others supported her and for a while a lively interchange of ideas kept her focussed and engaged until the chairman interjected and it was back to the note taking.

She sat by the window and looked out at the grounds. A large bird flew down and jumped across the grass. The freedom of its movement looked so inviting she began to wish she had taken the seat by the door and made an early escape. It was easy for the bird. It could fly away to almost anywhere even places hundreds of miles away. Over the past few years she and Ralph had travelled a lot. Luxury had become enticing and unsettling for them. When they were away they relinquished all responsibility as they moved from one hotel to the next, calling for room service, placing laundry in marked plastic bags, coming down to breakfast to choose from a variety of foods on long white linen table tops. A far cry from family life back home where everyday chores and the pressure of work rapidly eclipsed the laid back attitude and made the task of anchoring themselves to a normal routine increasingly more difficult to accept.

    The man beside her crossed his legs drawing her attention to her immediate surroundings. His shoes were highly polished, thirties style, straight laces, slightly worn across the instep. They had seen some service she thought. As he took notes Judith watched his hands move across the paper. They were large with pale well-kept nails. On each knuckle was a small plantation of hair, a few grey ones, mostly light brown. He wore a single gold ring but not on his wedding finger. Ralph had never worn rings. They would not seem right on his hands. She could feel the texture of them now. Dry, soft and firm. A black tunnel began to form around the lecturers' head and a warm buzzing caught an idea in her brain carrying it away like a bee from the hive. Edward. The hands had reminded her of Edward and like a genie from a lamp the image of him rose to fill her mind. Every day something provided the friction necessary to release him and he would travel through her thoughts summoning memories from the corners of her mind. At times their clarity would obliterate the present, leading her to some place once shared with him where she could re-enact the scenes remembering conversations like some well-loved poem. She could play and replay the past at will. The only thing denied her was the ability to fast forward because inevitably the future would always remain unknown. If she began to think of how things might be or attempt to predict outcomes she became swamped by frightening thoughts that she rapidly smothered and folded away. But today she could allow her mind to dwell a little on the future and imagine how the next few days would be spent. Today she would see him; the typed note left in her pigeonhole clearly stated he would be here, in Florence. She had read and re read the message unable to believe it would be so but she was not mistaken and at some time this afternoon he would present himself at the hotel and they would be together.

Edward had entered her life when they were both students in London. He presented such a different kind of character from those she knew. Coming from the north of England, a country boy, his voice displayed a hint of accent that was attractive to her. She had never known anyone before who had grown up on an isolated farm. His childhood had been solitary, his closest friends his dogs. And yet he seemed worldly and confident. More so than many of the young men she knew from the city or major university towns. It was exciting to be with such a unique young man. She saw him coming through the doors of the main hall at a student dance and had fallen in love with him. She looked at him from the other side of the room and, confident that he was too far away to notice, continued to stare at him surprised by the extraordinary sensations he evoked. Nobody had affected her that way before and as he made his way towards her she braced herself against disappointment in case he should ask her more attractive friend beside her to dance and leave her jealously watching. Incredibly he chose her and she placed her arms on his rather prickly jacket and danced a heavy rhythmic jive, aware only of his proximity and her desire to remain with him. That evening they deserted friends and escaped into the London streets where they exchanged their first kiss and, seated in a popular coffee bar off the Tottenham Court Road, talked long into the night. There had been an instant rapport and a shared sense of fun. For the days, weeks and months that followed she thought only of him, finding it hard to concentrate on her studies. Between their meetings she spent time wondering where he might be or when he would telephone. She would reconstruct their time together and dream of a future. She was extremely happy and their relationship seemed set to last but then one evening when they had exchanged rather heated words over a difference of opinion she was suddenly shocked to realize how different their views were and experienced a heavy feeling of disquiet and unhappiness that seemed to stay with her and became a kind of melancholia. At first she could not acknowledge why. She knew beyond doubt she was deeply in love with him and earlier she had hung on his every word but, as their relationship progressed, he would occasionally express views that disturbed her and as she, at that stage in her life, was a fervent socialist wanting to change the world and make all men equal, she could not accept them. He held strong opinions contrary to hers and planned a different future to the one she envisaged they might share. He was fiercely ambitious, keen to make his mark. They began to argue more and more over politics, attitudes, films, and the theatre. Often his disparaging remarks hurt and upset her. She would brood over things he had said alarmed that his ambitious nature would lead him down a route that smacked of ruthless insensitivity. One evening they had quarrelled and parted. In retrospect she permitted herself to think that maybe it was she who was insensitive but in her early twenties her ideals had become passions that obliterated sense. Once they were apart she busied herself with other men who meant very little but all the time she thought of Edward even missing their fierce disagreements but her pride acted like a guardian at the gate and prevented her from making contact.

Some time after breaking up with Edward she met Ralph. Ralph had been attentive and caring from the start. At the end of their first evening together he had shown her several of his poems and articles written for a magazine. She was flattered by his confidence and excited by his talent. Meeting Ralph was like being handed the ingredients of an interesting recipe which, when mixed, would result in future happiness. One evening as she walked to his flat, he came unexpectedly from the doorway of the local shop and she experienced a strong sensation of having found a man with whom she could live for a long, long time.

A burst of applause brought Judith back to the present and she found her hands participating guiltily wondering how much of the content she had missed. There was a rustling of papers and some one close by mentioned the word lunch. The lecturer, gathering an entourage of supporters eager to engage in conversation, made his way toward the exit with flushed cheeks and renewed confidence.

The man beside her stood up"Do you have anywhere to go to lunch?" he asked.

"Yes, thank you. I do." She smiled at him knowing she had no idea where she might go. It was important she remained alone for she did not know at what time or where Edward would join her. She wanted no other company but his.

"I think I'll lunch at the hotel. It seems to be o.k. and the firm is paying." He had not been squashed by her refusal and she felt glad.

Once into the streets she was enveloped in a delicious inner silence and aware that time, for a while, was her own. It was rather exhilarating to be here with only her to please. Independent time was relatively new for she had always been governed by the needs of the children or her career or accompanying Ralph on his trips for research. In general Ralph managed to shut himself away and protect his hours of work, keeping the world at bay. He was a prolific writer and now the publishers guaranteed everything he produced. When they were first married she encouraged him to find an agent. It had been the only subject on which they argued vehemently - his reticence to show his work. She had given over many hours when the children were small to allow him time to write. Had he not been successful she might have felt it all a futile waste. She remembered her burning rages of resentment each time she saw the completed manuscripts on his desk knowing they had sat there for many months. Finally he had plucked up courage and sent off a huge batch. One particular agent had liked his style and he had remained with him to this day. They were now both successful in their careers and there was no sense of competition. They set their paths to run in parallel, determined to succeed in their own particular way.

She stopped at the Ponte Vecchio and noticed a small restaurant with some vacant chairs. She took her place and picked up the menu, which looked promising. An enormously fat man was sitting on a small wall opposite resting and reading a city guide. His stomach hung like a canapé` of dough between his legs. He caught her eye and she looked away fearing he would sense her judgement of his size. She felt sylphlike in comparison and ordered lunch with lavish recklessness. The couple next to her were American and their voices reminded her of one other time she had sat alone in a café such as this. She was nineteen and had gone to Paris to meet an American film critic. He had presented himself as a wildly attractive figure, dashing all over the world from one film festival to the next. They had met at a party in Earl's Court and exchanged letters as he moved from one country to another. It was delightfully romantic to receive an aerogramme from Tel Aviv or a hurriedly written postcard from Cannes. He had interviewed Fellini and written articles for a New York publication. She had spent three days waiting for him in a hotel whose floor became a ballroom for papery cockroaches once the light had faded. She was terrified.

Walking back she saw a coach load of black North Africans pull up. The men, all tall and incredibly beautiful, emerged and began to lay high colored native rugs along the pavement. Intrigued she stopped to watch. Parcels of polythene followed from which were pulled hundreds of T- shirts. How bizarre. She had refused to buy them in England for one of her sons. A con she had said to charge so much for a little sign on a T-shirt. Yet here they were splayed out across the pavements, fakes no doubt but such a ridiculous price she was compelled to buy. As she paid the African he flashed an incredible smile that exonerated him in her mind from all things criminal. She continued on her way searching the crowds half expecting Edward to appear. She must be patient and wait. He could not predict at what time he would arrive but she knew he would find her.

The afternoon was spent in a small study group, the atmosphere heavy with discomfort. The room was hot and she could see silhouettes of another group moving behind a pastel blind. They appeared to be crawling on all fours. She thanked god she was not there to suffer the humiliation of so-called team building techniques.

As the group leader drew the session to a close muscles relaxed and smiles lost their wooden look. Leaflets and questionnaires were politely gathered up, knowing they would never be referred to again. Other flushed members of the conference filed out of separate rooms and the lobby echoed with exchanges. Judith looked on the agenda board and saw tea had been promised. A woman beside her suggested they go in together and she nodded in agreement.

"Judith!"

She turned excitedly to the voice. Her eyes became locked into those of a wonderfully familiar face and an overwhelming sense of pleasure filled her.

The woman beside her stood uncomfortably still. Judith became aware of her presence and of an urgent desire to be rid of her

" Do you mind if I join you later? This is a friend of mine I haven't seen for a while." She turned giving her undivided attention to the new arrival that leant forward to clasp her hands and kiss both cheeks.

"Edward."

They remained for a while without moving, their bodies pressed closely together as people passed jostling for access to the tea- rooms. The surrounding conversation became a distant sound track irrelevant to their ears. The need to free themselves from this situation sent them hurrying into the street where they stood taking stock of each other, both wishing to confirm the others reality.

Judith was the first to speak, her words falling in short staccato sounds as she endeavored to get over the excitement of his arrival. "I hope you realize your note destroyed any hope I had of concentrating today. I've been in a state of agitation ever since I read it" It was a relief to admit the presence of tension for now she could begin to relax and enjoy the time she had with him.

He laughed and took her hand, "You knew I'd be here, surely."

"Yes, but it was not knowing when or where. I was afraid of finding myself locked into a lecture, time running out, while you might be waiting on the other side of the door."

They began to walk, Edward leading the way. Judith was aware of herself metamorphosing into the persona of Judith with Edward. She glanced up at him still unable to believe he was there and felt the tense, wonderful excitement he always induced when she was with him. He was looking good, she thought. Slightly heavier but this suited him.

The hair at the back of his neck followed the line of his head. It had not been recently cut and soft side hairs joined to creep beneath his collar. His face was tanned and smooth, his eyes clear. There was a smile about his lips that pleased her.

"I had a terrible flight over. There was a hold up at the airport." He paused to guide her through a group of small boys talking loudly on the pavement. "We were an hour on the tarmac. All I could think of was that time was being lost and I might not get to you before you began the evening session."

They had arrived at a side street just off from the Via Porta Rossa. The area was strewn with tables and chairs, mostly occupied by foreign visitors but Edward managed to find a suitable place in the shade for them to sit. Judith was amused to see how he received instant attention from the waiter who moved forward speedily to help her to her seat and stood poised ready to take their order.

Edward sat back on his seat "What would you like Judith?"

"I'm feeling thirsty. I think a Peroni would be good"

"Perfect. I'll have the same." He watched the waiter as he scribbled rapidly on a small note pad then turned his attention to Judith. "I can't tell you how pleased I am to get away for a while. It's been so hectic recently. I seem to have been travelling from one country to another, waking up wondering where the hell I was."

"Don't make me feel guilty." Judith was quick to interrupt.

"Well," he gave a wry smile." I hadn't reckoned on Florence this week."

He held up one hand to ward off her protest. "But," he paused and his eyes twinkled with amusement "As soon as I knew you were going to be here I arranged to meet some clients of ours." He noticed the look of disappointment on her face. "No, no It's o.k. I'm seeing them this evening; I knew you'd be tied up too and I had to have some legitimate justification for this visit, didn't I? I'll take them for a meal but I won't let it run into the night."

"But Italian evenings begin at nine or ten." She whined. Her plans were being changed and a dull heavy pain began to creep across her chest.

"No, no." he laughed, reassuring her "Not these. These are Australians and as eager to get everything over and done with as I am."

The waiter arrived with their drinks and they sat silenced by his deft actions as he transferred the honey-toned beer from bottle to glass. Edward touched her glass with his very gently and as he looked across at her drew her legs between his knees beneath the table. "So my lovely, lovely lady. Here we are."

Judith felt a shock of pleasure run through her as the pressure and warmth of his legs held hers. She glanced hurriedly around unable to lose the fear of being seen with him and noticed a group of women she recognised as conference members. Instinctively she withdrew her knees. Edward looked both hurt and surprised and she jerked her head in their direction mouthing silently "Conference people". He leant back creating a more acceptable space between them and casually turned his head to confirm her observation. As his eyes returned to her he shot a wide smile to reassure her.

She loathed the sense of guilt that always reared its head. Even here, miles from home; she could not stop herself looking out for people who might destroy the secret and separate life she had. She so wanted to enjoy his company and, determined to do so, forced herself to take a deep breath and relax.

"It seems an age since I last saw you." He spoke quietly holding her gaze. "The other evening I was lying in bed in some uniform hotel room listening to the noises from the next room". He saw her smile knowingly, "No, no not those noises." He laughed and moved in his seat. "Just muffled conversation. The to and fro of a man and woman. There was a kind of emotional warmth in the timbre of their voices and even though I had no idea what they were saying I sensed how comfortable they were with each other and was overcome by a sense of having missed out. I wanted what they had and it made me think of us and feel a sort of panic."

"Why panic?" She sounded both surprised and curious.

"That we might never have the chance to really be together. Never just stroll along the street, go to the cinema or come home to spend time in each other's company without always being aware of the fact that the time we had was measured."

Judith recognised his thoughts mirrored hers and she resisted the desire to move across the table and wrap her arms around him. She wanted so much to console him but she knew the consolation would have little effect, as she was powerless to alter the situation. They had discussed leaving their respective partners many times but inevitably concluded it would be so damaging to so many, more so for her she realised, that it was preferable to keep things as they were. But, today she was aware of an increased intensity in his voice and a frisson of fear took hold. Fear that he might find the option of living without her less stressful than these stealthy meetings and decide to finish the relationship.

Edward pulled himself up straight and took a deep breath "But, but, but. We are here! We can't waste our time being melancholic." He swallowed another mouthful of beer and placed his glass between his hands gently moving it from one hand to the other. "You tell me what you must do and we can arrange our time around that."

"Well 'must do' immediately eliminates tea breaks and meal times. I'm not really sure of the group meetings. I can't remember the topics

I chose to attend. Nobody takes a register and I can probably pick up the handouts." She laughed. "They're often more informative."

Judith knew she would have to lie to her colleagues at home about the way her days had been spent but she knew she could not prevent herself from spending as much time with him as possible. She got out the programm of events from her bag and underlined the lectures that were most relevant and important. Edward would not return to the hotel until around ten, which left her free to play the dedicated professional this evening. She would take copious notes to atone. The fact that she would also have to lie to Ralph on her return was disturbing and she began to steer her conversation to recent events at home frequently mentioning his name as though by doing so she could exonerate herself by his inclusion. Edward also spoke of his wife Polly. They were always conscious of an unspoken need to keep each other up to date on family life. Referring to Ralph and Polly eased their guilt and helped in the pretence that this was just a casual meeting.

As they talked Judith found herself looking at his face or listening to the inflections in his voice almost forgetting to catch the content. She wanted to extend each minute knowing it would all too soon be gone to take its place inside her memory bank. When he talked of Polly she felt no resentment. She knew he cared for her. Polly was so different. She was always impeccably dressed, everything was right and looked right. She was very controlled and managed her life with apparent confidence but Edward claimed she was very insecure. By comparison Judith felt her own life to be something of a scramble. As Edward related an account when Polly and he were with some mutual friends she could not help wondering how the evening would have gone if it had been Edward and Judith rather than Edward and Polly.

News exchanges over they were left for a moment, their eyes trapped. The silence and the gap between their bodies became magnetized by a strong sexual charge that drew their hands together. She made no protest and Edward sensed her compliance.

"I miss you." He said and her stomach lurched in a rapid roller coaster of movement. The passage of time between their encounters varied from weeks to months. Each time they met they would continue to weave together the fabric of their relationship, the pattern emerging and growing slowly with the progress of time. It was far from complete as the intricacies of their other lives delayed the smooth interchange of threads. When they were apart she thought of him every day never knowing when next they might be together or when they might speak. The assurance he made of her importance to him shook loose doubts and inhibitions when she was with him but back in her world of family and Ralph she began to doubt. Today she was free to express the thoughts and longings suppressed in his absence. It was a cathartic release for the hours of secret dialogue she composed but could not share. Now her soliloquy could be transformed into dialogue where words like love and longing could flow from mouth to mouth and ear to ear.

"I know. It's ironic that we miss each other when in our minds we spend so much time together."

As they sat, they became unaware of time and their surroundings. To the outside world they were perceived as a pair totally engrossed in each other, viewed with envy by the silent elderly couples close by whose years of marriage had obliterated all passion. Within the portly bodies of the men or behind the wrinkled faces of the women there remained a permanent but hidden desire to love and be loved. This tender and amorous display of affection aroused jealous feelings and they found it more comfortable to turn their eyes away or stir the sugary remains of their coffee cups and drink the sweetened mixture in compensation for what they had lost.

The clock from a church nearby began to chime returning them to reality. Edward glanced at his watch.

"I have to make a few phone calls." Their hands remained locked and he made no effort to move. "And I must book a table for later. I'll make it early. There's a place not too far from you that will suit."

"I should be finished by ten." Judith was already delighting in the prospect and lifted his hands to her lips.

"I'll keep it short. They're both quite affable men and as they flew in this morning they should be tired and glad to get away. I'll ring your room when I'm through." He looked at his watch and then at her. "Are you coming back now?" He stood pushing back his chair and replacing it neatly beneath the table, waiting for her to reply. "I have to make my way to the Italian office but I'm happy to walk back with you." He made his way round to her side and placed his hands on her chair waiting to release her from her seat.

"No. You go. I'll walk myself back. I might call in to a shop or two en route and I'd hold you up. "She stood to kiss him and felt the gentle pressure of his tongue.

"About ten," he said and turned to leave.

She should have taken his offer to accompany her. She knew she was losing valuable time with him but wanted to savour the knowledge that he was here, close and available and that in a few hours they would be together with time to spare. The anticipation was intoxicating. She could spend the remaining conference sessions bolstered by this fact. She might even be able to face role-play. His parting left her with the smell of his skin on her hands and for a while she held them close to her nostrils breathing the aroma to resurrect his presence. She watched him walk through a crowd of teenagers knowing the irritation he would feel having his speed impeded.

The waiter came to clear away their drinks and the noise of people arriving at the next table broke her thoughts. Walking back to the hotel she paused in front of a shop window for a moment to collect herself and rein in the excitement she always felt when the prospect of Edward's presence was a reality. As she glanced through the glass into the darkened interior she found herself staring into the reflected face of a young man whose features bore a startling resemblance to those of Holoferne and a sharp splinter of fear punctured her buoyancy. Daring herself to look once more she was met by her own mirror image whose eyes conveyed an expression she did not care to acknowledge.

DOUGLAS — THE PAST

Douglas moved the large table a little to the left. The grain of the wood caught the sunlight giving a rich glow. It was to be delivered to a house north of the river tomorrow. It was lucky for them the table was still in the workshop and could be seen. Polly could not fail to be impressed. Patrick's cupboard looked good too. Perhaps he should have brought in more of the chairs from the back but that might produce a danger of overcrowding. Far better to display a few, well spaced choice pieces. He stood for a while letting his eyes sweep across the room before walking to the back to pick up the bottle opener. Everything must be right. Polly was a friend on his parents and he wanted to impress. The wine was chilling outside. Time now to bring it in.

He called to Patrick who was still working on an oak chest they were to deliver for a new client. They had found a wonderful supply of sand blasted oak several weeks ago that had swallowed a good deal of profit but business was increasing. Many of his old school friends and friends of Patrick were now earning high salaries and they knew it would take them a while to earn that kind of money but they were more than happy with the way things were going at present. Business was good and if they could just clinch a few more orders within the next few weeks they would be well on their way to profit.

Patrick appeared by the door and glanced round. "I thought she was here." He sounded aggrieved.

"No, not yet. I just wanted you to cast an eye. How do you think it looks?" Douglas spread his arms in an extravagant sweep.

"Great, but we don't really know what she has in mind do we?" Patrick walked across to where his cupboard stood and closed the door left slightly ajar. He hoped she would appreciate the work he had put into its making and placed his hand lovingly against the grain of the wood. It was smooth and sound. He was working on something slightly similar with different dimensions at the moment and hated being torn away halfway through its completion. He did not like to have his time wasted.

"True, but at least she can see the type of things we make." Douglas pulled the cuff of his sleeve to cover his hand and began to buff the corner of the table. He wished Polly would come soon; the anticipation of her visit was unnerving. He bent to pick up some wood chippings Patrick had brought in on his feet and for want of a better place, put them in his pocket.

"Well, as she's not here yet, I'll carry on." Patrick turned and disappeared into the workshop. Within seconds the silence was shattered by the scream of the circular saw.

Douglas was always impressed by Patrick's energy and how it repeatedly fuelled his own. A perfect partner, calm, inventive, and never willing to waste a moment. They had detected their kindred spirits at university and both felt slightly alien to a large percentage of the students. During the vacations they had discovered their mutual pleasure in carpentry. Douglas's mother happened to have friends who were disposing of some oak doors and he and Patrick wanted to make something with them. Typically, oak was the hardest of woods with which to work but they had gone to the experts for advice and between them made a small oak cupboard in a modern design. The response was extraordinary. His parents' friends had all expressed interest, asking if they could make other pieces and from there it had snowballed. Now they had their own workshop and show rooms in Battersea which they decided to buy rather than rent. If all failed they would sell up and make a healthy profit on the premises. It was unbelievable how much property had risen in the last few years.

Polly had telephoned him two days ago. At first he did not recognise her voice, as he had not spoken to her for a long time. He felt rather awkward talking to her in a professional way. Although he had known her for many years, he had little to do with her once he left home. Amazingly she said she was interested in putting some work their way and would like to discuss it as soon as possible. She was, he knew, a very successful woman and they both felt flattered by her approach. They were still relatively new to the business but he was confident they could rise to any challenge as long as it was realistic.

The doorbell rang suddenly causing Douglas to jump. He looked up and saw Polly standing outside waving to him. She tapped the glass with her fingernails and smiled in recognition. He had not remembered her being so attractive and was surprised to feel a small rush of excitement. He moved hurriedly to the door and as she entered the shop bent to kiss her cheek.

"My goodness Douglas, I had forgotten how tall you are! Am I late? I got caught in the one way system and had to drive right past."

She walked in quickly bringing with her a cloud of heavy perfume and a sense of occasion. She held her head like a member of the corps de ballet, her back very straight. Her hair was blond, her eyes an astonishing amber which seemed to draw his attention in a compelling way. Douglas could not remember how much younger she was than her husband Edward, around five years or so? She must be in her early fifties, he thought, and yet she looks so young and vibrant. She was wearing a very smart, tight pair of trousers, and a pale, wheat coloured cashmere jumper. Her overall appearance was stunning.

"It's lovely to see you, Polly." His voice was raised above the scream of the saw. "Hang on while I call Patrick. Take a look around. I won't be a moment."

As he moved away he was very conscious of the largeness of his hands and feet. Beside her he felt slightly clumsy. He made his way through the workshop, now filled with the aroma of her perfume, with a heightened awareness of her sexuality. He and Patrick dealt with many women clients and Douglas made a point of flirting if he thought it might help the deal along but just now, with Polly, he had felt awkward and gauche. He hoped he had not given that impression, as it was important for him to impress her and strike the right note if they were to secure this commission.

Douglas tapped Patrick on the shoulder. The saw ceased and there was a momentary silence. "She's here." He said.

Patrick removed his protective glasses leaving pink indentation on his cheekbones. He shook his hair free of sawdust and lay down his tools.

"Is she alone?" he asked wiping his lower lip. Douglas began to brush his shoulders and back vigorously sending clouds of fine beige powder into the daylight. Patrick held his breath until the wood dust had safely landed away from his lungs.

"Yes. She's waiting for us. I told her to have a look around. Are you ready?"

Patrick nodded and, as though they were both about to make an appearance on the west end stage, followed Douglas into the showroom.

Polly was sitting on her heels looking underneath the table. Her hand felt along the furniture sensing the grooves and joints. As they entered she continued to explore its contours before finally raising herself "This is beautifully made. I love the feel of the wood." She moved toward them.

"This is Patrick, my partner." Said Douglas courteously moving out of his way.

"Hallo, Patrick." She smiled and stretched out her hand. Patrick shook hands.

"Would you like a glass of wine, or there's coffee if you prefer?" He moved toward the wine bottle and ran his hand through his hair. A shower of fine sawdust fell softly to the floor.

"I think it's late enough in the day for a glass of wine."

"It's a Chardonnay. Is that ok?" Douglas was uncertain remembering the hours spent on its selection.

"Perfect." Her eyes moved around the room falling upon the furniture, revealing little.

They all stood for a moment, a little wary of each other. A warm smell of polish and wood provided a welcoming atmosphere to their surroundings. Polly was somewhat dwarfed by her two male companions but something about her personality gave her the greater presence. Douglas got the feeling she was gathering information to weigh and examine at a later date. He was grateful to have some thing to do as he poured the wine and carried it across to the circular table where he had earlier placed a small bowl of salted nuts. He drew back a chair and gestured to Polly. As she sat Douglas noticed how beautifully her hair was cut, curving into her neck to draw attention to a string of small black pearls resting against her pale skin.

Douglas and Patrick seated themselves opposite not quite sure of the procedure. Polly took the lead and raised her glass.

"Here's to our new business venture," she said and took a sip." but before we begin, I hope you won't mind if I use a little of our time to catch up on some family news. The last time I saw you was when Edward and I called in on your parents unexpectedly. I think we were lucky to have caught you there. You have a place of your own I know." He remembered he had been to ask his father for a loan and had to wait until they left before he could do so. He did not tell her. " Your mother and father had just returned from a trip somewhere. They both looked very tanned. I remember Hugh had gone with them and contracted some nasty virus." She continued to recall the visit and Douglas was flattered by how much interest she showed in his family. Eventually she became conscious of leaving Patrick outside the conversation and drew her attention to him, careful to pay him the same amount of time but, Douglas noted, took care to reveal very little of herself even warding off certain questions and subtly deflecting them.

Finally they came to discuss the new venture. Polly became very focussed and efficient laying down the facts. She was to open a new boutique in southern Spain in December. Work must begin by the end of September at the latest. She had drawings and plans of the layout, which she spread across the table. All the materials would have to be taken out to Spain. There would be a lot of planning .If they wanted to be part of this they must be willing to commit themselves one hundred percent and if this were the case, provide her with their plans, designs and estimates. If she found them acceptable she would engage Douglas and Patrick to fit the interior once the builders had completed their tasks. She was aware there were people in Spain able to do a more than adequate job but she wanted to experiment with this boutique and employ craftsmen who could bring something new and unique to the project. She had heard encouraging comments from people who knew their work and laughed as she saw their look of surprise. She had carried out some undercover research before approaching them and decided it would be far more exciting to have Douglas and Patrick complete the project. At the end of her explanation Polly lent back, closed her eyes and took a deep breath. For one short moment she looked tired. Douglas thought she looked troubled but the expression was so fleeting he was certain he had made a mistake.

She looked directly at Douglas "Rebecca has to be persuaded before formal contracts are drawn up of course. I don't think you've met my associate, Rebecca, have you Douglas?" She half closed her eyes and drew herself up in the chair as though gathering strength. " Rebecca and I joined forces several years ago. We both had the same taste in clothes and were encouraged by our friends to open a little boutique in Camden. The rent was very low and the lease short but we felt it was a good opportunity to try things out. It worked and now we have several outlets in England, two in France and now want to take our styles to Spain. Rebecca is busy today interviewing possible staff. It's a pity she couldn't be here but at least I can take a few photographs to show her your work if that's OK with you both?" She smiled a warm encouraging smile and rumbling through her large, soft leather handbag withdrew a small camera. "Douglas, would you be a dear and take some for me?"

Douglas had not been able to take his eyes from her face. She had addressed most of the conversation to him holding his attention in the darkness of her pupils. Each time she looked at Patrick there was the strangest sensation of having been abandoned and a strong desire to become the focus of her attention once more overwhelmed him. He stared, willing her to return to him and was rewarded when she flashed her eyes back to his. During their last exchange he had been confused for something other than mere eye contact had taken place. What was he to make of that look? If it had been anybody else he would have interpreted it as a precursor to seduction. Was she making a pass? This was a friend of his parents. Surely not. But as he returned her gaze their eyes were held for just that moment too long. He reached to take the camera and as it changed hands she wrapped her fingers around his. The blood in his cheeks rose to the surface and he was powerless to ignore the fluttering feeling that now filled his chest. Douglas hoped Patrick and Polly would not notice and proceeded to photograph the cabinet and tables close by.

A sudden breeze caught the glass in the window to divert their attention. Polly looked at her watch. "I should go now." She stood and looked toward Patrick. "Thank- you for the wine." She walked across to Douglas and took the camera he held towards her. "Perhaps Douglas, you could come with me to the car and point me in the right direction. I don't want to make the same mistake again." She began to gather her documents together folding them carefully into a large envelope, which she placed in her capacious bag.

Patrick walked with them toward the door. He stood waiting for them to make an exit and caught Douglas's eye as Polly turned to take a final look at the furniture on display.

"It really is impressive," she said as though surprised. As she looked away Patrick raised his eyes to the ceiling. He suddenly felt patronized by the tone in her voice. Douglas caught his glance and looked away not wanting to be seen to second this opinion. Suddenly he felt fiercely protective and did not want to acknowledge anything concerning Polly could warrant criticism.

"Thank you for your time, both of you. I've a feeling we'll work well together. I'll expect to hear from you in the next few days and once the price has been agreed we can begin." She stood between them adopting a very businesslike pose.

"No problem. It couldn't have come at a better moment." Patrick replied.

She raised herself to kiss his cheek. "Goodbye Patrick."

He held the door wide as both, she and Douglas, left the premises and watched them as they walked to the car. She seemed, to him, to be walking rather close. Perhaps knowing his family gave her the right to be so familiar but he could not dismiss the feeling there could be a little more to it than that.

As Polly pressed the automatic door lock she stood still. Douglas walked on and stopped, feeling a little foolish. He was annoyed with himself for his self-consciousness. It was something new to him. Without Patrick's presence his mind seemed to blank and he could think of nothing further to say. He retraced his steps to her side and looked down into her amber eyes. Again the jump in the stomach surprised him.

"I want you to come and have lunch with me Douglas. I 'm staying at the Compte Hotel for the next three days. I'll give you a call." She noticed his confusion. "Or may be, you would prefer to come for supper?" Polly gave him an inquisitive glance, slightly challenging his reply.

"No, no. Lunch would be fine." Why did he feel slightly fearful at the suggestion of supper?

She smiled a full, warm, inviting smile and placed her hands on his arms raising her face to his.

"Goodness Douglas, you are so tall! Bend down and I'll kiss you goodbye."

He lowered his face expecting to receive a kiss on both cheeks but Polly took his face in her hands and placed her mouth over his and applied gentle pressure. "Do give my love to the family, especially your mother. Tell her I'm so looking forward to Peter's wedding." She squeezed his hand before lowering herself into the car. As she drove away she waved and blew a kiss into the air.

Douglas stood, his lips smarting with the sensation of her mouth. Was that usual for her? Did she kiss other men in that way? She had spent so much time in Europe he would have thought she would be more inclined to kiss both cheeks but she had kissed him full on the mouth. He had been totally taken aback. What an exciting woman she was! Why had he not realised that before?

As he walked back to the workshop he resisted the temptation to shout out loud. He felt happy and exhilarated, but it wasn't only the prospect of the new venture that prompted his reaction. He closed his eyes and conjured up her face, those amber eyes, and such beautiful eyes. The memory of the texture of her lips still held and he passed his hands gently across his mouth as if to feel her.

Patrick was waiting for him on his return and poured the remaining wine into their glasses. The showroom had taken on a new prevailing mood of expectancy. The future could, conceivably, change radically and they were both ready.

"Here's to us Douggie, and our new employer." He tilted back his glass and took a large mouthful of wine. "She's quite a lady and, to be honest, I'm not quite sure how to take her but she's certainly enthusiastic and knows her mind." He refilled his mouth holding the wine for a second before swallowing noisily. "I can't quite believe it's us she wants though. I mean, she's had people working for her for years, why change? But, hey, we can make a lot of dosh here. Who cares?" He clasped Douglas round the shoulders and they gave each other a hug. Patrick pushed Douglas away playfully and looked hard into his eyes. "I know she is a friend of your parents, but did you get the impression she was coming on to you?"

Douglas laughed loudly. He felt relieved. "I did! But then I kept thinking I was imagining it." It was great to make a joke of it.

"A married lady, friend of the family Doug. You'd better watch your step." He grinned roguishly and punched Douglas lightly on the arm.

"She's asked me to lunch before she goes back to Spain." Douglas felt slightly guilty. Why had Polly not included Patrick? Probably just being polite for the sake of his parents but catching the look in Patrick's eyes, he could not help but share a guffaw of laughter.

"Whoa!" they laughed together

"She was only being friendly." smiled Douglas as he drained the wine from his glass.

JUDITH — THE PAST

On Judith's return from Florence the weather had turned. That soft heat, now left behind, confirmed the coming of autumn. She was finding it difficult to readjust to her normal routine. Lying in bed she allowed her mind to carry her back to the night spent with Edward. She had fallen asleep beside him listening to the rhythm of his breath, her arm across his body, her hand clasped in his. Earlier they had sat for a while talking but the need to touch soon drove them hurrying toward the bed. They had deliberately woken early to lie beside each other in the sunlight, limbs close, before making love one more time.

Judith turned to look at the clock. It was Saturday and the call of the alarm ignored. She could hear Hugh and his friend Jack laughing upstairs. Soon Hugh would enter the nocturnal world of his late teens and they would see little of him. Like Douglas and Peter, he would be independent once he went away to university. She felt a pang of nostalgia for those earlier years when they had all been home together, the house full of young men and women. It was no wonder Hugh was such a sociable being. He had never experienced loneliness and always seemed to hold center stage in spite of his difference in years.

"I've bought you tea," said Ralph pushing open the door with his foot. "I wasn't sure if you would like to lie in". He held a small round tray in his large hands, his gentle eyes looked out palely from behind his glasses giving him an intellectual air. He moved slowly allowing his limbs a kind of freedom that gave an overall impression of relaxation.

Judith pulled herself up to a sitting position and held the mug of tea between her fingers. She smiled as Ralph bent to kiss her cheek. "It's good you've had a chance to rest. I was awake at five thirty and knew I wouldn't be able to go back to sleep." he said and sat besides her.

They had been married for twenty-eight years and she still felt self-conscious when Ralph looked into her eyes. He could look at her in such a way that was so trusting it unnerved her. She had spent her married life in Ralph's company but could still be surprised by something he might say or do. She wondered what he really knew. Were there areas he dare not broach? It was heartening to know her own thoughts were hidden and she still found it possible to say one thing and think another without the slightest worry of causing him distress.

"What have you been doing?" she asked.

"I finished the article on Khiva. Perhaps you could read it later, tell me what you think. I read it through rather rapidly and noticed a few errors but in general I think it will do". He pulled himself back to lean on the pillows causing Judith to steady her cup.

"What about the novel?" She asked with slight trepidation. He had been pacing the floor rather a lot lately and had a distracted air about him she recognized as a lack of confidence in his work.

"Bit of a block there. It's difficult. I know what the publishers are after but it's not quite what I want. Not this time." He pushed her gently to her side of the bed as he rolled himself into a more comfortable position.

"I've heard that before."

"I know, but I have an idea." Ralph raised his cup to his lips and sipped the hot tea." It may be that..."

"Don't tell me" interjected Judith. She was woefully aware of the danger of Ralph talking himself out of many ideas in the past. It was far wiser to leave him to think alone. "Wait until you've really thought about it. I'm not really in the mood to discuss it now anyways. Too close to sleep. Sorry and all that but maybe later."

Ralph smiled "You're right. I won't say a word more."

They sat for a while quietly drinking the tea each with their own thoughts. Ralph placed his empty mug on the bedside table and squeezed her hand. "This won't do" he sighed as he raised himself from the bed and walked towards the window blocking the sun momentarily from Judith. He stood for a while in silence, his breathing just audible. "I ought to do something about the grass". The statement was directed at himself prompted by the sight of their neighbour removing his mower from the shed. There was little intention of carrying it through but it might be a useful procrastinating chore to carry out while his work was proving to be so difficult.

"I have to take Hugh into town to buy him some decent clothes for the wedding. Do you want to come?" Judith placed her mug on the shelf beside the bed and began to push back the duvet.

"I'd rather get back into bed with you." He turned, waiting for her reaction but seeing Judith continue to swing her legs across the side of the bed, he returned once again to the view outside the window. "The garden looks so beautiful this morning."

"Give Hugh a shout while I am in the shower and tell Jack his mother wants him home before ten this morning." She pulled on her dressing gown and walked across to the window. The garden was indeed beautiful. They were so fortunate to have found this house with its seclusion.

"Do you remember how it looked when we first came here? Douglas was only four and Peter six. I thought when the massive cherry tree came down it would devastate the view and yet, if anything, it's given the garden greater depth. We never did know what to do with all those sour cherries." Judith was aware of Ralph's contemplative mood and knew where it was heading. She should, she knew remain with him for a while and talk but her morning would be busy and she needed to get going now. Somewhat guiltily she began to gather her underclothes from the drawer and waited for him to speak. He remained silent however and Judith interpreted this as permission to make her way to the bathroom.

Ralph smiled recognizing her need to escape and continued to focus beyond the trees. He felt increasingly inclined to stand and stare even though every thing at present was "full of care". He must not let this lethargy take hold but it was all too easy to allow the minutes to pass, filling them with inappropriate actions of little importance. His constant companion was the thought of his computer idling on the screen saver. Perhaps if he went outside to mow the lawn, he would feel better but no, he knew he would not. Now Judith had left the room he was joined once again by a feeling of sadness. He couldn't quite understand this state that overtook him every so often. He was aware of a slight distancing between himself and Judith but there was no real concrete evidence that anything was wrong. It was probably this inability he had to goad himself to work. It was so easy to fritter the larger part of the day away. He still hadn't dressed and decided it was time to select something suitable for the coming day. He knew he would feel better once he was in his clothes.

Judith closed the door behind her and removed her dressing gown. She was aware of having left Ralph with his burden of work but short of writing the book for him, which was impossible, there was very little she could do. The bathroom was warm and receiving and as she prepared herself for the shower she found herself thinking of Peter's approaching wedding. She and Ralph had not wanted a church ceremony. At that time everybody was anti-church and very left wing. Unlike now, when all her children's contemporaries preferred traditional white weddings, no one of their acquaintance was willing to say their vows before God. Today even her eldest son, who had never or rarely been inside a church, had agreed to do just that. Yet even without a heavenly blessing theirs had been a very happy occasion surrounded by friends and family. They could never have envisaged their years together would be so harmonious.

She stood beneath the shower letting the hot water play upon her shoulders. Once home she became engrossed in her family and was carried along by their everyday needs. Whenever she was distanced from them she saw them differently. The Ralph she thought about when she was away was not the Ralph she found on her return. It was not that he had changed but his 'aura' seemed to dissolve. In his absence she could appreciate all his qualities, which, once home, she tended to take for granted. The long years together had enabled them to gauge each other's moods knowing when it was best to remain silent or when to proffer words of encouragement. They had become a kind of icon for their son's friends as living proof that marriage worked. This troubled her.

The water from the shower revived her and broke the connection with sleep. She was a late convert to showering and very rarely now chose to soak in a hot bath. She thought of the bath at the hotel in Florence, she had rather relished that. The temperature perfect, the perfumed soap. Edward. Hugh hammering on the door brought her back to the present rather abruptly.

"Will you be long?" He called and began to pace up and down. There was no reason as far as he could see to keep his mother in the shower for any length of time.

"No" she wailed. "Just a few minutes more". She was looking forward to her outing with Hugh and was willing to forego a few extra minutes. She would have to use a few encouraging tactics today on Hugh to get him to choose something appropriate. He showed little interest in clothes, unlike Douglas and Peter who only wore the most sophisticated brand names. Peter, now so particular about his suits and shirts, took his career very seriously and liked to look the part.

As she passed Hugh leaving the bathroom she gave him a hug. "Put on something reasonably tidy today". He hugged her back and laughed. His hair stuck upwards from the top of his head, the furrows of his fingers still visible. He had an open face that helped make him look younger than his years, a feature which caused great irritation when publicans refused to serve him.

"Go and shower. Is Jack still in bed?" Judith did not wish to be responsible for Jack arriving home late.

"Yes, don't worry, he knows about getting home". Hugh gave an enormous shout in the direction of his bedroom as he closed the door behind him and turned the radio onto full volume. Jack's response could just be heard and she was satisfied.

Ralph had begun to make the bed and she automatically moved to the other side to help. She wanted to mention Edward in some way to ease her guilt and avoid any slips of the tongue. Now seemed a suitable time

"By the way, Edward telephoned last night while you were out. It seems they might be able to come to the wedding after all. He thought they would both be out of the country when we first invited them. Apparently Polly is very keen to come. She hasn't seen the family for a while and says she's delighted there is going to be a wedding." Judith busied herself straightening the duvet cover.

"Peter will be happy with that and Kate will have a chance to meet them both". Ralph threw the big, white cushions across the top of the bed. The numbers for this wedding had grown so large he was sure another two would make little difference "How are they both?"

"Oh fine. We didn't really say much. If they do come you can bet Polly will turn up in something stunning. I wish I'd settled on what I was going to wear. I do so hate buying clothes for myself."

Ralph made no reply. He was used to her bemoaning the plight of females and clothing. She was only ever really comfortable in trousers.

Judith gave the pillows a final pat and straightened the bed cover. Her fingers ran across the surface and she remembered the day they had bought it. They had seen it in India in a small factory in Old Delhi. There were yards of vivid fabric running from floor to ceiling and they had stood beneath the swaying lengths of material amazed by the designs and colours. The creamy white cover was right at the end and seemed out of place. They noticed small circular mirrors sewn into the material, which drew them to it. The cost was small and they were happy to pay the full price. They had spent the rest of the day shopping and that evening she and Ralph had joined two fellow travellers and made their way to a hotel some one had recommended for supper. It had been so hot all day and the evening air was full of wood smoke. The idea of walking was out of the question and they had taken a motor rickshaw driven by a maniac. It had been quite terrifying. Ralph had been very confident and happy with the way his work was progressing then and found the journey hilariously funny.

Later as they all sat round the table eating he had entertained them with his traveller's tales for the larger part of the evening. He had looked so attractive in the candlelight and she had experienced a warm rush of love for him. She wished the confidence of that night would return to carry him through his recent difficulties.

"Do you want to come into town with Hugh and me?" She asked as she pulled off her bathrobe and began dressing.

"No thanks, I'll travel up later after I've done some work and call into the National Gallery." Ralph gathered up the empty teacups and made his way to the door. He paused, "There's a very good film on tonight at the NFT which I'd like to see if you don't mind".

"Not at all. I've no idea how long this clothes buying expedition will take". Judith was pleased to have the whole day before her to plan to her liking. She need not rush anything and could spend time with her youngest son. She rarely had him to herself and would relish the idea of an unhurried shopping trip.

Later that day she watched as Hugh tried on enumerable items of clothing. He had not yet grown to his full height and it was difficult to find a suit with trousers the right length. They had been laughing earlier at the number of women threatening their children in Hamleys. Judith was a good mimic and had used several of the overheard phrases to threaten Hugh as he dismissed suit after suit.

The sale's assistant was very attentive and sensed Hugh's discomfort. It was rare to find an assistant in most of the new outfitters. They had already stood in several shops waiting for attention, music blaring loudly, only to finally leave in frustration. When Judith was a child shopping trips with her mother were grand affairs. Her mother had a great interest in clothes but Judith found it a nightmare. The glare of the shop lighting, the pressing attention, all served to make her uncomfortable. As a teenager the styles had been hideous. The dreadful depression of suspender belts and high-heeled shoes, like her first period that ushered her into adult female life, were synonymous with discomfort and lost freedom. She envied the young girls of today who could wear large comfortable boots and flat shoes with almost anything they chose to wear.

"What about this Mum?"

Hugh stood before her in a dark blue suit. She caught her breath. How beautiful he looks, she thought. Had she made other decisions all those years ago he, would not exist. But here he was, transformed by this suit into a young man.

"Good heavens" Judith smiled and walked towards him. "How like Douglas you look. It's lovely Hugh".

"It feels quite good". He stood in front of the long mirror and pulled at the jacket.

Speedily the assistant stepped forward and tugged at the collar "It's a good fit. I doubt you will need any alterations." he said and stood looking admiringly into the mirror.

"It's time you had a suit," Judith said. "You'll need it for your interviews. What about a shirt and tie?" She pointed to another area of the floor where she had seen ties displayed in colourful rows.

Hugh walked further back into the shop and began to study the shirts. She left him to make his own selection. Now the suit had been chosen it was easy going. He had rather balked at the idea earlier but had obviously been won over by his own appearance in the mirror. When Judith first met Ralph he wore a suit with shirts and ties. He had progressed to large baggy jumpers when the boys were young. Most of their friends wore the same. It would have been bizarre for any of them to wear a suit. She knew of nobody in a suit. They were all illustrators or writers or college lecturers. They had their own uniformity, she could see that now, and yet at the time they all seemed so much apart from most working people. There was never any money for a start. as they were all "Freelance" which really meant sweating it out from one payment to the next. She had been very prudent then. And suddenly she remembered her money-box. It had once been a collecting box for the African poor in the shape of a straw hut and manufactured from some extraordinary substance. Perhaps it was papier-mache but it had a heavy, almost damp feel. It was impossible to open and eventually she had taken a chisel to its beautiful shape and prized open the base cracking the hut in two. That moneybox had taken them to France.

Judith was suddenly aware of her mobile vibrating in her coat pocket. She snatched it quickly from its place and checked the number. It was Edward. She looked towards Hugh and gauged the distance between them. She could take the call and speak quietly if she moved further down the department. His voice was urgent. He was in London, he had to see her, where was she, could they meet? She did not know what time Hugh would want to leave her or where he had planned to spend the rest of the day. He must surely be tired of the shops by now and she made a quick decision to see Edward later that afternoon. Immediately she recognized the tight band of tension beginning to form itself around her head. Why did he want to see her now, today, when she had planned to be with Hugh? Should she have refused, told him it wasn't possible? Why had she put him before her own son? Was Hugh beginning to tire? She looked across at him. He had finally made his selection, a shirt, a tie, and a rather sombre pair of socks. Judith was aware it was time for lunch and after they had dealt with payment and watched the assistant fold the clothes carefully into two large carrier bags she discovered Hugh was eager to leave. He was ravenous he said and hastily directed her toward a small Italian restaurant that he knew would provide them both with a suitable quantity at a suitable price. He had a passion for Italian food and had found the place a few months ago when he was out with one of his friends.

Judith's dilemma of need remained and she found it difficult to find the appetite to select a suitable item from the menu. Days like this were few and far between, but she had to be sure Hugh was off and away before the afternoon was out. That would leave her time to sit for a while in some coffee-shop and prepare herself. It was still relatively early and she would wait before asking Hugh what other arrangements he had made for the day.

Judith ordered a filling dish for Hugh and decided on a salad for herself. They had found a table just at the right time for now there were no spaces. The place was obviously popular with the young who used it daily for their lunch breaks. Everybody seemed to know each other. They waited rather a long time to be served, prompting Judith to check her watch anxiously and surreptitiously, mindful of her later engagement. There would be time. She could relax a little and when the food arrived she sat back and allowed Hugh to entertain her. He spoke amusingly and enthusiastically about his friends, his plans, his chances at University and Judith absorbed his news gratefully.

Hugh sat beside his mother driving his fork through the pasta wondering how he would tell her his friends were waiting for him at Covent Garden. He had said he might be late and he didn't want to rush away as soon as he finished his meal but he would have to say something soon. Best to skirt round.

"How are you planning on spending the afternoon?" Hugh asked. Judith looked up suddenly trying to gauge the correct way to reply. She did not want to appear dismissive of his company but he must not be around when she met Edward.

"We ought to see about a pair of shoes to go with your suit." The look of dismay on his face told her that was not such a good idea.

"I can easily get those mum. In fact my present ones would do if I gave them a lick of polish." He looked hopeful.

"Well that's all we really need to do together. We could go to an exhibition if you like, or take in an early film?" Judith waited anxiously for his reply. She was counting on a refusal but it might just be possible to squeeze in before meeting Edward. Her stomach was beginning to tighten.

Hugh suddenly felt it was time to throw caution to the wind. "Actually mum, I'd rather not. I know a few of the group are coming up to central London today and if you wouldn't mind I'd quite like to join them." He looked rather sheepishly towards her as he placed the last mouthful of his lunch in his mouth." But if you really want me to stay, I will." He threw her a beatific smile and waited for her reply.

Judith laughed and reached across to squeeze his hand "No, no. You go and meet your friends. I'm sure you won't want to traipse around the shops with me. I might have a look for myself now. I had intended to do so anyway and it will be a lot easier. Would you like a dessert or coffee?" She felt all the muscles in her body settle and relax. It was all working out.

"No thanks. That was delicious." He checked his watch and pushed back his seat. "I don't know what time I'll be home tonight, We're all going across to Clapham to watch a video then out for the evening, but I'll call if I'm going to stay out. O.K.?" He walked round to her side of the table and kissed her cheek. "Thanks mum for the suit. It's great."

Later that afternoon she was left with the parcels and a picture of Hugh in his suit in her head. It was rather typical she should be left with the bags. She supposed it was reasonable of Hugh not to consider taking them and, she thought, she would have worried he might leave them somewhere. As she walked along the wide pavements, Judith passed a shop window displaying wedding gowns. A picture of Kate came into her mind. Kate would become such an important part of their lives now. Peter's marriage would mean his separation from the family. It was hard to accept the notion that Peter's wife would know far more about her son than she could ever know. The truth of this statement was painful and hard to admit. He was lost to her and all that love so easily metered out in his infancy and childhood must now be held in check, for who could kiss and hold a son in manhood as one had done in infancy?

Douglas too had gone. His lifestyle, so hectic, it was unusual to see him more than once a month. She and Ralph always advocated freedom for their children. To beware the evils of routine, no must for Christmas or Easter. It had worked and they maintained excellent relationship with all three boys but Judith was still left with an element of nostalgic longing to have them back once more. She had been so involved in their day- to -day activities but what did they remember of those times?

The traffic now was building and her arms began to protest at the weight of the bags she was carrying. There was still some time to go before their meeting. The lights in the shops were being turned on and the street took on a warm familiar glow as the crowds wove in and out, each with their own purpose for being there, each in their own thoughts. She could run for a bus but her energy was low. The small coffee shop to her right looked inviting, it would be a relief to sit down right now. Judith walked across and selected a table by the window that allowed her a clear view of the road. She would tell Edward where she was and have him pick her up. She gathered her parcels around her and got out her phone. Their conversation was brief but he was happy with the arrangement. She did not permit herself to ask any questions and knew she must wait to discover what he wanted to tell her.

Judith relaxed as she drank her coffee. Ralph would probably be coming out of the gallery and making his way to the N.F.T. He would walk around for a while and then get something to eat. He would not be coming in this direction she was sure. He hated shopping and crowds. Hugh and his friends would be on their way to Clapham.

It was difficult maintaining these separate lives. At times she would repeat the same thoughts in her mind trying to reach a decision that never came. She accepted she was weak. She was also greedy. She had what most women wanted, why could she not accept it and be grateful? She knew the reason. She could not stop herself from loving both Edward and Ralph. She loved them differently; she and Ralph had so much yet she truly believed she was a better wife and a better mother for having Edward. Surely it could not be a case of selfishness or indulgence if she could not prevent herself from loving them. It would be as difficult to stop loving one as the other. Living with Ralph meant everything was on tap. He was there; she had no need to live on memories. She could sit in the chair at night and see him, she could talk to him, make love to him. He was there. But Edward spent so long away from her that their meetings became precious and memorable. Her feelings for him were different, more passionate, for the long intermissions allowed her to feast upon their actions in tasty morsels .She could sit in her car and think of him. She could lie awake at night and conjure up events, savouring details of the conversations they had. She could ignite herself with nostalgic fuel.

A car hooted loudly and dragged her back to the present. The car slid alongside the kerb and she looked through the glass front of the café at the driver. It was Edward. She gathered up her belongings and hurried out into the street. A gust of wind blew her hair across her face obscuring her view. She cursed as she lifted the heavy bags to pull it from her eyes. She heard the whine of electric windows opening. He lent across "Get in quickly, I'm holding up the traffic".

He unclipped his seat belt and stretched across to open the car door. A car hooted impatiently behind them. Without hesitating, she moved forward and placed herself awkwardly in the passenger seat. Her parcels filled the space and she clumsily drew the seatbelt across. Edward removed several of the bags and pushed them toward the back. "What on earth have you been buying?" he said, and turned to look at her. The locking mechanism of their eyes engaged.

"Oh all sorts." she paused "what on earth are you doing back here so soon?" She settled herself more comfortably into the seat

"My plans were changed and they sent me across to discuss with the people financing one of our new projects." He glanced into the rear mirror and pulled into the busy traffic. The radio in the car was playing a rather jangly tune and he lent to turn it off. "I needed to see you. We have to talk"

Judith's face registered alarm. Edward stretched his hand across to touch her face reassuringly. "Not here, not right now. I need to concentrate on the traffic. Tell me what you've been doing today"

"I've been helping Hugh choose a suit - for the wedding. He looks rather good in it," Judith tried to keep her voice light but she was already worrying at the suggestion they had to talk. What could that mean?

Edward's eyes turned from the road to sweep across her face, "I still can't believe the years have passed so quickly. I suppose it is time he had a suit but I still think of him as a young boy."

Judith laughed. "He is in many respects but he is more or less out of our hands now. He hardly seems to be home. Douglas and Peter are beginning to include him in their social scene, which he loves, of course."

Time had passed so rapidly, Edward was right it did only seem to be a few years ago that Hugh was a young boy holding onto her arm when they went anywhere, always eager to be included. Edward had re entered her life before he was born and watched, all be it from afar, his growing up. She remembered how she had stumbled across his whereabouts all those years ago and how that particular day had made its mark on her life. She had gone to the British Library to follow up on a research paper she was preparing for her Doctorate. Before settling into work she had found a quiet corner and opened the newspaper. The paper was still held together by small indentations from the printing press and she turned two pages at once arriving at the business news section. Her eyes made a quick scan of the headlines and finding little to grab her attention was about to turn back to the Art's section when she found herself looking at the photograph of a familiar face. The copy beneath revealed that Edward Ashton (above) had been appointed to a senior position in a large London based company. He was the youngest man to have ever taken a post of such high responsibility and it was this fact that had made him something of a celebrity in the financial world. Judith felt a rush of excitement. He had made it. His ambition had served to steer him in exactly the direction he had hoped. He was successful and, no doubt, wealthy. She took from her bag a small pair of nail scissors and much to the fascination of her neighbouring researcher, began to cut carefully around the edges of the article before folding it into her bag. For the rest of the day she had been unable to concentrate. The newspaper cutting sat like a persistent knocking at the door to draw her back to its contents and encourage her thoughts to wander into Edward territory. He was in London. Where? Was he married, did he have children? She looked again at the photograph searching for clues. The name of his company was there. She did not know where he lived but now she knew where he worked. She gathered together her notebooks and returned the books she had been using. She would go for a walk and think. Later as she wandered round the periphery of Regent's Park she made up her mind to contact him. She merely wanted to pass on her congratulations there could be no harm in that. Her decision set she made her way to Paperchase and purchased a suitable card. She was careful to add her own address and telephone number as she could not deny a pressing need to see him once more. That evening she showed Ralph the cutting and later that evening had hidden it in an old purse where it remained to this day. Within two days the telephone rung and she found she talking to Edward in an old familiar way and made arrangements to meet the next day.

For a few brief seconds she could not identify him but then his features became familiar and from that moment they were unable to take their eyes from each other. The same rush of emotion she had felt on their first meeting was renewed with all its intensity and, without her being able to take any kind of control, the loves she had unknowingly held dormant for several years reclaimed a prominent position. Edward had confessed he had thought of her ever since they parted. He had always been aware of a sense of loss and incompleteness in his life but had not sought to contact her again because he believed she no longer loved him and would not want to see him. He could not face rejection. Her card of congratulations had overwhelmed him and he had thought of nothing but their meeting ever since. He had thought so often of what they might say, how they would explain away the hurt they had caused to each other. When he left her at the station he had kissed her passionately and said they must not part again. Judith had told him of her marriage, her two boys and her love and respect for Ralph and they had made a pact not to destroy that. Edward had recently married Polly and did not want to hurt her. They were trapped but not captive. For now they would accept the fact they might not see each other as often as they would like but they would always know where the other was. She returned home on the train with the pressure of his lips on her mouth and her heart beating so violently through her chest she thought the whole carriage would ask her to be quiet. She was terrified to go home carrying such a sound in case Ralph would hear and she would be forced to tell him exactly what had happened that afternoon. From that day Judith had kept her feelings for him hidden from everyone, even her closest friends.

That same evening she had told Ralph of her meeting because she did not want Edward's name to be forbidden or unmentionable and by speaking of him in an open way she could place him, in Ralph's eyes, in the category of "friend" and slightly ease the uncomfortable sense of disloyalty. He was after all a friend from the past, somebody she felt Ralph would like and several weeks later they had all met, she and Ralph, Polly and Edward and surprisingly, had become friends. It was disturbing sometimes to see Polly sitting close to Edward or to watch her kiss him when she was unaware they were being observed. Judith hated to acknowledge the presence of a jealous heart.

They were approaching Piccadilly Circus. The crowds were waiting to cross. A taxicab cut in abruptly causing Edward to swerve slightly. He drew in his breath.

"Bastard. He nearly clipped my wing."

"Those taxis are built like tanks. That's why they swing them about so recklessly," laughed Judith. She was aware of his tension and tried to make light of his irritation.

"I'm not amused." he turned to look at her. "I have to be somewhere at 9.30, can you stay that late?"

His tone of voice surprised her and she answered rather defensively. "Ralph is going to the NFT and won't be back until later. I can always ring and leave a message. I'll have to tell him we met, he'll be surprised but I'd rather surprise than suspicion. I told him you and Polly were hoping to be at the wedding. He hasn't seen Polly for ages and is looking forward to it."

She positioned herself more comfortably to turn towards him. "I had no idea I'd be seeing you today. Ralph may find it hard to believe in a coincidental meeting but I can't think of an alternative". She pictured herself arriving home and seeing Ralph come to kiss her. She would tell him straight away.

"Just tell him I contacted you. It's easier to tell the truth. I phoned and finding you were in town, asked to meet." They were turning now into the Strand. "I'm going to see if it's possible to book an early table at Simpson's. Would you like that?"

"It would be lovely" she remembered a family outing she and Ralph and the boys had two years ago to Simpson's. The atmosphere was delightful and it was such a joy to be treated so well by everyone.

"Well I certainly fancy roast beef" Edward pulled into the kerbside and retrieved his phone. Judith watched as he made the reservations. "Great, all settled, a table at six. That gives us time for me to find a parking space".

"We some times find one just off the Embankment. It's not far to walk from there and it'll be convenient for me for Charing Cross."

Before moving off he turned and held her head between his warm hands. He searched her eyes for a brief moment before kissing her gently. Judith felt sadness in this kiss, which triggered once again the tension on an already tight knot of anxiety she was trying to ignore. She fought the urge to ask him then and there what was wrong.

They entered the wide doors of the restaurant holding hands. Edward was greeted like an old friend and with a great deal of respect. Judith handed over her coat and looked across at Edward. He smiled and took her hand leading her like a child as he followed the rather suave looking receptionist taking them to their table.

Settled in a side table, relieved of coats and parcels, Judith looked around at the comfortable brown panelled room and breathed in the aroma of roasted meat. The tables were covered in crisp white linen that sent small circles of gentle light upwards into the faces of the seated diners. Waiters walked purposefully between the aisles ready to administer to their every need. The atmosphere was settled and solid giving an air of tradition and respect. The darkness of the walls enclosed them in discrete shadows from where they could observe. Judith watched as a trolley containing an enormous piece of beef was wheeled from table to table and marvelled at the expert way in which the waiter carved slices of the most succulent meat. There was a party of Middle England ladies on the centre tables, excited to be away from home and so obviously enjoying the food. Later they would fill a row of seats at the theatre and be shocked by the language.

When their food arrived Edward delighted in the cabbage and piled his plate high. "It's early to be eating but I skipped lunch and I'm ready for this. Are you hungry? "He looked somewhat guilty.

"Yes, I didn't think I would be but the smell has triggered something. It's all so delicious." She cut through her Yorkshire pudding watching him eat and suddenly panicked over what was to come. She leant towards him and before he could begin to speak asked, "How is Polly?"

As soon as she put the question Judith suddenly felt afraid that there might be bad news. Polly had recently been hospitalised having initially contracted a viral infection. She had refused to believe herself ill and continued to work, eventually collapsing with pneumonia. It had taken weeks for her to fully recover and the doctor had insisted she take time out and go somewhere warm and dry.

"A lot better but she's been behaving rather strangely. I think she may have taken on too much" Edward swallowed and put down his knife and fork. "She's decided to open another branch of her shops in Spain. There seems to be a big market for high quality casual clothes along the coastal resorts so she and Rebecca feel it's time to expand."

Judith remembered Rebecca. A tall elegant dark haired woman with extremely blue eyes. She had been the driving force behind the shops. They had begun with one tiny cubby-hole of a shop in the South of France. Their clothes were distinctive and word got round. The next shop was further along the coast and now they had half a dozen. Polly was always travelling from one to the other. She and Edward often spent weeks apart. His job as financial director for a huge chemical company sent him to many different countries in the world and they often found themselves crossing at airports.

"They've built quite an empire over the past few years. But I'm glad Polly's involved again. She seems to feel working will get her back to strength." The waiter stopped to enquire if everything was to their satisfaction. Fast on his heels came the wine waiter who refilled their glasses with adroit movements of his gloved hand as though performing a magical trip for an audience of thousands. He paused for a moment as though considering his next few words. Judith waited expectantly and then rather surprisingly he asked, "How is Ralph?" as though he were duty bound.

"He's having problems with his latest novel. He says it has to be finished by the winter but what with the wedding and his commitment to the newspaper, time is running out." Judith wondered for a moment if he had managed to do any work after she had left home this morning.

"I read one of his reviews last week. He's doing well." He moved uncomfortably in his seat and looked away.

"Yes, he is, and at last he's receiving recognition. I wish he could feel more confident at the moment." Oh dear thought Judith, we are talking like strangers, someone has to make a move. She sat back in her seat and took a deep breath. "Edward, I can't stand this. Why are we talking like this? For God's sake tell me what all this is about".

Edward wiped his mouth with the heavy white napkin and made himself more comfortable. He was relieved Judith had forced the issue and had been thinking their strangled words were bordering on the ridiculous. He was afraid to bring up the real reason and she could not be fooled into thinking he had rushed half way across London to see her to ask after Ralph. He ceased to eat and looked at her intently. She felt her face flush with anticipation.

"They want me to take up a posting in Australia." He took a long breath as though relieved the truth was out.

Judith looked up quickly from her plate, her face registering shock. Australia! The vision of a world globe flashed into her mind. She saw Great Britain and the necessary twist it took to find Australia. There were thousands of miles in between. The impossibility of their being able to meet was unimaginable and deeply disturbing. "How long have you known this?"

"Just for the past few days". Edward looked as troubled as Judith. "I've tried to get out of it but there's nobody else capable of running the company over there. Judith, I don't know if I can let you go again. How could we ever see each other?" Edward encircled her legs beneath the table and held them tight. His hold was painful but she could not move.

"What does Polly think?" She did not really care what Polly thought but other deeper and darker questions had to be pushed to the back of her mind. "I can't imagine Polly wanting to leave everything she has spent the last few years working for to Rebecca." Judith was afraid now. Afraid of his decision and all it could imply. Polly might jump at the chance to open a new string of shops out there. She was a woman who always had business in mind and she was after all, his wife.

"I haven't told her yet. Things are somewhat strained between us just lately. We've hardly spoken and when we are together she seems curt and off hand. I suppose she'd have to remain in Europe for a while. She's so involved in her business. She could always come out every so often to visit I suppose. It's difficult to tell at the moment what her reaction will be. She might even like the idea. I don't know. She has a choice but it's us Judith, how will we cope?" He breathed heavily, "At least they've given me some time before making a decision." He ran his fingers across the table and picked up his desert spoon tapping it with nervous rapidity on the back of his hand. Looking up he caught Judith's eyes and replaced it. "It's going to be so difficult." He lent to take her hand. For a moment nothing was said.

" And what if you said no? What then?"

"I'm not sure but I know they are relying on me to go. It's important for the company that some one very senior is seen to be there. It does virtually make it impossible for me to say no. If I refuse I'll be handed the kind of work that doesn't really interest me, if I go I know it will be a fantastic opportunity. I know all that but how can I leave you?"

"How long are you going to be in London?" Judith was aware of a heavy lump forming around her heart. This morning the world had been such a happy place and now she knew it to be otherwise.

"Maximum four to five days. I have a lot to clear. A good deal of the Australian business is tied up with this transaction. Will we be able to meet?" His faced was tight with anxiety.

"I have to work on Monday until quite late. There's a new child I have to see. His family are hostile to the idea of psychologists and it may be lengthy. I'll need to look in my diary for the rest of the week. I do know it's pretty full." She was under a great deal of pressure at work. Her client list was long. Her conscience would not permit her to cancel appointments. She knew many of the parents and children had waited months for their chance of assessment. Perhaps she could call in a Locum. Whatever happened she would work something out. She could not accept the thought of not being able to see him.

Edward lent back in his seat as the waiter removed his plate. Judith waited until they were alone before continuing. "Ralph is home all week. Maybe you could come down and see us both if I can't get away. He's bound to find it odd you not coming to see him while you are here. At least I could see you." Judith saw the look of despair in his eyes. She knew it was not what he wanted but any chance of seeing him held value for her, especially now.

She took the desert menu from the waiter on his return and glanced at the list. Bread and butter pudding, apple pie, steamed pudding. "I don't know if I can manage any more. Can you?" The news of Australia had dulled her appetite.

"I hate to pass up the chance of bread and butter pudding but right now I have no appetite." He smiled at the waiter who nodded and went away.

The ladies in the centre table began to stir. They were anxious not to be late for their entertainment. Chairs were pushed back and a large lady in red laughed loudly and clasped the woman next to her as she rose from her seat. "Oh, Anita, how on earth can you remember such detail? Did I really?" Anita assured her she did.

Judith looked around at the other tables. There was an elderly couple to their right who were dressed in the most uncomfortably smart clothing. The woman wore a heavy bracelet that banged against her thin wrist. The man wore an enormous watch that seemed to be planted amongst a forest of thick wiry hairs. They had eaten rhythmically, periodically wiping their mouths with their napkins, almost as though to a beat. What did they store in their heads as they sat? Maybe they had lived together for years finding little need to speak as their thoughts ran parallel. They obviously had money. Judith hoped they enjoyed it but there were no visible smile lines around their eyes. What did others make of her and Edward as they sat together? Could they appreciate the enormity of the news he had just passed on to her? The young couple further to their right had glanced over several times and catching eyes had looked away. Could they know? Did everybody else in the restaurant assume they were a married couple enjoying a meal together? She could usually identify between the married and the unmarried. Often the married did not speak. She and Edward had so much to say but this news had cast a silence between them and made them mute just like the couple she had watched. She had often thought that had she married Edward all those years ago nearly everything familiar to her now would be nonexistent; certain people eliminated from her group of friends, the houses in which she had lived unknown. Her whole attitude and outlook on life might be totally different. Perhaps she would have been a better person, perhaps not. Would she have pursued the same career? What might she now be? So many times she had counted her good fortune, her family, career, friends. Yet even so the fascination remained to toy with the idea that Ralph could be her Edward.

Edward broke the silence first. "We still have time to go for a drink when we finish here." He placed his napkin on the table and brushed a few crumbs from the cloth. "Or maybe you'd prefer to get home?" He looked miserable and dejected as though the news he had imparted had already separated them.

Judith looked around the restaurant before her gaze met his. She continued to stare at him. There was a brooding heaviness between them that she wished to break. His blond hair fell thickly across his head and she noted the white of his temples. It was late in the day and tiny pin pricks of blond and ginger hairs could be seen on his cheeks. His mouth fell in a soft curve. How lovely he was, she thought, how could she ever stay away from him.

"Take me for a drink somewhere. I really can't face going home knowing you are here in London. Ralph won't expect me. He knows I like to make the most of a day out."

"I've got the use of a friends flat. We could go there. We have time. Please say yes. I can't face the evening without you. Suddenly every minute matters"

As she agreed she felt the tension lift. They had some time. He had not gone yet. Something happened to alter his plans. Who knows.

THE PAST — FAMILY SUNDAY

Judith placed the telephone on the hall table. "Hugh," she shouted, "Are you up?" She stood for a moment waiting, listening for a response. "Hugh, it's Simon on the phone. HUGH!" She coughed, having strained her throat and returned to the phone. "Simon? He's still dead to the world. What time did you all leave last night? Well, I doubt we'll see him before midday. I'll tell him you rang."

Sundays tended to follow this pattern. The phone was constantly ringing and it was always for Hugh.

Ralph sat in the kitchen, newspapers spread across the table. He looked up "You should just let it ring." He looked tired. Judith knew he had been up for hours unable to sleep. Last night he had returned around 12.30 and she had arrived home first. She had faked sleep and turned out the light preferring not to talk. He had gone up to his study and she had not been aware of his coming to bed.

"Would you like a coffee?" she asked and pressed the switch on the kettle. The air that day was crisp. Soon the nights would draw in and with it the feeling of enclosure. Once darkness fell it was more difficult to raise oneself from the sofa and be active. Judith loved the long days of summer bringing the garden and house together. This year all the flowers seemed to appear in May so rapidly. She wanted to call stop, wait, I haven't had a chance to appreciate you all. The long lawn was broken with shrubs, walkways and quite areas. It was unusual to have such a secluded garden in suburbia. She had planned it carefully, making sure the plants and shrubs followed each other through the year to provide an altering pattern of colours and shades. Ralph hated gardening. He was obliging and mowed the lawn when necessary. He certainly enjoyed sitting outside but he became irritated by the swiftness of weeds and their eternal reappearance. They had thought of employing a gardener when things had become too hectic for Judith but had found it incredibly difficult to find one. None of the boys were interested now. As children they had their own plots. Judith could not remember whether they had actually grown anything or merely dug deep mud holes for their toys.

She looked out of the window and noticed how bright the geraniums looked against the earthenware pots. The huge cat from two doors away sat, defiant, on their garden table. She had learnt it was pointless to protest. He had won all the battles. She caught his eye and held it. Eventually she looked away. She had succumbed again.

"Yesterday was quite extraordinary" she began. Ralph left a finger to mark his place on the paper and looked up. "I had just left Hugh, we got him a splendid suit by the way, when my mobile rang. It was Edward"

"Edward! I thought he was abroad some where." his face displayed surprise.

"So did I, but he is over here on business. For a few days, he said. It's odd isn't it? We haven't seen him for months."

"I can't remember the last time he came down here. Is everything alright?" He lowered his head to the newspaper.

"He's fine. Looking good. When he discovered I was still in town he offered to take me for an early supper at Simpson's. I knew you wouldn't mind. It was really delicious. He says he may be sent to Australia." Judith knew she was trying very hard to keep the tone in her voice natural and calm. She held the coffee pot tightly for fear her hands might give her away.

"With Polly?" He looked up questioningly.

"Maybe but Edward thinks she might want to stay behind and build up her business. She's doing extremely well at present. New shops opening and more recognition." She passed Ralph his coffee.

"Well, I'm glad we don't have to make decisions like that. All that uprooting and starting again isn't for me. I'd hate to go away on my own for two months, let alone years." He shot her a somewhat sheepish smile and Judith was struck by his boyish expression. She laughed and took her coffee to the table.

"He might call in while he's here. I expect he'll ring." They sat for a while in silence and Ralph returned to the newspaper. Judith looked across at him realising the news held little impact for him as he continued to scan the pages for book reviews. She waited as he read wondering whether to elaborate or leave it there. Sensing her scrutiny he looked up.

"I shall be at the book fayre on Wednesday don't forget." He held the coffee mug to his lips and tentatively sipped, the steam forming beads around his top lip. "My publisher wants me to be seen as much as possible at the moment."

"Will you be doing any book signing?"

"Probably." It was always a boost to the moral having people line up, waiting their turn to ask for some kind of personal note to be added beside his signature. It was quite entertaining and at times surprising. Ralph regretted not making a note of some of the more bizarre requests. He could have used them as conversational pieces.

They both paused and looked at each other as they recognised the sound of the front door lock being opened, followed by three short rings. Peter and Kate. Judith looked at the clock. The morning was racing along and she had done very little. She would have to finish her assessment reports tonight. For a while she would forget work and enjoy the rest of the day.

"Hallo darling" Judith walked towards Peter and hugged him tight. It was always a joy to see him. "Hallo Kate, how are you?" She lent towards her and was pleased to feel the spontaneity in Kate's kiss. We're just having coffee. Would you like one?"

"Hmm, please. Hi Dad."

Ralph stood pushing back his chair and scraped the floor. He smiled at them both as they moved towards him. The boys had always kissed Ralph and Judith was pleased they had not fallen into the habit of shaking hands, as had her own father and brother.

"It was murder getting here," said Kate. "There was a march of sorts and one of the bridges had been closed. We set out really early." She checked the time, "Not too bad."

She began to remove her raincoat. Ralph came forward to collect their clothes and took them to the lobby. Kate stood for a while before Judith signalled for her to be seated.

Peter, feeling very much at home went to the cupboard and took out two mugs as Judith refilled the coffee pot. "We had a great evening last night" he said, "We met up with Harry Sears and his girlfriend."

"Harry from university?" Asked Ralph returning to the kitchen. "Nice chap".

"Yes, he is doing really well. Has a job in marketing. His girlfriend Nicola was there. They're getting married next year."

"In the South of France! A huge affair. Makes ours pale into insignificance". Kate smiled at Peter. "Bit of a hustle getting everyone accommodated in hotels or B&B's."

"At whose expense?" inquired Ralph.

"Theirs, I believe. Her parents are loaded."

The telephone began to ring and both Ralph and Judith moved towards the hall. "I'll get it," said Ralph.

"We have finally settled on the menu," said Kate. She picked up a large soft leather bag and began to delve into its interior. "Peter said to bring it down".

"Oh, good. Do let me see." Judith had heard so much about the plans and knew the effort that had gone into selecting food suitable for a variety of palates.

From the hall came a shout for Hugh. They heard Ralph move to the stairwell and shout again. "Hugh, its Jeff" This time some sort of reply was forthcoming.

"Is Hugh here?" Asked Peter. "He wanted me to help him with something before the end of the month".

"Yes. He's been in bed all morning. Late back last night"

Peter laughed. "I know the feeling."

Ralph returned with a smile on his face. "That was Jeff," he said "for Hugh. He has such a dry sense of humour."

"Well, at least he has the power to raise Hugh," said Judith. All these years of teenage boys had been such a mixture of frustration and pleasure. At weekends one never knew who might be around. Ralph had often exploded with rage in the early hours of the morning when eight or ten youths had returned with either Peter or Douglas "to finish the evening." Total strangers either late at night or early morning frequently passed her on the stairs, a cursory nod acknowledging her presence.

She returned to reading through the menu. It seemed good.

"This all looks perfect" she smiled and handed Kate the paper.

"I think the evening food should be just right too."

Peter interceded and took up the menu. "The caterers wanted us to add all manner of extras but I'm sure this should suit everyone". He was also sure they could not afford any further expense.

The door opened and Hugh entered still filled with sleep, his crumpled T-shirt fell awkwardly above his pants. He went straight to the fridge, paused as he noted Peter and Kate. "Oh, hi, I'd forgotten you were both coming today." He moved across the room and gave Kate a kiss and as he passed Peter gently punched his shoulder. "How you doing?"

"A lot better than you, judging by the look of you." Hugh laughed and returned to the fridge. He stood before the open door. "Any chance of breakfast?"

"We'll be eating in an hour or so. Don't have anything huge" Judith wailed.

"Did anyone stay here last night?" asked Ralph." You must have got back very late. I didn't get to bed until well after two."

"Nobody stayed. I was going to stay with Alex but he had to get up early this morning to go somewhere with his parents." Hugh began to busy himself with his breakfast opening and closing cupboard doors.

Ralph was pleased. He enjoyed the company of his children's friends but it was always so good to have just family around him. He loved Kate, she was different, and looking across at her realized how much a part of the family she had become. She had changed Peter over the past few years and he was far more confident now his future and Kate's were assured. Thinking of the future Ralph felt a sudden rush of panic remembering the book. Tomorrow he would get up very early and stick with it. He thought he had known how the story would unfold but, suddenly, last week he found himself leading the main character into something totally unplanned. He needed time to rethink.

He's lost again, thought Judith as she noted Ralph fall into a hypnotic stare. If only he would talk about his work as he talked about his research. He would never allow her to read his fiction until it reached publication. It had developed into a kind of superstition that she supposed she could understand some writers read their work to their wives in daily instalments but Ralph had never wanted to.

They all began talking of mutual friends as Judith busied herself with lunch. Douglas had said he would be down a little later but definitely to eat. Hugh, who, having burnt his toast, picked up the pieces of blackened bread and began to scrape them slowly with a knife into the sink, suddenly shattered the ambiance. Judith remonstrated with him loudly.

"For heavens sake Hugh don't scrape it here. Throw it away for goodness sake. You've made everything stink of burnt toast. Open the kitchen door and let the smoke out into the garden. Why on earth do you have to turn the toaster up so high? It always burns you must know that by now!"

Peter began to sing "Gee, but it's great to be back home" as he was reintroduced into the chaos of life with Hugh.

Ralph looked across to him and laughed. "You were the one that got away." He stood by the kitchen door to breathe in the fresh air and was aware of the song of the blackbird sitting not two feet away. Even through the chaos there was calm.

As the morning progressed they sat together to finalize the wedding arrangements. The table was spread with brochures and papers as lists were made. The numbers had grown to a frightening size but as each guest came up for elimination there was inevitably a reason why they should remain. Peter seemed amazingly relaxed about the whole thing. He and Kate constantly reassuring each other. As they moved and shuffled the papers Ralph looked at Kate respectful of her youth and beauty. They would make a striking couple on the day. He hoped these plans, so carefully made, would all contribute toward making the wedding a hugely successful event. They certainly deserved it to be special.

Lunch was ready and, as usual, Douglas was late. Judith knew he had spent yesterday meeting somebody. He may well have returned late and maybe, this morning, overslept. She was aware he and Patrick travelled a lot looking for oak all over the countryside. They were still at the stage when they could not afford to turn anything down. It had been very difficult for them both as they struggled to start their business. Initially Judith and Ralph had helped financially to get things moving but over the last few months they had a run of orders and were now busy. She and Ralph were proud that both Douglas and Peter had decided to go it alone. Peter's own advertising studio had started with nothing but his reputation from his first job had followed him. He now employed several people and his future was looking bright. Peter and Douglas had displayed high levels of motivation and commitment, unafraid of long hours at work. Hugh, as yet, was an unknown. But he too possessed great confidence. They suspected there was a competitive spirit between the three of them, unspoken but present, which fuelled their ambitions but did not in any way sour their relationships.

As Ralph was opening the wine for lunch the doorbell rang. A lengthy ring. Hugh, who was now respectably showered and dressed, went to the door. There were shouts and scuffles as mock boxing took place between Hugh and the newly arrived Douglas. They came, laughing, into the dining room, Douglas filling the room with his size and smiling happily at them all. His blue eyes settled on each of the occupants with a loving gaze resting finally on his mother whom he bent to kiss. She squeezed his hands and he flinched. Judith lifted them together and saw a deep graze across the knuckle of his right hand.

"Douglas, what happened here?" She cried with some concern.

He brushed the graze lightly with his left hand "It's getting better now but God did it hurt. Patrick and I were taking an old oak beam through a doorway last night when Pat slipped on some old roof tiles. I swung to one side to keep my balance and grazed my hand against the old lock on the door. I thought I might have to get it stitched but it seems to be healing. I'm fine." He looked around the table "Where shall I sit Mum, I'm ravenous. There wasn't time for breakfast." Ralph held up a wine glass "Yes, please."

He sat between Hugh and Kate, pulling his chair close. Although Douglas had not lived in the house for several years he still referred to it as "home". As soon as he walked through the door he was enveloped in his past. The house had scarcely altered since his departure, the odd change of colour scheme in some rooms, a new piece of furniture, but in general he could return to his roots and feel the rich, brown earthy nutrients of family life.

The table was filled with vegetable dishes, roast beef, gravy and horseradish, Yorkshire pudding. Judith passed the dishes around and was pleased to see that Ralph, at last, was looking content. The boys always managed to enliven him and he so enjoyed their quick banter. Hugh, too, could certainly hold his own. There was a considerable amount of general catching up on mutual acquaintances and the conversation gathered pace. For Judith and Ralph, this was an opportunity to learn a little more about their children's lives as now they no longer lived under the same roof things could happen and they would not know. It was also an occasion for their sons to confess to small, or sometimes not so small, misdemeanours in their past feeling bold now that the passage of time had reduced all worries of recrimination safely outside the perimeters of parental judgement. Had Judith and Ralph been aware of these actions at the time, they might have been alarmed but now, amidst the banter of the Sunday dinner table, the news could be accepted and passed off as a stage in their development.

The sun suddenly broke through the clouds and shone into Judith eyes. She moved her chair and helped herself to potatoes, gesturing to them all for another helping. As she lent across to pass to Kate she was jolted back into the conversation hearing Douglas mention the name Polly.

"We will probably go down there and work on the premises. Patrick is keen and the money should make it very worthwhile." He concluded excitedly as he helped himself to the last of the vegetables.

Ralph placed his knife and fork down and lent back in his chair "When did all this happen?" He was somewhat bemused by the project.

"Polly rang me last Tuesday, or Wednesday, can't remember which, and told me she and her partner were opening a new boutique in Southern Spain. She'd heard we worked in old oak and wanted some sort of design drawn up for the new premises. She called into the workshop actually to have a look at the work we do. I'm meeting her next week to discuss in more detail but if we think we can do it we could move right away. Patrick says after this present order there is nothing too pressing. At the moment we've plenty of stock." His eyes were full of expectant hope. "This account could make us. We've built the business to this level and we're now ready to accept something more challenging to push the boundaries up a notch or two."

"Polly? Polly has been to see you?" Judith tried to keep the surprise from her voice. Edward had not mentioned Polly seeing Douglas.

"Yes, mum. It's not all settled yet. She said they would be discussing it."

He looked around the table for the wine, lifted the bottle and asked, with his eyes, if she wanted more.

"No, thank you. They? Who they?" She was aware of asking a little too rapidly as five sets of eyes focussed, with a degree of surprise, upon her face.

"Polly and her partner. Why?" His blue eyes shot a quizzical look at his mother who busied herself with her table napkin, wiping her mouth, preparing to answer but Ralph intervened.

"Your mother saw Edward yesterday. Did he mention any of this to you Judith?"

"No. He said she was opening a new place in Spain. That's all" Judith hoped she was expressing the correct amount of interest as her mind formed questions that she knew she could not ask.

Kate put down her knife and fork and addressed the table "She has such lovely clothes in her boutique. I'm surprised she hasn't thought of opening one here. Peter and I went to one of her French branches. There were some lovely things but very expensive." She looked to Peter for confirmation.

"Kate looked good in everything she tried on. Pity was Polly wasn't there to let us have them at cost price. Perhaps next time Kate?" Peter laughed and lent across to touch her hand "when we make our fortune."

"I'm going to be the first millionaire in this family." Their gazes fell on Hugh. "Alex and I are working on a piece of software." This comment was delivered so positively that for a few seconds everyone was silent. Judith could not help but wonder if this was the reason he had done so little work over the past few months. She was about to comment but thought better of it.

"Well, you better keep it under wraps. Don't reveal any secrets to anyone. They may take the idea" Ralph surprisingly spoke this with conviction. Years ago he had written a short story that was later plagiarized by a so-called friend on the radio. Subtle differences here and there made accusations difficult and it had rankled for years.

"Were you surprised to hear from Polly, Douglas?" Judith felt compelled to enquire. She did not want the conversation to alter direction just yet.

"Very. I can't remember the last time I saw her."

"One of Mum's or Dad's celebrations. Birthdays or anniversaries probably" said Hugh. "I remember she didn't stay long at your last do"

"We saw both, Polly and Edward, together a few years ago. They had just bought a place in Italy. Your mother and I stayed close by for several days." Ralph recollected the time very well. The heat had been stultifying. Polly and Edward were keen to show them the new villa having just completed the furnishings. The surrounding landscape was spectacular with tall Cyprus trees and vineyards that ran down the hillside towards a wide river. The local town in the distance sat huddled on the other side like a sleeping dog curled within its basket. The heat shimmered through the air breaking the outline of the vines into fragmented segments of greens and browns. It was like a living canvas whose brush strokes were constantly being reinvented as the sun rose and set throughout the day. In the afternoon Judith and Edward had gone to look at some architectural wonder leaving Polly and Ralph for a while. She had been very enjoyable company. He smiled to himself as he remembered the vast quantity of wine they had consumed. They may well have been slightly drunk when Judith and Edward returned. It was a good time.

"I've yet to meet them both" said Kate "Peter says they are likely to be at the wedding."

"That's why Patrick and I have got to make a decision on this quickly. I can't be away for the great day. The first of my brothers to wed. Family history being made, I couldn't and wouldn't miss it for the world" Douglas said this with great emphasis draining his glass in a gesture of mock toasting.

Judith stood and began to clear the dishes. Ralph stacked the plates and passed them across a table that was now strewn with empty dishes

"Do you need any help Mum?" Peter moved as though to stand. In his position as non-resident son he felt obliged to offer but hoped the answer would be negative. It was so good to be with his brothers, sitting round the table and enjoying the conversation. It was not always easy for the three of them to get together. He had not realised at the time of leaving home that the facility of being together everyday was lost. Like leaving school, having his friends around constantly was very short lived and never appreciated. It was only when he tried to gather the old group together he realised how difficult it was for everyone to be available on the same day.

"No, no, I'm fine. Stay there." She carried the plates to the kitchen and began to place the desert on to a large wooden tray. Why did she feel uneasy about Polly contacting Douglas? It was most unlike her. Polly had not seen the pieces of furniture Douglas had made or his designs. He had never, as far as she knew, fitted out a shop of any kind. Polly wasn't the type to take risks. Why hadn't she told Edward? Judith was pleased for Douglas of course and it would be a huge boost to his career but she could not dispel a slight feeling of unease as she busied herself and fought the temptation to phone Edward as soon as the opportunity arose.

On her return the topic of conversation had changed. Ralph was informing Kate how Peter, as a small boy, refused to accompany him on a fishing trip to Scotland because he could not bear the thought of killing the fish. Kate always enjoyed discovering a little more of Peter's history when she was visiting and Ralph welcomed a chance to reminisce.

There was a lot of laughter and further talk that became more serious as coffee was served. Eventually the need to move and stretch their legs drew them to the sitting room where newspapers were spread across the floor. Kate took the review section and curled onto the sofa. Hugh decided the time was right to visit a friend and Douglas fell asleep. Judith and Ralph invited Peter to walk in the garden to see the new area of shrubs that had recently been planted.

The air had a slight chill causing Judith to shiver. Above them a plane was gaining height. The sound of its engine brought her a momentary feeling of excitement. Where was its destination? She pictured the passengers, locked into their seats, the stewards enjoying a brief moment of rest before the endless round of meals and duty-free. "Have you booked your flights yet Peter?" she asked.

"Yes, I did it on Friday. We should arrive in Istanbul at around seven in the evening. It will give us a chance to sleep in after the wedding. We'll have four nights there, then down the coast for the remaining ten days." Peter paused beside the cherry tree and turned back to look at the house. "Kate doesn't know yet but I booked us into a wonderfully secluded hotel right on the hillside overlooking the beach. She thinks we're staying in the town."

Ralph grinned at him and continued to walk ahead. "It should be wonderful" he was delighted to hear this. Peter did not always reveal his emotions. Including them in his conspiracy caused a warm rush of filial love. "You both seem very relaxed and happy at the moment"

"We are, dad."

Judith placed her arms through both men and pulled them toward her. She felt happy. Some children in a distant garden were laughing and calling to each other. She wondered if Peter and Kate would want children early in their marriage. The idea of grandchildren was immensely seductive. She and Ralph had waited four years before having Peter. Perhaps another four years, then?

"The garden is looking great Mum. I like the colours of the shrubs here against the yellow brick."

"I think I've finally reached the end of the landscaping. I still hanker for another water feature but it involves too much digging and your father has neither the time nor the inclination."

"It all looks right now to me." replied Ralph defensively. "You need time to sit and enjoy it."

"You're probably speaking the truth, but I will still keep it in mind"

They stood for a while close together and watched the fish swim in the pond. Here and there tiny newts swam to the surface using their tiny hands to force them up for air. The dark, clear water had a mesmerizing effect upon them as their eyes refocused to distant vision.

In the silence Ralph's thoughts turned to his novel. He knew he would have to sweat this one out. The blank page could be both terrifying and exciting. At times words would spill out causing sentences to fall upon each other in rapid succession but, as with a full jug that inevitability becomes empty, his head became depleted of vocabulary leaving him to sit staring at the keys of his computer.

Having the family here today gave him a genuine excuse to leave his room but tomorrow he would shut himself away.

Peter looked at the back of the house remembering how he and Douglas used to fight in the garden with broom poles. They had saved their pocket money for weeks to buy them. Some TV programme had prompted it. His thumb had taken quite a crack. They had spent many hours at play in this garden. Then it had been laid out differently. Much more lawn but still quite a few good hiding areas. When they had first moved into the house Peter was old enough to remember the enormous bonfires they had burning all the old linoleum left by the previous occupants. The thick black acrid smoke had risen high into the air carrying with it the claims of the last inhabitants. Those raging flames that stretched and bent against the wind would not be allowed today. He raised his head, almost expecting to see the flat black particles of burnt lino that colonized the garden for weeks fluttering from bush to bush, and noticed the light in the sitting room had been turned on. Kate was still on the sofa reading the paper. Would they, he wondered still be together in twenty years? The majority of his friends' parents had divorced. Judith and Ralph were very much in the minority. The idea of them separating brought with it such a sudden flash of pain; he was amazed by its intensity. Even though he was an adult and totally self-supporting he still needed the reassurance of their being together. He and Kate were very sure of each other and he knew he loved her. There should be no reason why they could not remain content with each other's company as his parents had for all these years. She looked up and waved to him. He unlocked his arms from his mother and waved back.

Peter's movement caused them all to stir and they made their way inside. Time for a cup of tea, thought Ralph, and time, still, to continue catching up on his children's life.

Later that evening as they were all leaving Judith reached up to kiss Douglas goodbye. "Do let us know the outcome of your meeting with Polly."

"Yes, of course I will. I'll give you a ring once I know something."

She and Ralph stood at the door and watched them drive away. It was dark now and the streetlights threw a yellowish circle across the front lawn. The houses opposite were similar in design, large, double fronted with ornate wrought iron around the windows. They were good, solid, family homes built at the end of the nineteenth century at a time when a bedroom housed a fireplace with plenty of room for a double bed and furniture. There was space to walk around. One of the reasons they had remained in the house for so long was the inability to find other houses that could match bedrooms of this size, their boiler room being larger than many they had seen. As they waved a car drove by momentarily blocking their view of Peter and Kate. Douglas followed behind in his very old Mercedes estate; its diesel engine dry and rasping for a while until it took control and roared with satisfaction.

At the end of the day, as they lay in bed reading, Judith allowed her thoughts to return to Polly. Who had told her about Douglas? Of course Polly knew he was involved in making furniture, but he was still relatively unknown. Had she mentioned it to Edward when they were at the conference? She didn't remember. Perhaps she had. Polly was always so cautious and exact. Could Douglas and Patrick work with her? Douglas seemed confident enough. It was just so unexpected. Somehow having one of her own children working with a contemporary of hers seemed to rock her timescale. Generations became squeezed into straight lines. Edward would probably think little of it but nevertheless it was odd he had not thought to tell her yesterday. Surely Polly would have wanted to discuss it with him? The thought of Edward raised the question of Australia. She had looked on the Internet for information. It was an amazing country and under any other circumstance she would like to see it for herself. How could she reconcile the huge distance that would be placed between them? A rush of wild, mad panic coursed through her as the words in her book began to form one large greying mist of print.

Ralph turned down the page and reached for the light. "Don't feel you have to stop." he said and settled himself into his sleeping position. Bed was a delightful place to be these days. As he stretched and turned his neck into the pillow he said to Judith "I love you".

RALPH — THE PAST

Ralph lay on his back against the wooden floor. He had succumbed to the hum in his head. The delicious dip into the unconscious had become part of his working day. He thought of his father who used to doze behind the newspaper, ashamed to admit tiredness. Ridiculous. Judith could never understand how he could sleep anywhere. Like Churchill, just a few brief moments could refresh him for the rest of the day. He had even slept on the crook of his arm, balanced on a narrow wall. He had sat at his desk for three hours this morning and written nothing. He could not even remember what had occupied his thoughts. It wasn't depression. There were a great many things for which he was grateful. It was more a kind of inertia. He wanted to be pulled along. There was no impetus for him to push. He'd felt Judith was somewhat preoccupied at present and even she hadn't the usual energy to spur him on. Perhaps he should go away for a few days. He could go to the book fayre for an ego boost and then continue north to Edinburgh, take in some culture and try a little solitude. His family was vital to him but sometimes separating himself from them exaggerated how important they were and refuelled his powers of creativity. He was so desperate to get back and immerse himself in all that was familiar that work became much easier. The warm September sun fell across his face reminding him of hot, continental days. One year Judith and the boys had gone to Italy. They had camped in a small seaside town close to Venice. A hugely energetic young German couple had befriended the boys and taken them to swim. It was only hours later, when they went to find them, they realized the sea was awash with sewage and that their stomachs were already alive with bacteria Later that evening they begun to vomit and were ill for the rest of the night. Poor Hugh continued to be dreadfully sick for days and they cut short their holidays fearing for his safety. Their holidays were always eventful and often exhausting but the chief joy was being together for a long stretch of time, particularly when the boys were in their early teens. They had spent many very happy times and the mishaps had provided them all with amusing anecdotes for friends. He suffered the discomfort of campsites for the sake of the children and, he could not deny for economic reasons but as a child Ralph had often gone away with his wealthy grandparents who indulged him and taught him to enjoy comfort and service. After that being on a campsite could never quite measure up.

A strange man wearing a large green hat suddenly walked across his mind. He was showing him something. He moved closer. It was a large basket of aubergines. Ralph marvelled at the purple, shining, objects and reached forward to take one. As he moved the man with the basket stepped back and pressed a button on the cuff of his sleeve. A bell began to ring intermittently. Ralph was aware of the ringing and then it ceased. The air in his study now resounded with rhythmic breathing as he descended into a deeper level of sleep. Fifteen minutes later he was roused by a knock on the door and glanced up to see Judith enter with a mug of tea in her hand. He focussed on her face and felt his mind reorganising into wakefulness.

"Were shall I put this?" she asked. She was dismayed to find him lying on the floor obviously asleep. She had imagined he was hard at work.

He raised himself, with some difficulty, into a standing position and took the steaming mug carefully from her hand. "Thanks." He averted his eyes knowing they would be filled with the telltale signs of sleep.

"Edward rang a few moments ago. I'm surprised you didn't hear the bell. He planned to come down on Wednesday to see us but I told him you would be at the book fayre. I have the afternoon free though and he wondered if I might like to go to the cinema or something. What do you think?" She looked across at Ralph as he placed his tea beside the computer keyboard.

"Well, I certainly won't be able to get back and I doubt Hugh will mind getting something for himself. It's always the way, isn't it? You can go for days with few engagements, then up come two on the same day. I'll be sorry to have missed him. Will Polly be with him do you think? She's over here too, isn't she?"

"I really don't know. I know she's meeting Douglas some time but whether she's staying on with Edward for a few days, I'm not sure". Why had she said that? She knew Polly was around. Edward had just told her but he had not mentioned anything concerning her intention to employ Douglas and Patrick if she found their work satisfactory. Judith had decided to say nothing at present. Perhaps Polly wanted to keep it to herself for a while. Until Douglas confirmed she would not bring the subject up unless Edward did.

"I know she's very busy organising her new venture. Edward said he'd scarcely seen her He'd also said he'd been amazed to see her on Sunday. He thought she was in Italy with Rebecca interviewing staff". She had barely mentioned her plans, rushing here and there and

Edward said he had little time to spend with her. He rarely involved himself in her business ventures anyway only occasionally helping with setting up the accounts. He knew Polly and Rebecca were both very capable business- women. Their independence relieved him of any responsibility and he had no desire to participate.

"He did mentioned Polly had arrived with an armful of clothing from some young designer they were hoping to promote."

Polly was the kind of woman who was prepared to sponsor new ideas, Judith thought, while Rebecca was more cautious. Edward had mentioned Polly's heightened enthusiasm about the Spanish boutique and must have persuaded Rebecca to help her look into it.

Ralph sat at his desk and swung his chair to face her. "Well, whatever the case, I can't cancel. You'll have to go for the pair of us. As a matter of fact, I was wondering about having a few days out myself. I'll be halfway to the north on Wednesday evening. I could just as easily continue on and spend a couple of days in Edinburgh. Would you be happy with that?"

She could hardly believe the timing of such a trip. She recognised his restless state but never imagined he would want to go away. She knew he was struggling and was overcome with guilt and love.

"That's fine by me, Ralph but are you sure you want to be away? I have a pretty full day on Thursday and Friday. Hugh will be out with the CCF on Thursday evening, so you wouldn't have had a great deal of company but," she paused "Where will you stay?"

"I thought in that small hotel by the station. They know me and I can leave the car there and everything is within walking distance. A brisk walk to the top of Arthur's seat should help aerate the mind." He took a large gulp of tea from the mug swallowing loudly.

"You haven't had time out for quite some time. It should be fun. Will you call in on anybody on the way?"

"No, a few days alone should set me up" He reassured her but felt anything but reassured himself. He knew he would not enjoy being on his own after the first night. Try as he might he could not find comfort in his own company. He was ashamed of this weakness and continually pushed himself into situations demanding his absence from home, He supposed his childhood growing up with two very protective sisters and never spending time alone until he went to university probably turned him into something of a home lover. He liked nothing better than to lie in bed and hear the sound of his family around him.

Judith glanced at the computer screen. "Are you still having problems?" She endeavoured to keep the note of anxiety from her voice. She could not recollect such a lengthy bout of inactivity on his part. Even his room held an inert, heavy atmosphere. Perhaps the introduction of the outside air might stimulate she thought, as she moved to the window and threw wide the catch.

"Yes, there's nothing there at present. I need a kick start from somewhere." Ralph cupped his hands around his mug of tea taking comfort from the heat as a waft of cool air blew across his shoulders. He moved to his desk and sat down placing the tea on a pile of papers, a pile that had not grown in height for many days.

"Will the publishers give you more time?"

"Probably not but I'm not going to panic yet." This was true. He would not. Somehow he would regain the impetus.

The telephone began to ring. They looked across at each other wondering who might make the first move. "I'll go" said Judith and left him swinging his chair from side to side.

She ran down the stairs with the picture of the empty computer screen on her mind. She wished she could help. Ralph had experienced blocks before and as suddenly as they came, they went. He said he had an idea when she came back from the conference but that seemed to have been rejected. She would offer to talk through some ideas later in the day even though he preferred to hold back discussions until the work was complete. It was worth suggesting. As she reached the phone it stopped ringing. "Damn!" she cried and pressed the "yes button" "Hallo, hallo" her voice came over the answer machine. "Don't hang up" It was one of her friends inviting them to supper later in the month. She gathered the calendar and pen and began running through the engagements. Judith always felt embarrassed as dates were suggested and then rejected because of a prior commitment. She and Ralph had weekends they tried to keep free. The pleasure of sitting in front of the television on a Saturday, tray on lap and a chosen video was delightful. Or, as this Sunday, have just the family. Having managed to select a date, mid week, which she hated, the early morning start next day hanging over her mind; she fell into an easy conversation. Her friend, Susan, had a sharp wit that Judith enjoyed. They might mention a word which then took on an amusing significance only they appreciated and laugh spontaneously or enjoy each other's descriptions of recent events. She placed the telephone back in its hold still smiling.

She had finished work early today and brought home several assessments to write up. Fortunately, they followed a basic pattern and certain areas applied for any child. All that was required of her was to insert names or scores. The difficult part was working out the best way forward. It was all very well to say a child needed specialist, one to one, tuition. Getting it was far more difficult. Half of her work was with a private practice. The children she saw there were the lucky ones. Their parents were keen for practical help as soon as a diagnosis was made. They could afford to engage specialist's teachers or even pay the enormous fees charged by an independent school able to provide this help. The poor children in the State sector had to battle through the process of "statementing" and even then only get a meagre amount of teaching time per week allocated to their needs. Money should be poured into schools by the bucket load. She was grateful they had only Hugh to educate now. They had been able to afford school fees, the alternative being pretty dire. Both, she and Ralph, pitied young parents with children who had no chance of choice. It was what was in the catchment area and no alternative.

Judith picked up her mug of tea, which had gone cold, and poured it down the sink. She re-filled the kettle and stood waiting as it boiled. The clock ticked rhythmically against a low background hum of London traffic. Their next- door neighbour banged shut his side door. The sun suddenly reappeared from behind a cloud flooding the kitchen with light.

Judith felt uneasy. She experienced a sensation from time to time that would wrap itself around her shutting out the many positive things in her life to leave her with an unwanted feeling of fear. The image of herself falling into some huge gaping fissure in the earth would sometimes project itself before her eyes and the sensation of a tremor beneath her feet prompted her to check the floor for cracks. The kettle clicked off to break the spell and she set about making a fresh cup of tea helping to rid her of the sensation. She scooped a handful of nuts from the tin and began to eat them noisily. Almonds, somebody had once said, contained some vitamin that was enormously beneficial and relaxing. She and Ralph had taken them on board and had a tin full at the ready. As a child Judith had been fascinated by the soft green, velvet almonds, which grew on a tree at the corner of her road. The blossom in spring formed a cloudy mass of papery pink flowers that transformed the view and heralded the confirmation that the grey damp days would soon be gone. As the year progressed, the nuts would form. She and her friends would sneak along the garden wall to steal them from the tree, running as fast as they could to hide somewhere out of sight. Their teeth would bite into the outer green casing and become incredibly dry. It was virtually impossible to break through and even more impossible to obtain the inner nut. At Christmas time her parents had a large bowl of nuts for after dinner eating, the almonds, however, were the last to go, standing no chance beside the walnuts and brazils.

The front door opened and Hugh was heard throwing his hefty school bag onto the floor before pushing wide the kitchen door.

"Hallo, darling. Had a good day?" Hugh brought with him such an abundance of energy altering her mood in an instance. His smile, strangely tilted to the left, was infectious and engaging. This he knew and used it to good effect.

"Yeh, not bad, not bad at all. I did rather well with my French essay." He walked to the sink collecting a glass on the way and poured himself some water which he drunk in noisy gulps.

"I've just made tea, would you like a cup?" It amused her to see him behaving as though he had just returned from the desert.

"No, no thanks." He refilled the glass to drink again. "I needed that! Will you be busy tonight Mum?" He let out a gasp of breath before drinking again from the heavy pint glass.

"Fairly, I've a couple of reports to finish, recommendations, why?"

"I've got to get my UCAS forms sorted. Do you think you could give us a hand? I've virtually decided on what to put but I'd really like you to read it through with me." He walked across to the bread bin and removed four slices of bread.

"Oh Hugh", Judith cried anxiously "Don't eat too much now. Your supper will be earlier tonight."

"That's ok" He stood before the open fridge, selecting. "Will you have time?" He helped himself to the ham and balanced a large piece of cheese on top.

"Probably. If you draft it out. Fill everything in pencil and then we can go through the lot. Have you made a final decision yet?" Judith knew he had been deliberating, spending time pouring over each University prospectus fluctuating between enthusiasm and despair.

"Probably Leeds. Though quite a few are going for Edinburgh or Bristol. I know a lot of people in Leeds." He carried everything to the table and began making his sandwich. "Pass me the pickle, please, Mum"

"Are you going to go to some of the Open Days?"

Judith found herself searching for the pickle jar and placing the butter before him. The table was already covered in crumbs. She went to the sink for the sponge and gently wiped around the food gathering them up in her hands to throw in the bin.

"Yeh. They've given us a list of dates. I'll need quite a bit of cash for the train fare. It'll be worth my while getting a student rail card." He pressed the enormous sandwich down with his hand before taking a bite. "Can you buy some more pastrami when you do the shopping?"

"Please"

"Please! God, we had such a row in the lunch queue today. Younger boys, pushing and shoving. I sent two of them to the back and they refused to go. Luckily two of us were on duty so we used a bit of force. I loathe lunch duty." He ate with such ferocity. His appetite was insatiable these days. His growing body constantly demanding fuel.

"I hope you weren't physical!" Judith cried with some alarm. She pictured the smaller boys compared to Hugh. To them he was a grown man.

"No, of course not. We just stood about an inch away from them and were persistent in our demands".

Judith automatically began to wipe the table once more and went to find a plate for the remaining sandwiches. "Your father may go away for a few days on Wednesday. What are your plans for the week?" She held him by the shoulders and guided him to a chair. "Sit down while you're eating for heavens sake".

Hugh lowered himself onto the seat and began on the next round of bread. "CCF on Thursday night, Wednesday I may stay late for band practice. Alex will probably want me to go back with him afterwards, if that's ok. Friday, we're all meeting up for Giles' eighteenth party". He chewed hard on the last mouthful and drank the remaining water from his glass before bringing his eyes to rest on Judith's aware of the recriminating look they might hold "I know, when am I going to do any work? I've got several frees over the next few days and I'll go to the library and work through the lunch hour. It's this UCAS form that's urgent". He lifted his plate and glass and walked to the sink. "I've been thinking about it a lot, so it shouldn't take too long. I have to make myself sound worth having. So that makes it pretty easy." He grinned widely at Judith and gave her an affectionate hug.

"Give me a couple of hours and I'll be free." She kissed his cheek and made her way to the study, stepping over Hugh's ample bag as she went. The weight he carried to and fro each day was ridiculous. They all seemed to do it. On music days he could scarcely get outside the door. Lord knows what it was doing to his shoulder blades.

Taking out her reports she began methodically to read the notes. This poor child had been at a school that would not accept he had difficulties. Give him time they had told his parents. Time, she knew, was of the essence and she remembered the look of relief that had passed across their faces when she had informed them of his dyslexia.

At last they had a reason and at last the child could see it was not his fault, neither was he a dullard. Fortunately, he was seven and with the right tuition could be taught the correct strategies to help him cope. She wrote down the recommendations checking his scores once more.

Looking from her window she watched one of her neighbours walk along the road. He had a long easy gait and Judith was reminded of Douglas. He had not rung yet. Had the meeting with Polly been cancelled or might it not yet have taken place? She was aching to know but could not bring herself to phone. She wondered once more why Edward had not mentioned Polly. The trouble was there was nobody she could confide her fears to as she had actively decided not to involve even her closest friends in her relationship with him She felt it would demean Ralph and her desire to protect him from gossip strengthened her resolve. Maybe, if she rang Peter he might have something to report. She had to prepare supper soon and a break now would be appropriate.

Kate answered. Peter was working late today and would not be back until nine-ish. Kate had just heard of a possible job vacancy coming up and thought she would apply. It would mean an increase in salary and the firm of architects were beginning to make a name. It had been a long haul gaining her degree and she certainly deserved success.

"Any word from Douglas?" asked Judith casually.

"No. He may have phoned Peter but I haven't spoken to him today."

"No matter. Love to Peter. Bye"

Judith looked at the receiver. She was desperate not to appear intrusive. Douglas would want to tell her but he would have no idea how impatient she was to know. If he had been a daughter, she would have been in contact as soon as the meeting was over. Her fingers pressed the button and just as she began to dial she heard Hugh. He was on the phone and she would have to wait.

Returning to her study she glanced at the photograph of Ralph. He was then in his early thirties looking very like he looked today. She felt a rush of love for him. He was such a good man. All they had shared together so inextricably linked their lives. How could she contemplate losing all that? They were both so pleased Peter and Kate had decided to marry. Ralph adored Kate and it was a novel experience for them both to be in the company of a young woman. Ralph hugely enjoyed meeting current girl friends of all the boys but when Kate arrived they both knew she was somewhat special.

The coming wedding had galvanized them all in different ways. For Judith and Ralph it had brought delight and importantly, a future daughter in law, but it had also set the timer for their own mortality. This would be the start of a new stage in their lives and within a few years their home would house only the two of them. It had brought them up short. The value of time and its use took on a new meaning. She and Ralph had discussed this the evening Peter had announced his intention to marry Kate. The oncoming years would be different and important and they would have to spend them wisely. The frightening manner in which the years had passed with such rapidity drew them to a mutual conclusion. If there were dreams they could fulfil they were to follow them. If they recognised a yawning gap in their development, they must fill it. They must not be left with a series of regrets for it was important to be able to look back on their lives with satisfaction. They acknowledged the need to diverge on occasion might arise but the notion of sexual diversion did not enter the discussion. Judith knew it was an area that still remained taboo and, as far as Ralph was concerned, would never enter his mind. They would follow their interests and if it took one off or away for a while this would be acceptable. Before this if Ralph had expressed a wish to spend a few days alone in Edinburgh she might have felt a little slighted but now she understood his need and knew his need would always bring him home. Her needs however would never be understood. It was not acceptable to love two men.

Judith heard Hugh laugh. He was still on the telephone and her work was not yet complete. She must wait.

DOUGLAS

The pavements were wet and shiny and Douglas took care not to step into the large puddles that had formed so rapidly. As he walked he could see into the windows of the shops and offices. They were alight with electricity and a yellow glow penetrated the rain. He was very aware of his own apprehension. He knew this meeting with Polly was to involve discussion concerning the future project but he also knew it might involve more. Why had she not invited Patrick? He felt somewhat ashamed of the care he had taken that morning in choosing his clothes. The dark shirt and tie, the jacket he had recently purchased. He was, after all, going to meet her in a rather swish hotel. This justification was weak, he knew. Patrick found the whole thing amusing but was also somewhat wary, warning of mixing business with pleasure. This idea seemed preposterous when Douglas reminded himself of the relationship between Polly and his family. In her eyes he was probably still the small boy she had bought sweets for one summer. She and Edward had no children of their own and they had looked upon Peter, Hugh and himself as close relatives.

A bus passed and shot water from the curb into a splintered water cascade. He jumped aside automatically and in doing so stepped into a deep puddle. He could feel the water ooze into his shoe and he cursed. He had almost reached the entrance to the hotel, there was little he could do but squelch his way forward. Polly had instructed him to go to the reception desk and announce his arrival. He checked his watch; it was one minute to twelve. He was on time.

The foyer was very quiet. A single gentleman was sitting with hands on his knees staring out into the rain. He had an empty coffee cup before him on a small, highly polished, table. Douglas could not help looking at the joinery and thinking how much better one of his own tables would look in that corner. The lift door opened and a couple with a child walked toward the reception. Douglas waited as they made enquiries as to the location of the "British Museum". Best place to go on a day like this. His parents had often taken them all on wet Sundays to wander around. His first visit was in a pushchair and he had screamed with delight as they entered the large hall containing sculptures. Any museum now would give him a frisson of pleasure as he entered the doors knowing so much was there to see. He approached the desk and smiled at the receptionist.

"Could you inform Mrs. Polly Ashton, Douglas Farrington is here, please?" His voice echoed in his ears disconcertingly.

The receptionist turned to the computer and typed in Polly's name. He was smartly dressed in a dark suit that sat around his shoulders. His tie was very flamboyant in bright greens and blues setting off the pale blue shirt. Gold cufflinks showed beneath his sleeve, and Douglas noticed how pale his wrists were. He pressed the buttons on the internal phone and glanced at his watch.

"Good afternoon, Mrs. Ashton. A Mr. Douglas Farrington is here in reception."

Douglas could hear Polly's voice in the background and heard her request he be sent up right away. He had not really wanted that. He had hoped she would have been waiting for him in the foyer and they could then have gone straight out to lunch.

"Mrs. Ashton says to go up Sir, room 242."

"Thank you." Douglas turned toward the lift. The man with the coffee cup stood and glanced toward him. "Terrible day", he said and shook his head.

"Yes." replied Douglas somewhat lamely and was reminded of his soaking wet foot. He pressed the button for the lift. It was very quiet in the foyer, almost churchlike. The air was warm and held the faint perfume from the flowers that were placed in elaborate arrangements all around. There was something very attractive about hotel life. He adored all the little freebies left in the bathroom, especially in one hotel in which he had stayed where they had provided toothbrushes, paste, razors and shaving cream in a sealed pack. There was always the urge to take them home rather than use them. He had managed to leave with four such packs after his stay and had found them of enormous use when he went away for the odd night.

The lift made a whirring sound throwing open its doors. It was empty. Douglas stepped in and pressed 2. As the lift rose he could not avoid looking at himself from all angles in the mirrored walls. He brushed his hand across his chin checking for smoothness and bared his teeth. His hair was thick and wiry standing in awkward clumps. As a child he had been blond but now his hair had turned light brown. His girlfriends were always surprised when they saw photographs of him as a child. A few years ago he had dyed it white blond, and been greatly admired, but he grew tired of the frequent visits to the barbers and had grown it out. He noticed the dampness of his clothing but there was little he could do. The sleeves of his jacket were creased and would have to remain that way. Inside the lift were menus advertising two restaurants. The prices were pretty pricey he thought. There were also two bars. Maybe Polly would want to stop there. As the lift bounced to a halt he looked back into the mirror for a final check on his appearance before stepping out into the long silent corridor.

Room 242 was to the left. He knocked and waited. Polly threw open the door and held wide her arms.

"Douglas, do come in." She stood on tiptoe to kiss him and again avoided his cheeks. It was a brief kiss but his mouth held the sensation. She seemed even shorter here in the room and taking him by the hand led him to a small sofa. He was impressed to find Polly had a suite. There was a door to the right that was slightly ajar and he could just define the end of a large double bed covered in a heavy linen, deep blue counterpane and averted his eyes rather rapidly. The room in which he stood was furnished tastefully with matching furniture. Beneath the window was a small kneehole desk upon which Polly had placed a reading book. The atmosphere was cool and opulent.

"You are very wet Douglas." she said as he sat and ran her hand across the top of his hair and shoulders. "What a miserable day. Would you like to dry your jacket on the radiator?" She laughed. "Don't look so frightened. You have a very attractive shirt beneath."

Her infectious laughter helped him relax somewhat but he hated himself for having made so gauche an entry He stood rapidly noticing the damp imprint of his trousers and removed his jacket, shaking the drips onto the pale carpet. Polly laughed again and jumped clear of the spray. Douglas apologized as she took it from him to drape carefully across the radiator. She rubbed her hands together in a drying action and walked across the room toward a small round table on which was set a silver tray. Resting on it were two heavy whiskey glasses and a bottle of Lagawulum.

"I may be wrong Douglas, but I rather think a wee tot of whiskey would go down rather well right now."

"To be honest, I hardly ever drink it" He was aware of how unworldly this must make him seem to her. His desire to impress was becoming more improbable by the second as looking down towards his shoes he noticed the splattered, mud stained spots of rain on the lower leg of his trousers.

"Well, this is a particularly good single malt and I'm sure once tasted will become one of life's small pleasures" She lifted the bottle and poured a good inch and a half of the golden liquid into each glass.

"We will have it "on the rocks", shall we?"

Before Douglas could reply she had lifted the lid of a small ice bucket and, using the tongs, placed four large ice cubes into their tumblers. A rich aroma of whiskey filled the air. It was almost like T.C.P. Douglas thought but decided to keep this to himself.

"Do sit down. Would you like a towel for your hair?" Polly asked and reached towards his head gauging the dampness with her hand. Douglas prevented himself from rearing back attempting to look casual and unaware of the discomfort the rain had caused. Part of him though was rather grateful for the degree of intimacy it provoked .He raised his hand to his head to feel his thick damp hair. The back of his collar was wet against his neck. He did not relish the idea of sitting with raindrops intermittently dripping down his face and but he might feel slightly embarrassed drying it in the full gaze of Polly.

As though she had read his mind, she added. "There are plenty of dry towels in the bathroom Come along" She took his hand and led him across the room. "Dry yourself off and come through"

Closing the door behind him he was grateful for this time. As he rubbed his hair he realised how excited he felt. It was as though something had happened and yet, of course, it had not. He took the opportunity to remove his shoe and dry his foot. The sock was still uncomfortably damp but at least it would not make an embarrassing squelch. By the hand basin was an array of make up. Mostly Clinique. His mother liked that too. He also noticed a man's leather sponge bag, zipped closed. Douglas fought the desire to inspect the contents. He raised his head and looked into the brightly lit mirror. How long had he been in here? He suddenly panicked. Had he been too long? He must go out now.

"That's better, I'm sure," said Polly and as he advanced across the room following her motioned instructions to sit besides her. She raised her hand once more for a final inspection of his hair and, satisfied to find it sufficiently dry, settled herself into the sofa cushions.

"I've brought some drawings with me for you to see" he blurted out. He knew he was behaving like some immature adolescent in Polly's presence. She was so very much in charge of the situation. Douglas wanted to redress the balance and lent across for his portfolio in a purposeful manner and placed it beside his legs. Polly passed him his whiskey and took hers toward her lips. Just before she took a sip she touched his glass and looked deeply into his eyes. "Here's to our new relationship"

He returned the gaze and found himself once more thinking how very attractive she was. Her amber eyes almost matched the colour of the whiskey. He touched her glass lightly and threw back a mouthful of the liquid. The powerful warmth it gave to the sides of his throat instantly affected him. He felt his shoulders relax as he placed the drawings onto the small table in front of them. He and Patrick had spent a good deal of time over the last few days discussing designs and had both agreed finally to be somewhat bold. As he spread the drawings carefully and cast his eyes across the finished product he felt proud. They could not have improved upon them and if she rejected their ideas today they had decided to use them and approach others they believed might be interested. They had never thought of retail design before and if all failed Polly had opened a new avenue of possibilities that they would not hesitate to explore.

The table was soon covered. Douglas took another gulp of whiskey and sat back. He hardly dared glance at Polly for fear of finding a look of disappointment. She moved closer and placed her glass upon the carpet beneath her feet. He dropped his gaze, waiting, watching the curb of her back as she stretched forward to look at the designs. The bones of her spine could just be seen beneath her pale linen blouse. There was an elegant air about her that distanced him and held him slightly fearful and yet, he reasoned, beside his bulk she was frail and vulnerable. She sat up rapidly and turned to him bringing his thoughts sharply back on line.

"Douglas, these are very exciting!" Her eyes sparkled and she smiled broadly. "What a clever pair you are. The shelving is so attractive and unusual. I love the shape of the stock cabinets. Will the wood all be reclaimed?"

"Yes, we have plenty to work with. The timing couldn't be better." He felt absurdly happy. She liked the designs.

"The scale is so right. Rebecca will love it" Polly threw back her head and took a deep breath. "I knew this would work," she said almost to herself.

"Will you need to show her before making a decision? I can get copies and fax them to you tomorrow if you want." Douglas was eager to show their commitment and ability to act quickly. He was prepared to do anything to gain this contract.

Polly turned again to look at the plans and moved closer. She leant across to pick up one of the drawings and as she drew the paper toward her slid her hand gently across his thigh.

"That's a splendid idea" she turned to him. "And now we must talk money. Do you have an estimate?"

The estimate was in the front pocket of his portfolio and Douglas was unwilling to move. She was so close now he could feel the warmth of her body and the pressure of her legs against his. He would have to stand he knew and reluctantly stretched himself into standing and stood looking down at her. The skin across her cheeks was exceptional. He would have liked to remain there looking at her, committing to memory the contours of her body. The whiskey must be having an effect, he thought and rapidly moved to collect the envelope. She had loved the designs but would she agree their price? They had tried to be realistic but it was a big assignment involving travel and time out of the country. They had agreed on employing somebody to look after their premises should they go. They could not really afford it but neither could they afford to lose this commission. He passed the envelope to her and drank the final mouthful of whiskey. The ice had now weakened it considerably but he still experienced the warmth.

As Polly took it from him he sat down making sure to sit as close as he could. She made no move to alter this proximity as he watched her open the estimate. She flipped her hair back from her face, bent to retrieve her glass and took a small sip. She held the piece of paper in one hand, her finger and thumb holding the page wide.

"How sure are you both of keeping to this sum?"

"We are reasonably confident. We have to be realistic and keep hidden extras in mind, but I would hope we could remain very close" He knew the consequences of being over budget. There were firms he knew who, as a result of not remaining within the estimated price, had turned their relationship with the client sour. He and Patrick would not want such an outcome and as neither of them was extravagant or careless with money he could see little reason to go over.

"I think it's fair. Again, I must consult with Rebecca, but I can't foresee any problems." She leant forward and kissed his cheek. "Well done, I'm very keen to get everything underway. We'll discuss this fully when I have the all clear but I can't see any reason why you and Patrick shouldn't start to get everything organized."

"That is fantastic! This is such an exciting project for us both. Thank you". He was delighted by the outcome. The alcohol and her enthusiasm boosted his confidence and before he could consider his actions he returned her kiss and hugged her. "I feel so good about this"

Polly did not recoil. They broke apart and she squeezed his hands. "We must have some lunch. You must be ravenous" She stood up and went across to the radiator to feel his jacket. "It is still a little damp."

"I don't mind" He raised himself from the sofa and began to pack away the drawings. His fingers were shaking and he could hear his heart pounding against his ribs as he took the jacket from her. She held it open and he pushed his arm through the sleeve. She was taking control again.

"Now, where shall we go? I don't want to eat in the hotel. Do you mind if we walk a little? The rain has stopped. There is a delightful French restaurant not too far from here." She crossed the room toward the bedroom and out of sight. Before waiting for a reply she called to Douglas "How is your mother?"

"She is fine, very busy at the moment." Douglas remembered her telling him she had a heavy workload right now.

"Does she spend much time at home?" Polly could just be seen retrieving her handbag from a glass-topped table.

Douglas looked slightly bemused. "Well, I imagine so. I don't live at home now."

"Of course, you don't. Your mother is a very clever woman. Successful at work, even though she had to look after you three boys." She laughed. "Such a lucky lady".

"Lucky? I don't think she would agree with you" Douglas was certain she would not. His parents had always impressed upon him to rely on ones own actions rather than luck.

"Lucky to have such a lovely family" Polly entered the room smiling warmly at in him. She was wearing an incredibly stylish raincoat with a pair of dark brown expensive high-heeled shoes. Her perfume filled the room in intoxicating wafts. He forgot the dampness of his shoulders as a rush of emotion ran through him. She moved and took his arm. "Are you ready, Douglas?"

"Yes" he replied. "Yes, I am."

JUDITH AND EDWARD

Judith caught the train earlier arranging to meet him outside the station. Thankfully he was there on time as the rain was heavy and she would have got very wet. Edward's upbringing had instilled in him a keen sense of manners. As he saw her run to the car he leapt out and, before greeting, opened the passenger door. She pulled her raincoat across her knees making sure to place the dripping umbrella away from her legs and sat down. He closed the door quickly and ran round the bonnet to his side.

"It's supposed to stop soon," he said settling himself into the driver's seat. Before pulling on the safety belt he lent across to kiss her. It was fierce and passionate taking her breath away. "What a morning I've had. Sometimes I long for a small place in the Outer Hebrides"

"Plenty of rain there" laughed Judith recovering.

"I wouldn't mind. At least it would be peaceful" He turned to reverse the car. Judith noticed the whiteness of his shirt cuffs against his jacket. His hands held the steering wheel lightly as he manoeuvred the car. He was a confident driver. "We'll go to the hotel for lunch. We can grab a drink first in the bar, if this traffic isn't too bad. I booked a table for one thirty. How does that sound?" He spoke decisively.

"Fine. My day is free." Judith sensed a need to calm him. She would not tell him the difficulty she had encountered in organising this meeting. It had been somewhat stressful to say the least. One of her colleagues had phoned in sick. Naturally everyone assumed she would step in and cover and normally she would but today she was determined not to miss the chance to be with Edward. At the last minute a Locum had been found leaving Judith to depart in somewhat of a rush, just catching the train with minutes to spare.

"Great" He took one hand from the wheel and squeezed her knee. "I'm beginning to feel better already."

As he concentrated on the fast flowing traffic Judith settled back to enjoy the comfort of his car. There was a delightful smell of leather and a sense of order. She stared out into the traffic, comforted by the rhythmically swipe of the windscreen wipers and the warm ecco system heating. People hurried along, heads bowed against the rain. A group of backpackers stood against the grey brick frontage of a bank eating beefburgers, unaffected by the rain and the weight of their wet, heavy rucksacks. They talked and laughed together, united by the desire to see the world and all its varied climates. In Judith's youth it was considered daring to Youth Hostel in Switzerland at the age of sixteen. She had gone with a group of friends exhilarated by the freedom, their social life suddenly filled by young European males eager to make their acquaintance. There had been two, very shy, Swedish boys who spent their time taking photographs of the surrounding scenery whilst making sure Judith and her group were somewhere in the composition. She often thought how they must have returned to Sweden with a completely fabricated story of their relationships with "the English girls" passing round the photographs as proof.

"I wonder where they have all been, or are going to?" She was thinking aloud.

"Who?" Edward slowed at the traffic lights and looked around.

"There was a group of backpackers. We passed them just now. They looked well travelled"

"The best bet these days is Thailand. Almost statutory for today's middle class youth"

"How old were you when you first went abroad, Edward?" She was eager to hear of his past attempting, with each contact, to fill many of the gaps that still remained.

"My parents took me to Italy when I was about seven. It was both exciting and oppressive. Exciting to see the trains and take a boat across the channel but after that we spent so much time in silent hotels or, what where then to me, museums full of dark paintings and uninteresting ceramic artefacts. Over the years, they took me all over Europe but it wasn't until I went away with my school friend, Mark Barns, I really began to enjoy travel and realized how clever they were in sowing the seed" Judith pictured him as a young seven year old, a solitary child among adults. Did he then possess the same air of confidence? Inhabiting hotels at such an early age (her own family had always rented houses or stayed with friends. She was well into her late teens before experiencing the delights of hotel living) had obviously paid off. He could always ask for and be shown to the best table in a restaurant, catch the eyes of barmen before others and know exactly the correct tip to give whatever the occasion. Being with him in these situations gave her an air of importance that, since they were relatively rare, she found exciting. She once overheard an elderly man remark "He looks like he ought to be somebody". Edward, she felt, was.

They were nearing the hotel as Judith asked "Is Polly here?" She knew she was in England. Edward may have told her of their meeting as she had told Ralph. The four of them, might have had lunch. It could have been a possibility she supposed.

"She is, but you won't see her. She told me this morning she had an important business meeting that would take up most of the day. I left very early"

He pulled into the curb beside the hotel. Before he was able to leap out and open the door for her, the doorman stepped forward and with great courteousness helped her out careful to protect her from the rain with his bright green umbrella. Edward handed the car keys over as he escorted them to the main door. Once in the foyer Edward pointed in the direction of the bar "It is twelve forty five, we have time for a drink."

Edward steered her through a small groups of hotel guests preparing to brave the rain to see the sights. Judith was sorry they would not see her city in full sunlight and hoped they would return home excited by what they had seen in spite of the weather. She was conscious of the pressure from his arm as they made their way along the long heavily carpeted corridor to the bar. As they pushed open the door and found a suitable place to sit Edward turned to her. " Thank goodness it's not crowded. ". He reached across to help her remove her raincoat and placed it on the chair beside him.

"If I'm going to be drinking wine with lunch I'll have a glass of fresh orange juice now, please"

"Are you sure?" He looked surprised.

"Quite sure. It is the middle of the day. I'd like to stay awake for the rest of it!"

They settled themselves as he ordered a whiskey for himself and the orange juice for Judith. The bar man brought a small tray filled with an assortment of savoury treats arranged like a small work from the Tate Modern. Their interest aroused they reached to select one each breaking the symmetry of the plate and stimulating their palates with the sharp, sweet taste. Edward reached for a second and looked around.

"I like this bar. They seem to have got everything right. No loud music, no hot smokey atmosphere. It's Good." He smiled across at her and took her hand. "Do you like it?"

"It is perfect. I hate crowded bars. We can talk without having to shout." Judith felt very comfortable. They would be left discreetly alone with space enough between the tables for her to feel their conversation would not be monitored. They could talk with confidence with no fear of recognition. There was no one there they knew just a dozen or so other people spread around the tables and engaged in talk. A single man at the far end of the bar sat looking at some typed A4 sheets of paper, one hand supporting his forehead. He looked across at them from time to time in an abstract sort of way. His drink was almost spent and Judith imagined he would soon depart.

They soon became engrossed in their own company, the conversation flowing from one to the other, broken by occasional bouts of shared laughter. As Judith paused to sip the last of her juice Edward fell silent, the composure of his face tightening. Instinctively she knew not to speak waiting with some degree of expectancy for the content of the words that were to come.

"Judith, I've had a bit of a reprieve" He looked at her earnestly, leaning closer.

"What on earth do you mean?" She was suddenly very alert.

He leant back placing his hands on his knees. "Well, I've managed to tie up a lot of business transactions in the last few days. For a short while the heat is off and they've given me more time to consider

Australia. Polly was adamant I remain here for the wedding. She's really looking forward to it. It seems to have cheered her in some way. With a bit of luck I might have a month or two to decide."

Judith's face lightened. "You'll definitely be around for Peter's wedding!" You will be close to me for a while longer, she was thinking.

"It seems so but we both know what it means if I accept. My trips back to England would be infrequent, days like today impossible to arrange." He took both her hands in his and searched her eyes." It's such a long way. I don't know that I can bear to be that far from you."

"And Polly?" She could not let herself forget that Polly was also to be considered.

"She'll be in Spain for a while but will be back to see Peter married. She mentioned it only yesterday. She says she's very fond of Peter. Fond of them all, in fact." He looked slightly wistful. Judith was reminded of Polly's inability to have children. Edward had always been sympathetic but she knew how much he had wanted a family in his earlier years. When they had discovered Polly's infertility they had both turned to their careers in compensation.

"Did you ever think of adopting?" Judith hoped she had correctly guessed his line of thought. He had not reacted with surprise at this sudden enquiry but merely allowed his eyes to rest long enough on hers for her to detect a sadness she had not seen before.

"Polly didn't want to. She wanted her own. We never talked about it again. Not much point really once she had made up her mind". He picked up his glass and drank. "I did feel resentful for a while, even found myself thinking of leaving her, but then I realized how painful it must have been for her and how selfish I was being. Our careers became our children, I suppose". He took another gulp of whiskey.

"Anyway, don't let's get maudlin. That's all in the past. There's still time before committing myself to Australia". Edward dropped her hands and ran his fingers through his hair. "Lets talk of happier things. Tell me about the family"

For some reason Judith could not bring up the topic of Douglas. She wanted to ask Edward what he knew but was under the impression he knew nothing. So far he had mentioned no word about Polly meeting Douglas. Perhaps Polly was keeping it a secret wanting to surprise him? Though it was hard to imagine what purpose it would serve. She couldn't imagine Edward being impressed. Perhaps she would wait for a day or two. Polly would by then have definitely engaged him and would surely tell Edward. She herself had not yet heard from Douglas, it might come to nothing. It was ridiculous, she knew, not to just say "What a surprise, Polly taking on Douglas and Patrick to fit out her new boutique in Spain" but she could not. Instead she talked of Ralph and his work, of Peter and Kate, of Hugh. Finally, she came to Douglas. Somewhat lamely she talked of his social life leaving out all reference to his business. As she finished speaking she glanced at her watch. "Did you say you had a table booked for one thirty? We should go now." The moment had passed. As they made their way across the bar to the lift the topic changed and she felt safe. She would definitely bring it to his attention when she had a more positive and detailed account. For the moment they would talk of other things.

The lift stood open as they approached. Edward and Judith stepped inside quickly expecting the doors to close. The restaurant was on the top floor. As they began to ascend Edward pulled her close to him. "There is a wonderful view from the restaurant, we have a table by the window. Do you realize we are having our second meal together in one week? People will talk," he whispered pressing his mouth and body against her to take advantage of the seconds it would take for them to reach their destination.

As they left the hotel, Polly moved close to Douglas linking her arm. The difference in height made this gesture awkward. Had she been his girlfriend he would have taken her hand, but Polly was, after all, a friend of his parents. The rain had stopped leaving a shine everywhere. The traffic made a slight hissing sound as tyres picked up water from the road. The streets were busy with people. Looking at passing faces Douglas noticed the enormous racial mix. It pleased him to think people from all over the world should be here. He loved London forever thanking his parents for choosing to live there. They had enabled him to spend such a full and interesting childhood among the museums and parks. His adolescence was spent in clubs and pubs with a wide circle of friends who would travel for miles across London on the promise of a good party. His parents had been reasonably tolerant. Hugh, now, was submerged in this lifestyle. He sensed a twinge of regret for its passing but life was far more controllable these days and until recently he had managed to keep his emotional life in check. Work had taken over and, he was surprised to admit, he had been happy with that.

Polly pulled on his arms steering him toward a shop window that displayed nothing more than two very elegant frocks. Their recognisable quality expressed the style and superiority of what was to be found within. Through the glass Douglas could see three sales assistants fussing with the clothes. Everything smacked of money.

"Are you ravenous, Douglas?" She asked peering beyond the shop front toward the interior.

He was aware of an emptiness in his stomach but sensed this was better not revealed. "Not at the moment" he replied.

"Splendid. I want to choose something to wear for Peter's wedding and I rarely get the chance to come to this particular shop. The opportunity's too great to miss." She released his arm and he moved forward to open the door. The assistant looked up in expectation as Polly walked toward a short row of frocks hanging by the door. She passed her fingers delicately across the fabric pushing the hanger back for a better view. Douglas stood somewhat uncomfortably by her side aware of his clumsy masculinity and of having lost her interest.

"Why don't you take a seat over there, Douglas, while I search through." Polly suggested. She was fully engaged in her mission to find the perfect frock and wanted no distraction.

One of the assistants came forward. Her skin was pale, her ears heavily weighed down by large, gold, droplet earrings. Douglas noticed she exchanged a knowing look with the other assistants before giving him a bold stare. What message had been conveyed in that glance? Did they think he might be Polly's son? He could have been - just. Maybe they saw him as her Toy boy. He wasn't very happy with that idea.

As Polly and the young girl busied themselves Douglas settled himself in the seating area. Two large leather club armchairs were placed on a rug. Between them a coffee table on which several magazines were fanned. He was relieved to find some were suitable for men and selected one to read. As he lowered his head in the pretence of being absorbed by its content, he listened to the conversation. She was looking for a classic style suitable for a wedding but also suitable for other occasions. No, she did not like that colour, too bright. Perhaps she could try this.

"Douglas" she called "do you like this?" He jerked his head away from the page. Oh God, what would he know about selecting a fashionable frock for a woman of Polly's age? She held a straight, sleeveless piece of material, its colour a deep aubergine. What could he say? How would it look on her? Probably amazing. All of her clothes were so well cut and designed. He was about to praise the frock when she cried "Hideous colour! Awful" before replacing it on the rail. "Ah, this is much more me". She placed a frock onto the outstretched arm of the assistant and began again to search the rails. Finally, with a pile of different styles selected, she followed the dark haired girl into the changing rooms.

"Would you like a coffee?" A somewhat dreamy sales girl moved toward him. She was younger than he and he felt his confidence return. A coffee would be perfect he thought and settled himself back in his seat. This was obviously going to take some time but he was beginning to feel more at home with his surroundings. They might even bring him a biscuit or two if he was lucky. At least he was warm and dry and more importantly he was assured of Polly's company.

For the next three quarters of an hour he watched Polly emerge from the dressing room. Each time he was able to study her appearance, her movements and facial expressions. Her charisma affected the sales staff as she encouraged them to put forward their opinions and they became animated and enthusiastic. There was much praising and touching; almost a reverence prevailed as they helped her in and out of the frocks that impressed Douglas. This woman among women was obviously held in esteem and as she turned, walked or gazed into the mirror, he became more and more intoxicated by her. He had never known anybody in this league and was flattered by her frequent request for his input as she made her selection. He felt it gave him added kudos in the eyes of the other women and felt foolishly elated, dismissing his hunger that was now making itself apparent by occasional embarrassing rumblings of his stomach. Finally, a decision was made. Polly's slender, beautifully manicured fingers passed over her platinum card in exchange for an extremely smart carrier bag containing the carefully selected items of clothing. He rose to meet her and she squeezed his hand. "How patient you have been, Douglas"

"Not much help, though" He took the carrier bag from her.

She laughed. "Indeed you were. I could read your face. Your taste is admirable. Together we have chosen the perfect frock." She thanked the young woman, smiled a warm genuine smile and waited for Douglas to open the door. Douglas was amazed at his actions, with her he was completely happy to carry bags, open doors, offer up seats. Polly did not demand this of him but somehow released an old seam of gentlemanly manners that had previously remained untapped.

Once outside the shop Polly paused. "It's getting late" she said. "Let's forget the walk and take a taxi." Douglas stepped forward in his new masculine role to hail a passing black cab.

RALPH

It was early November. Leaves had fallen from few of the trees. The geraniums were still in flower. Weathermen talked of high temperatures for the time of year. Peter and Kate hoped it would continue until the twenty forth. Bonfire night had passed yet the odd explosive firework could still be heard in all the suburbs of London. Ralph found himself seated besides the pond in the garden enjoying the late sunshine. Behind him an urban squirrel ran to and fro remembering the burial site of last year's nuts. Judith had encouraged them with handfuls of peanuts placed on the kitchen windowsill. They were vermin but they had charm, unlike the foxes that bore the scars of mange and left loathsome turds around the lawn. They often stood, staring defiantly into the house, staking their claim. Ralph was always determined to stare them out. Their response was to lift a leg and leave a pungent dry smelling scent.

He had made himself a pot of green jasmine tea. One of their friends had extolled its virtue as an antioxidant and they had thought to buy some. Ralph was intolerant of food fads, people with passions for organic food, brown rice, Soya milk, but he had found the tea refreshingly differently and enjoyable, especially at times like the present. The bench seat was a little damp causing the cloth of his trousers to stick but he felt a momentary wave of contentment. He had managed to wheedle extra time on the book and he had organized his mother's annual accounts. It was always a relief to know it was done. She lived in the southeast of England in a small village where, amazingly, a true sense of community survived. People still "looked out" for each other. If anything were to go wrong, he would be contacted immediately. He must remember to book her onto the train. She was coming to the wedding. Was adamant it would not be too much for her. He admired her spirit. Their relationship was strong, although, sadly of late, they spent little time together. He telephoned her two or three times a week to exchange news. She still had an engaging way of relating incidents and they shared the same sense of humour. His sisters lived closer and could be on the motorway to be there before him but she was still a distance away from any of them. She had a full social life and would not hear of moving closer to any of them.

The volume shifted on his personal stereo. He realized he had lost several minutes of the afternoon play on Radio 4. The small earplugs were pressed hard into position. As he attempted to pick up on the plot, he looked back at the house. Hugh could be seen in the top room pacing the floor, one hand held around the phone. Ralph could not help but compare his own adolescence with that of Hugh. His had been a far lengthier metamorphosis. He was the youngest child, the only boy. His parents were very liberal in many respects, certainly more so than any of his friends, yet they still exerted power over his whereabouts, friends, interests and arrival times back home at night. Hugh, as the youngest, had behaved at fourteen as had he age twenty. Ralph felt he had little control over Hugh's social life. Fortunately, he liked his friends and did not see them as potentially threatening. Hugh was very streetwise knowing the best times to walk through darkened streets, bus routes to avoid, and how to appear courageous in front of aggressive young men. Life in the city was both exhilarating and unnerving.

He raised his cup, sipping the tea and sent up a finger of steam from the hot liquid that misted the base of his glasses. He closed his eyes, unwilling to retrieve the tissue from his pocket to clean the lenses. The play was about an Irish family struggling through their disadvantages. There were so many good Irish writers. Judith particularly enjoyed M. J. Farrell's books. He listened as the characters argued, their voices harsh and angry, unable to reconcile. What a dreadful way to live. How soul destroying to be constantly at odds with the person with whom you have chosen to share your life. It was a blessing now divorce was nowhere near as complicated a process as it was fifty years ago. Couples of his parents' generation often spent years in penury rather than face the procedures. But, he knew, it still remained an arduous, emotionally draining event. He had witnessed several of his friends undergoing the strain. Perfectly pleasant people could turn into unbelievably cruel, selfish and embittered characters. Personality traits emerged never before imagined. A friend had once shown him an enormously large suitcase he had in the attic demanding he, Ralph, lift it from the floor. He had just managed to raise it an inch or two before banging it down. "Divorce papers! Page after page, sheet after sheet of solicitor's letters! Every typed word, sentence and paragraph has cost me a fortune. Not only did I lose my wife and house but half my capital went to the solicitor. I should burn the lot but I'm still plagued by the nagging fear my ex may want to trawl the evidence, hopeful of another handout." He had spoken with such venom and loathing, his voice adopting a new violent tone never before witnessed by Ralph.

How did the loss of love begin? He thought of Judith. What had caused him to love her? In his mind's eye he saw her walking across the kitchen, standing in their hallway removing her coat. She moved with a great deal of grace. Her shoulders held straight, head balanced equally between. He had noticed how her posture distinguished her from the group of young women she was with when first they met. He had looked across at her and known she was the woman with whom he wished to spend his life. What an extraordinary conviction. He still felt the same now. They had been married for an eternity. He could not imagine life without her. She took on many of the responsibilities and in the past had allowed him a great deal of freedom to follow his career. He owed his success to her. She had tirelessly built up his confidence and kept him on track when he was ready to pull out. People who lived alone for years found the idea of sharing their lives, altering their homes and being answerable to another increasingly difficult. For him to adapt to a changed way of life would be virtually inconceivable. Lengthy relationships could be restricting but for Ralph it provided him with the confidence to tackle most things that came his way. It was interesting to observe other long married couples. How divisions of responsibility evolved. Judith always dealt with the bills. He sorted out the cars, did the Sainsbury's shop. His friend had admitted to never having ironed anything before his divorce and now found it the most pleasant of domestic activities.

Ralph glanced again at the house, each brick, window and door, so familiar to him. Whenever they returned from a holiday he would walk through the front door sensing the atmosphere seeping once again into his skin. He was received back into the fold. At night the click of the radiators soothed him. People visiting the bathroom closed the door gently with a familiar double click. He could pace the stairs in a certain way knowing where his feet would fall, how his hands would feel against the warm, mahogany wood of the banister. They had not changed the use of the rooms a great deal over the years. Just the top attic that had become the room of departure for the boys, each one spending their late teenage years under the roof preparing for their maiden flights. A sort of "rite de passage". The last years were spent in sound proofed privacy away from Judith and himself. All current friends could make their way to the top of the house knowing restrictions were held to a minimum. It was Hugh's room now. Perhaps, when the time came for him to leave, he, Ralph, might claim it for himself. His own study was overfilled with books and manuscripts. How would it be to have no children around? Ralph rather avoided thinking about this. He and Judith loved to have the house full. Perhaps by then Peter and Kate would have provided them with grandchildren. Peter had never expressed any feelings one way or the other as to his becoming a parent. Ralph's own parents had been so utterly devoted to their grandchildren. It saddened him immensely that his own father had not lived long enough to see his grandsons reach manhood. He compared the age of his own sons measured against that of his mother. If Peter and Kate produced a child in a year or two he, Ralph, unless cut down by cancer or heart attacks could look forward to around a further twenty-five years or so. The brevity of years shocked him and he was very aware of the swiftness of their passing. How would he spend them? Was this it? Would each day unfold here, in this house? Family events come and go, birthdays, weddings, anniversaries, would that be enough? He had achieved some sort of status professionally and escaped hospitalisation, war or oppression, being lucky enough to have been born in a civilised country where political parties changed hand without a bullet being fired. But, twenty-five years! What should he do with those remaining years? He must think about unfulfilled ambitions? This forthcoming wedding was more than the union of his son with Kate. It had, he realized, released something unexplainable which was gathering momentum, forcing him to delve more deeply into his own values, motivations and ambitions. He knew his next quarter century must be as satisfactory or more satisfactory than as his last two?

He had totally lost the thread of the play. Easing the small earphones from his head he wound the wire neatly around the radio and placed it in his top pocket. He raised himself from the bench and stood for a while staring at the gently moving surface of the pond. He should go in and do some work.

Picking up the small tea tray Ralph carried it carefully back to the house. He jumped suddenly as the rasping rattle of a teaspoon against a rusty tin can assailed his ears. It was the refreshment call for their next-door neighbour who was busy planting or preparing the garden for next spring. The children had always been amused by this method of communication but had to admit, it was remarkably efficacious. Ralph pictured sponge cake and sandwiches, a traditional tea. Something that passed their household by. His mother made wonderful cakes. She would bring them on her visits and be shocked by the speed at which the boys consumed them. One minute there, the next gone.

On entering the kitchen he encountered Hugh pouring himself a large bowl of porridge oats. The table was littered with bread, butter, milk and sugar.

"Hi Dad, do you want anything?" he asked adding a spoonful of sugar to his bowl.

"No, I don't think so. Thanks. Make sure you clear everything away. Don't eat anything we plan to have this evening?" Hugh's body was like a furnace which constantly required stoking. He was growing at a rate comparable to a hyacinth bulb brought into the warmth.

Ralph wondered if he would match his own height or even that of Douglas. He remembered the clumsiness he had experienced as a boy of thirteen when he suddenly shot up. It was a weird sensation that he could still vaguely remember. His sense of spatial accuracy had been almost lost for a while.

Hugh pulled a copy of "Metro" from the other side of the table and sat down." There's a good film on down the road. I might go and see it tonight."

"Hugh, you really must get down to work. There is very little time left. Once term ends you have mocks immediately after Christmas." Ralph was concerned at the lack of urgency displayed by Hugh when faced with academic pressure. "The wedding will take up quite a large chunk of one weekend. Don't waste this chance. It is never as easy again". He found it difficult to impress upon Hugh the importance of his approaching examinations. He had never seen him anxiously pouring over his books for any of his end of year exams as he had done when he was at school.

"It's ok Dad. I have plenty of free periods at school. Can I have this?" He had opened the fridge and held a portion of cold quiche between his fingers. Having just recalled the constant feeling of hunger when he was Hugh's age Ralph nodded assent.

"Peter phoned when you were in the garden. He wants you or mum to give him a ring"

"What about?" Ralph asked hoping it was nothing serious.

"Didn't say. He sounded fairly cheerful."

They were both suddenly aware of the sound of footstep and of the front door swinging open. A familiar call announced Judith's return and Hugh hurriedly began to clear away his mess. There just remained time for him to make everything appear presentable before

Judith entered, her arms laden with files and carrier bags from the supermarket. Hugh moved quickly to relieve her. "Hi, Mum"

"I'm exhausted! Marks and Spencer was unbelievable. It's ridiculous. I went in for two or three items and ended up with all of this. Put the kettle on Ralph. I'm parched"

She began removing her coat laying it neatly across the chair back. "It's been beautifully warm today" Hugh made a space for the carrier bags as his mother began to place the contents in the refrigerator. He noted with satisfaction she had bought several appetising items.

"Yes, I took advantage and sat in the garden." Ralph busied himself with the tea and glanced at the clock. "It was difficult to leave. I rather overstayed my time and no work was done" He was annoyed at himself for admitting this. "I'll make up the time before supper." Judith gave him one of her looks and his annoyance transferred to her.

Judith sat down pulling the "Evening Standard" from her bag. "Well you've plenty of time. I've bought ready made for supper." She looked across at Hugh "What on earth are you eating?"

"Dad said it was ok"

Ralph feigned ignorance as he poured the tea and placed it beside the newspaper. He bent to kiss her head and squeezed her shoulder. "If you don't mind I might try to spend an hour or so upstairs" She nodded her assent and continued to read.

As Ralph opened the door to leave he remembered Peter's call "Oh, by the way Peter phoned. Can you give him a ring?"

Judith looked up "What did he say?"

"Hugh took the call." They looked enquiringly across at him.

"I think he wanted to ask you something. It could be about the wedding. Everything's about the wedding at the moment. He said he'd be in all evening." He smiled widely at them both "They've probably decided to call the whole thing off."

Judith and Ralph refrained from a reaction as Hugh picked up his glass of fruit juice and followed Ralph from the room.

Later that evening Judith settled herself on the sofa. She had been reading earlier and almost fallen asleep when she remembered Peter's call. It was close to ten o'clock, not too late. Peter answered within two rings.

"Peter, it's me. Sorry to have left it rather late"

"That's ok, Mum"

"Is everything alright?"

"Yes, yes. It is just that I had a telephone call from Polly and wanted to tell you"

"From Polly!" Judith felt her heart rate increasing. "Is Douglas alright?"

"Yes, nothing to do with him. A bit odd really. She was asking me about place settings for the wedding. Where would she and Edward be? Actually Mum, we haven't finalized them yet. We're so worried we might offend people. I had no idea it would be so difficult trying to put certain people together. I told her they would be close to the top table. That's O.K isn't it? She seemed keen to be near you." He sounded weary.

"Did she? Don't worry darling there are lots of the guests she and Edward have met before and they're both sociable beings used to fraternizing with all sorts of people. Polly certainly wouldn't need me to give her confidence." Judith felt a mixture of pleasure and surprised flattery yet there was an underlying current of unease that she could not explain.

"She asked about the order of service and at what point Kate and I would be leaving for our honeymoon. She was very interested in everything we had planned. We spoke for quite a while. Kate and I thought it was kind of her to take such an interest."

"Yes, it was" It was also slightly out of character she thought. Did Edward share this interest? Would it matter to him where he sat?

"She said how much she was looking forward to it and that they would send us a cheque rather than a gift. She wanted us to buy something we really wanted with the money and let them know. She didn't say how much but the cheque was in the post."

"That's very kind of them. I'm sure it will be quite a substantial sum. It's so lovely they can both come isn't it? Polly is very fond of you and I know how thrilled she'll be to be able to share your day. Why don't you put Edward and Polly on a table with your uncles and aunts? They are sort of family aren't they?" Judith did not want to keep Peter on the phone for too long and was about to sign off when he asked in a somewhat stressed tone.

"You couldn't help us with the seating could you mum? Kate and I have set them out so many times. We can't agree on certain combinations. Does it matter if you mix the age groups? Kate says we should put grandmas with grandmas, and uncles with uncles and I say let's mix them up. It all seems to be getting on top of me."

He sounded tired. Organizing this wedding had become as complex as a state occasion. Judith had spent several hours organising the flowers with Kate and it had been weeks before the final menu was agreed. They had remained remarkably calm throughout but perhaps now, as the last few weeks drew near, they were beginning to run short on energy, their patience running out bringing to the fore emotions that had previously lain dormant. Kate's parents were financing the giant share but had left the organisation to them. She and Ralph offered to help with the expenses but Kate's parents would have none of it. It was a rather archaic tradition to expect the bride's parents solely to take on such a costly event. Judith and Ralph had agreed they would finance the honeymoon and by doing so had relieved their guilt. It was, after all, to be an extremely joyous event.

"I'll come over whenever it's convenient. Don't worry too much. Most people will be busy eating and listening to the speeches to mind their immediate neighbours. Once the formalities are through everybody will begin to mingle. Polly probably hoped to be near for easy access to the family. You and Kate will be the centre of attention all day and won't notice who is sitting where. It is all going to be wonderful." She was relieved to hear his laughter.

"You're bound to say that, Mum, but thanks"

"Of course. It's going to be such a fantastic day. One you will remember for the rest of your life. Not long to go now so try not to worry. Everything will run like clockwork I'm sure."

DOUGLAS

Douglas could feel the sweat trickling down the furrow in the small of his back. Patrick's face was set in deep concentration as he placed the spirit level against the new shelves. They were virtually on schedule but it looked as though they might need more oak to complete. Perhaps, when he returned to England in two weeks' time he could bring back the van and transport the required amount. The shop door had been sand blasted, thank God. He stood up for a moment and surveyed the space. It was looking good. Patrick was such a fantastic craftsman. He had managed to fit cupboards into a very difficult alcove. Polly would be so pleased, he was certain. The area was spacious but long with fitting rooms to the back. The location, on the sea front, was bound to catch the eye of the browsing public. Polly and Rebecca had chosen the town after a good deal of deliberation and research. They had been attracted to the neighbourhood by its reputation for shops of quality and taste. They had waited for premises like these to become vacant for over two years.

People passing looked inquisitively inside unaware as yet as to the nature of its use. There were restaurants, boutiques, hairdressers and gymnasiums, all catering for those with money to spend. To the front a tall row of palm trees spread their leaves to top the crisp, dry trunks wrapped in their history of growth. The sea, a myriad of moving light, could be heard lapping gently against the sand as it dragged back its flat, small "It's looking great." Patrick raised himself from his squatting position for a better view, his face red with heat and exertion. "I must admit we should be feeling proud of ourselves" He looked at his watch "One o'clock, Doug, how about a break for lunch? Where shall we go?"

"Well, actually, I've arranged to have lunch with Polly" Douglas was conscious of the look of disappointment in Patrick's eyes. He should have told her he could not go but she was so insistent. He also knew nothing would keep him away. Over the past two days, he had been able to think of little else but Polly. He and Patrick had spent some time with her but now he was desperate to have her to himself.

"She is only here for four days. There is a lot to discuss. You should be there. Come with me?" Douglas could sense his tension as he waited for Patrick's reply. Inviting him helped his pretence that nothing was personal, that there was little between them but a flirtatious escapade that he could take or leave. Already two days had passed. He had seen her each day but never alone and he was beginning to recognise a sense of urgent frustration within himself that could not be quelled. Today they had arranged to meet in her friend's apartment overlooking the harbour. The very thought of it caused his body to react with a delicious wave of anticipated pleasure.

"I don't think so, thanks." He placed the spirit level down carefully and rubbed his hands together. "I'll give you an opportunity to be alone with the great blonde boss" Patrick straightened a smile and gave Douglas a hard stare. "Just be careful, eh. There's a lot at stake. We don't want to mess up this assignment. She's not yet paid in full".

"I know, I know, but you must admit she is quite a lady but she's also my employer, sorry, our employer, and years older than I am. You don't honestly believe she sees anything in me other that her employee. She's just keeping me sweet." But how desperately he wanted this not to be true and how fiercely he longed for it to be otherwise he withheld from Patrick's gaze.

"Don't underestimate your charm, mate. I've been watching from the sidelines these past two days. There's definitely some sort of charge between you."

Douglas felt insanely pleased as though he had just received the chemistry trophy at school. He made an effort to dampen his emotions once more before he spoke.

"It's merely fun. Once this job is complete I probably won't see her again for a year or two." The thought sickened him.

"Well, don't get too involved" Patrick looked around "I think we should concentrate on the till area next. It needs to blend with the background. There's a lot of glass to fit. Is it all here?"

"It should be. It would be as well to do a little stock taking later today. Check everything is here or on order. I can make a list of items to collect."

They began to clear. Douglas grabbed the straw broom and made large, circular movements gathering up saw dust into separate piles. The sun was hitting the glass of the shop front spreading itself into coloured shards against the white wall. He had not really got used to the heat of the place. Neither had Patrick, but they both admitted to loving the gentle evening heat and the proximity of the sea. Usually, at lunch times, they would down tools and run straight into the water. Their work clothing becoming bleached by the combinations of salt, water and sand. They had found a small bar close by which served wonderful sardines, bread and salad where they could sit in the shade and relax enjoying the opportunity if gave them to talk and be together.

Patrick was such a good companion; being with him twenty-four hours a day over the past weeks had served to deepen their friendship. In the evenings they sat discussing politics, religion, books or films and often their philosophical views on life. He was something of an intellectual with an alert and receptive mind but he had abandoned a life in academia to work with Douglas. He was happiest now working as he did with wood. The career into which he had immersed himself provided him with the opportunity to be creative. He would like to believe in the future people would cherish the furniture he made and that, in time, his name would be associated with quality. In years to come he hoped his creations would grace the homes of people unknown to him and to be considered important pieces by the Antique dealers of the day.

Together they locked the tools into the back cupboard and surveyed the premises. Nothing left to grab the eye of an opportunistic thief. Other workers in the area had warned them to be careful. Douglas juggled the set of keys and found the one to the shop door. He looked at Patrick "Ok?" And together they left.

Outside the full impact of the midday sun hit them. It was still unusually hot for this time of the year. Sahara wind had been blowing bringing with it a fine deposit of sand that lay across the cars like mist. The main shopping area was quiet with most people now seated in the cafes and restaurants nearby. A group of smartly dressed women, their feet surrounded by elaborately designed carrier bags, looked across at them archly taking note of their attractive young bodies. Douglas, tall with ambling gait, Patrick, short and compact, his hair bleached by the sun. His features were unsymmetrical, his nose just a little too long but the combination resulted in a strikingly handsome face. His personality was warm and generous, Douglas knew of no one person who disliked him. Patrick nodded a greeting and they waved. "Probably fancy a bit of rough," he whispered to Douglas. "How do you rate my chances? The dark one in blue looks keen enough."

Douglas laughed, "I reckon she is all yours." He turned to face Patrick "Where are you going for lunch? Are you sure you don't want to join me with Polly?"

"Quite sure, I'll pop down to the local, then head back to the flat and send a few e-mails. What time do you want to start this afternoon?"

Douglas did not want to commit himself. He might only be there for an hour. He felt his stomach lurch at the alternative. Was his interpretation of Polly's behaviour correct? When they had left each other in England, she had again kissed his mouth, her lips resting against his for just that length of time to imply more than a friendly departure. Later here, in Spain, when she had arrived, she had constantly held his gaze. The first meeting they had together with Patrick she placed the side of her leg against his for most of the evening. He had spent the rest of that night aware of the scorching ardour it had unleashed. When Patrick had gone to buy the drinks she had continued to discuss business related topics, never once letting her eyes stray from his. He had found it difficult to drink his wine; aware only of the inner turmoil she was creating. Every moment since he had thought only of her. He could not eat, for every time he raised the food to his mouth he would think of her and his stomach sympathetically rose then sank. Since his London encounter with Polly he had a weird sensation as though being watched, as though everything he did was for Polly's sake. This morning on his way to the shop his senses were heightened. He knew it would be lunch-time soon enough and he would be making his way, as indeed he was now, to Polly. He had shaved so carefully. How stupid, he thought, since I am now bathed in sweat, my clothes crumpled by the morning's work. He cursed his inability to plan ahead. Why had he not suggested they finish work at twelve? He had been so totally obsessed by the idea of seeing her; he had blinded himself from practicalities. He looked again at Patrick. How did he look? Was his unkempt appearance a reflection of his own? Patrick shot him a quizzical look. "Well?" asked Patrick.

"What?"

"What time do you want to get going this afternoon?"

"Oh, I don't really know. Why don't you take the keys? If I'm back earlier I'll come up to the flat and we can walk down together. Otherwise you stroll down when you are ready." He handed him the somewhat cumbersome bunch of keys, relieved he would not now be tied to any time restrictions.

"Ok, fine, I'll see you later." He tapped Douglas on the arm "Make sure you let her know we may have to increase the budget if she wants the fitting rooms exactly like the drawings. Those mirrors are expensive." Patrick continued in the direction of the bar thirsty now for a glass of beer.

Douglas nodded his assent and began to walk in the direction of the harbour. The air was filled with the sound of sail cleats clanging against masts as boats bobbed in the water. Enormous yachts were moored end to end. At least two thirds were wrapped tightly in protective tarpaulin waiting for the return of the owners. He read the names of those close by. One was called "Rush Hour Blues". What story lay behind that, he wondered? He had never liked sailing. Perhaps the sheer size of his frame increased the discomfort but even as a boy he had not enjoyed the odd times friends of his parents had taken him to sea. Most of the yachting fraternity here appeared to spend their time sitting on the decks, peak capped and cross legged, reading magazines and drinking. The real sailors only spent a night or two in the harbour replenishing supplies, over anxious to be off. Maybe, most of these yachts were holiday hires. Rather cramped some of them would prove to be.

He looked across at the shops to check his bearings. The apartment was not too far. What should he do? He looked at his watch; he was on time, which meant no time to call in anywhere to check his appearance. How lucky Peter was now with Kate. They had reached that stage in their relationship when everything was secure, or so it seemed from the outside. They were perfectly at home with each other, sure enough to want to commit themselves in marriage. How long did it take, Douglas wondered, for them to realize this? Relationships took up so much of one's time. Each new woman he met meant going through the preliminary questions, revelations and discoveries. Often this was exciting but they had all led to the unenviable stage of boredom. Not with Miranda Henchley. He had really enjoyed being with her but last year she was seconded by her company to Boston. It was difficult to maintain contact as he was too lazy to phone or send e-mails and never quite got his head around the time difference. But this, today, with Poly was totally new. He had always felt in control before. Now, he was in some Kafkaesque situation not knowing which route to take or where he might find himself. Polly knew all about him, had watched him grow up, what did he know of her? She and Edward had been married for quite a while now. Douglas could remember visiting their house in Hereford once and being given some very expensive Wellington boots for his birthday. He must have been around seven or eight. They always gave great presents to all of them. His mother had once admitted, on a return journey in the car, how clumsy she felt when in Polly's company. Polly being so immaculately dressed, she felt they had little in common other than Edward. His mother, he knew, liked the company of academics or people in the arts. She was somewhat stopped in her tracks by very feminine women like Polly. But Douglas had found her to be immensely warm and sympathetic. He had been touched by her interest and the way she made him feel valued for the craftsmanship he displayed.

He was now at the entrance to the apartment block. He was to look for the name "Heath." The main door was heavily coiled with ironwork. There were elaborate birds in the corners with leaf like shapes below. The brass boxes, for post, glittered in the sunlight each with its own identity plaque beautifully scrolled. Douglas pressed the appropriate bell and waited. A slightly crackled "Hallo" from Polly was followed by his "It's Douglas". The door buzzed, clicked, and finally opened to reveal a marbled hallway, mostly white, with large grey and white slabs breaking the walls into glamorous shape. There were Turkish rugs scattered on the floor and several large leather, club like sofas, strategically placed. Toward the back of the hall was an oval window inside which had been placed an enormous spray of white flowers. His mother would have approved the flowers, he thought, as he waited for the lift. He turned his head to look back at the gates to see a small dog stop inquisitively and lift its leg. It was a Dachshund with such an audacious look of cheek Douglas found himself laughing aloud.

The lift door wheezed open to reveal Polly and as he turned he was almost choked by the rush of excitement experienced by her unexpected appearance. She looked stunning in a pair of beautifully tailored, navy blue shorts and a soft lawn cotton white blouse. Her arms were bare causing the delicate gold of her bracelets to sparkle as she lifted them in greeting.

"Douglas" she kissed his mouth and held him at arms' length. "What has amused you?" "That dog" he answered and pointed at the door just in time to see the back half of the dog disappear from view. "It rather abused your wrought iron work, I'm afraid."

"I couldn't wait to see you" Polly pulled him inside the lift that was scarcely high enough for Douglas. She placed her arm around his waist holding him loosely. "Have you been working all morning? I am sure it is all going to look fantastic" She stood back looking up into his face.

The skin around his waist became electrically charged and he suddenly caught his breath. The lift was full of the smell of her. Confined by the space, their bodies touching, he was overwhelmed with desire He bent his head to look at her raised face wondering if this might not be the time to kiss her properly, so strong was the urge. No more messing around with ambiguity. She would either allow him to do so or object, but, at least, he would know how things stood. She was looking deeply into his eyes and seemed to paralyse all movement and mental control. Before he was able to drag himself from her mesmeric power the lift glided to a halt on the third floor and she broke the spell by removing her arm from his waist to take his hand and lead him out and across the hall.

As they entered the apartment Douglas could see Polly had prepared lunch. It was set out on a glass table on the balcony. A blue and white striped awning provided the area with a soft shadowy light. There was a bottle of champagne on ice to the left of the table.

"No doubt you're ready for lunch, Douglas. Do you want to eat straightaway?" She led the way to a large, airy, room furnished in pale yellows and whites. Here and there strong green cushions or plants contrasted sharply. The air conditioning was humming gently in the background. There was a feeling of peace despite the busy street and harbour being in such close proximity. Nothing was out of place and the newness of the fabrics alerted Douglas to his own slightly grubby appearance.

"I would really like to take a shower. I must admit to feeling uncomfortably sweaty." Normally, he would never be aware, particularly at this time of day, when he would be planning what to eat, of his own bodily discomfort. He knew now exactly what it was he wanted and the path he must take. It was as though he had been walking in a maze for a long time and had now found the centre. The Polly he had known was evolving into the Polly of the present day. She was leaving behind her familial history and he was shedding childish memories. He no longer saw her as his mother's friend for as he continued to look at her, he was aware of a change in her features. There were two tiny moles to the left of her mouth, her nose perfectly proportioned, one eyebrow was slightly higher then the other. As her eyes focussed onto his Douglas saw an expression of deep, wounded, sadness, pass across her face .For one brief second it pierced him through but then she flashed a smile, took his hand, and it was gone.

"Of course, I thought you would want to do so. The bathroom is through here. There is a towelling robe on the back of the door." She held the door ajar as Douglas entered. It was then he bent and kissed her. She lent back against the shower door, letting her hands drop loosely to her side. His kiss was gentle and slow, his chest filled with the pumping of his heart. He pulled her closer to him and closed the door. Polly raised her hands and, with mouths still in contact, began to pull his shirt free and undo the row of buttons. Douglas thought of the films he had seen where couples came together in a frantic sexual rush, tearing at clothes, falling against each other in a frenzy of passion. With Polly now, it was as though, the present, this minute, was holding them both. They moved together in this amazing erotic choreograph which involved the removal of clothes, entering the shower, exploring their bodies beneath the tepid water, hands sliding graciously. Discovering. In retrospect Douglas could remember no awkwardness as they began to make love. Her body had so rapidly and easily become a part of his. In spite of his bursting heart he had managed to control his desires. He had lifted her comfortably, being aware of the soft, roundness of her form. Her hair had fallen in damp strands across her face that he kissed, over and over again. It was a unique experience that he would, he knew now, never forget. They had climaxed together and fallen breathlessly against the dampened glass cubicle. Polly had taken the sponge and washed him gently, kissing his body, kissing his mouth. She smiled when she saw he was becoming erect. "I had forgotten the passion of youth", she said, and pushed open the shower door to reach for the towels. He wanted to begin again, to relive the experience, to wallow in this sensation of lust and love. Squashed in this tiny cubicle he wondered how they had so gracefully slid together. He bent his head to allow Polly to dry his hair and shoulders, then taking the towel he wrapped her tightly inside "I have captured you" he said, then, realising his mistake, "No, you have captured me" Small beads of water hung about her eyelashes which he bent to kiss. The whiteness of the towel caused the amber of her eyes to shine like candled lanterns. He wrapped the towel tighter and drew her close. Now the thought of leaving this glassy bower dismayed him but Polly laughing struggled free.

"Take the robe and sit on the balcony. I'll join you in a few minutes."

Douglas caught her again and lifted her to reach his mouth. Her lips were soapy and as she returned his kiss he slowly lowered her to the floor. "I feel like Samson," he whispered. At this her eyes flickered for a brief moment. Once again Douglas experienced that strange second of disquiet he had felt earlier before they had made love.

Polly turned to leave. As she collected her clothes from the floor she bent, loosening the towel, which fell around her ankles. She stood, her arms full of clothing, her body naked. "And I shall be your Delilah" she said.

Douglas remained still watching her leave. There could be no doubt now. Polly had wanted this to happen as much as he. She could be anything she wanted. All Douglas wanted was to be with her, to touch her, to look at her, to become a part of her life, to be important to her.

Judith felt the floor of the car with her feet for her handbag. Her lips were dry. She snapped down the passenger mirror and reapplied her lipstick. The traffic was abominable. Luckily Ralph was fairly even tempered in the car, refraining from oaths and curses every time something occurred. It was a very masculine thing to make derisive comments on the driving skills of others and to take umbrage when criticism was directed close to home. They had volunteered to organize the white, heavy cotton, chair coverings for the wedding ceremony and reception. Kate had a friend who could supply them at a slightly less astronomical cost than the central organisation. The covers were made to fit a certain type of steel chair transforming their shape. Ralph had a list of instructions.

The length of the guest list still alarmed her. When they had first decided to marry it had begun in a rather modest way but as names were committed to paper other names followed for fear of upsetting people. The list had grown reaching well over one hundred guests for the afternoon reception and a further two hundred for the evening. Everything had been planned most carefully. Judith knew Peter had become just as involved as Kate and wanted the day to run smoothly but Kate had very strong ideas and was determined every last detail should be perfect. From the moment the decision had been made as to the type of wedding they wanted, Kate had set about researching. They had chosen the Barbican. Initially Judith had pictured the tall concrete flats and concert hall and wondered how they had arrived at such a conclusion but Kate had shown them photographs of the inner atrium filled with tropical plants and palms trees that would provide a lush and exotic area for guests to mingle. The actual wedding ceremony would take place on the upper floor where the tops of the tropical creepers and trees would provide the perfect backdrop. Another talented friend of Kate's had offered to arrange and select the flowers.

"We should have allowed ourselves more time for this," said Ralph uneasily. "If this kind of traffic keeps up, it could take us an hour to get there"

"Kate said somebody would be there all day until six. I don't think we need worry too much about being punctual."

Judith had taken two days' leave in an attempt to organize her own household. Ralph's mother and two of Judith's friends would be staying with them the night before and possibly after the wedding. She was sorry her parents had not lived long enough to see this wedding. Her father would have so enjoyed the company, especially the young friends of the boys. Her mother would, no doubt, have been the centre of attention, laughing and engaging people with her warmth and sense of fun. People loved to tell her things. She had the knack of probing discreetly. She listened well and shared the conversation.

Judith noticed more and more how selfishly some people conducted conversations. They were only interested in revealing their own life history and gave no time for others to contribute something of their own. She wondered on the content of their thoughts, for after such a singular dialogue what could be left with them for reflection? They asked little and discovered nothing. Judith preferred to remain silent when in such company. This was not difficult as she had never been inclined to pour forth her life story to someone she scarcely knew. Often, at work, she was amazed at the degree of intimacy the parents of her young clients were prepared to share with her.

"I wish now I had taken the Lower Road. I suppose I could turn right up here somewhere." He turned to look at her as he spoke. It was a habit of his that Judith found unnerving. Once, in America, he had almost killed them both by keeping his eyes on her rather than the road during a conversation. They had laughed about it afterwards, but as the car went spinning toward the ditch it had frightened them.

"Look at the road." Judith said pointing her finger at the windscreen. "It could be just as bad when we hit the bridge. We might as well stay on this route."

The Old Kent Road had changed over the last decade. It was no longer full of boarded shops. At night coming home from the theatre, the road was alive with young people, cars lining the pavement, double-parked. There was an air of festivity and life. Judith loved this nocturnal vibrancy. It excited her to see so many people filling the streets. At almost any hour of the night the roads were busy. As their car halted at the traffic lights a group of young boys sped across on skateboards, jumping the kerb and landing with a hard, dull, smack. They wove their way along the pavement, lifting the board from the ground as though glued to their feet, the group rumbling noisily on, then twisting sharply round the corner and out of sight.

The sky had not yet made a decision as to the kind of day it would be. Judith searched for a patch of blue big enough to make a pair of sailor's trousers. It was there, even two sailors might benefit. Perhaps, it would become more positive as the morning progressed. Ralph's sisters always made much of the weather. Before any news could be imparted, they would provide a detailed report on the area. In Tessa's case it was understandable, she and Tom ran a farm, but Anne, a local GP, must have acquired her taste for descriptive weather conditions.

"Did Anne confirm she would be free for November the 24th?"

"I was just thinking of her" their thoughts synchronised. "She has managed to organize her off duty and hopes to finish on Friday midday." Judith enjoyed the company of Anne and Tessa. As a child she had longed for sisters and brothers. Luckily her close friend came from a large family who drew her in. Being accepted by them appeased her longings. Meeting Ralph had provided her with two virtual sisters of her own. They all enjoyed each other's company, their children growing up together. They were lively interesting women who managed to pursue a career and bring up children without making a meal of it. They were both endowed with a dry wit and great energy. After spending time with them Judith felt renewed and inspired. They laughed a lot finding humour in unlikely places.

"I was going to ask you if you could take some leave once this is over."

Judith registered surprise "What for?"

"I've been nurturing an idea for a new direction my book could take. You know how uncreative I've been recently. I re-read the work I've completed so far and it suddenly occurred to me what might be needed. I'll have to do some extensive research, because I want it to be as authentic as possible, and being in the right location is important. One of my characters seems to have highjacked the plot and I like it. Since I am coasting right now and can't seem to make progress it seems like a good idea." He paused and turned to check her reaction. He raised his voice above a passing lorry determined she should hear. "I want you to come with me. Do you think you could?"

Judith's mind ran like greyhounds. There were two tracks of thought. Edward had not yet decided on Australia, if he were to go she would want time to spend with him at least to say good-bye. She could not just let him go, waving him off in the company of others. It would be too cruel to be away prior to his departure. There was also her work to consider. She visualized her schedule. It would mean handing over several of her new clients to Felicity. She would lose money, quite a considerable sum, if Ralph's plans meant weeks rather than days.

"How long were you planning to be away? Where do you want to go?"

"I need to go to the East Coast of America. To the small towns north of Kennebunck. It will be pretty cold and stormy along the coast-line at that time of year. I know it might not be much of an interesting place for you, but after all these wedding preparations, I thought it would be a good idea to escape completely into another environment. You could get on with your research papers and we can explore the coast right up to the Canadian border. The history in many of the small towns is fascinating. I'd like to use some real life scenarios. It will be set in the 19th century and there are several small museums I know of which hold a substantial amount of first hand reporting of life at that time." His head turned back and forth from Judith to the windscreen. "I really do believe it's where I need to go. I'd probably require around four weeks, stopping for three to four days in each place".

"When would you want to leave?" The idea of being away for four weeks was virtually impossible. Judith ran her thoughts around her calendar. Perhaps she could join him at the tail end to meet somewhere half way. It would depend upon his departure date naturally.

"As soon after the wedding as is practicable. I have to take my mother back first of course and see that she's settled. How long are Beth and Angie staying?"

"Just over night."

"Well, once we had sorted the house, we could be off."

Judith's mind was scrambling in panic. Ralph had obviously been planning this secretly for some time. At any other time she would have found it something of a release to go away and shelve her responsibilities but right now there were too many intervening circumstances and she wanted to leave her path clear. She searched her thoughts for possible reasons to hold them back in England.

"What about Douglas? Polly's opening is set for the 7th of December. I had thought we might drive down for it. Douglas and Patrick would like us to see their work. I know how proud they are of their craftsmanship." A few days in Spain would have provided the perfect break for both of them. Polly and Edward might be there together. If Edward had decided to go to Australia he would, no doubt, feel some sort of obligation to support Polly. If Judith went with Ralph she would undoubtedly miss the occasion and that would be a pity. She wanted them to be supportive and be there for Douglas.

"I know, but we can see that at any time in the future." He readjusted himself in the seat altering the position of his hands on the steering wheel. "The timing is just right for the kind of weather atmospherics I'm looking for." He was developing an edge to his voice.

They would, she knew, have an enjoyable time together. She was always pulled into Ralph's research and had, over the past few years, learnt a great deal. He was able to immerse himself completely, reading pertinent books, fiction and non-fiction, keeping note cards, taking photographs. He would read short extracts from his source books aloud to her, coming down the stairs to share his discovery and they would spend time engaged in lively conversations exchanging their views. Ralph, always, with an interesting angle. This pursuit of detail was becoming his trademark and readers often wrote to him congratulating him for his eye for detail.

"We could still be away for Christmas," he added. "It might be fun, just the two of us. If we go up as far as Bar Harbour we should be in for deep snow across Mount Desert and Arcadia National park. The American's really go to town at Christmas. We'd see all those amazing house decorations." He was warming to his subject.

Judith felt a second sinking. She would not see her family for Christmas. Realistically, Hugh was now their only responsibility but even he was virtually independent. He could go to Peter and Kate, she thought. No doubt, Douglas could go there too. It suddenly struck her with something of a shock that this might be the year in her life when she relinquished her matriarchal headship and passed on the responsibility of festive family celebrations to the next generation. In some ways she welcomed the idea thinking she and Ralph might spend time with his sisters if they were not away, but at this moment she could only worry where could Edward fit into this scheme? She wanted to be free to see him and she wanted to go with Ralph, but she could not commit herself either way. She despised herself for not having the will or more truthfully, the ability to make a choice. It was like choosing which child to save from drowning when all three were in peril. How could she decide?

"It would be quite a long time for me to be away from work."

The hesitation in her voice irritated Ralph "You've had that kind of time off before. I can't see why, with plenty of warning, you can't get in a locum or something." She was always making excuses lately and it was beginning to annoy him. This was the time in their lives when they ought to be able to take off. He did not want to be restricted in his actions by her work. It was selfish of him he knew but every so often the idea that maybe he was taking second place crept in and he felt wounded.

Judith sensed the reprimand and began to backtrack. "It sounds interesting though I'm not too happy about the temperatures we might encounter. Next time round perhaps you can locate your characters somewhere warmer and closer to home. Give me some time to work things out." Judith hoped she had kept the disquiet from her voice. She was conscious of the support Ralph needed right now and did not want to give the impression of holding back. She had not said yes neither had she declined.

Ralph pulled across behind a coach load of children. He waved his hand in return as four young girls smiled down at him. They giggled and hid below the seat. "Shouldn't have done that," he groaned, "Now we're stuck with them." The girls bounced back waving and smiling, moving their heads from side to side. Judith noticed the outline of their teacher approaching. She tapped the central child on the head, obviously reprimanding such behaviour. They were now all hidden below the seat line again. Ralph laughed. "Thank you, Miss" he said "and praise be for seatbelts. I'll start looking up various towns on the website. That in itself will be a therapeutic exercise for me. We still have some time and once you've decided, I can go ahead and start to book flights and hotels." Ralph resettled himself into his seat and re-adjusted the rear view mirror waiting for her response.

"Give me a few days." Still she would not commit.

"O.K. but not for long. I want you to be with me and rather hoped you would want to be with me." He knew he was using emotional blackmail but was determined to win his round.

They were now approaching Trafalgar Square. The address they had was for West Hampstead, at the far end of Abbey Road. Judith continued to torture herself as her loyalties and emotions clashed in battle. Inappropriate questions loomed which she could not put to Ralph. The timing was so inconvenient. Maybe he could go first, she later, giving her time to see Edward on his last few days. Felicity would know there was something amiss if she gave her the work and remained in England. Hugh would think it odd too and wonder why she remained behind apparently doing nothing. Hugh, they could not leave him alone in the house for that length of time! He would love them to, of course, but he was of an age where unthinkable and unspeakable damage could be done. Parties, overnight stays, kitchens littered with ringed coffee mugs and sticky jam infested knives. They had gone through all this with Peter and Douglas.

"I don't think we should leave Hugh alone for that length of time. Remember the gate-crashing incident with Peter and Douglas?" She hoped this might add some strength to her obvious indecision. "He also needs someone behind him to check on his revision"

"I had thought of that." There was an element of steel in his voice "Hugh is not a child but I know we would both sleep easier if we knew he was being supervised. Maybe David and Carol would move in for the period. They always enjoy a stay in London. David gets on well with Hugh and wouldn't be afraid to turf out miscreants when necessary." David was Ralph's closest friend who had left behind the stresses of city life, installing himself and his wife in a small stone cottage in the Welsh hillside. "They are coming to the wedding, staying at Carol's sisters, and could move straight in. I'd have to give them some warning of course but they would both be very responsible. I know Carol would be quite firm with Hugh over revision. It might even be the best thing for him."

Judith was reluctant to let this loophole go. "He smokes a pipe. I don't know that I like the idea of the house reeking of tobacco on our return." Ralph released a rush of exasperated breath. "Alright, alright. It's a possibility but don't ask him yet. I still feel uneasy about leaving Hugh at this time." This was perfectly true. Judith knew how easily Hugh could be distracted. His mock A levels followed hard on Christmas festivities. She could not imagine he would be more inclined to work for Carol. Short of entombing him in some crammer's college for the next few months she could not see how anyone or anything could make a difference. She had been like Hugh herself at that age; believing an exam could be passed sufficiently well without having the necessity of work.

"Well, what ever you decide, I feel I ought to go " His face displayed dissatisfaction as he clutched the steering wheel too firmly stretching the skin tight across his knuckles.

Judith knew Ralph hated to go on long trips alone. The days he filled researching but in the evenings, sitting in restaurants and later watching foreign TV stations in his hotel room, brought disenchantment. He would walk long distances to find public telephones, hotels were always phenomenal expensive and it gave a purpose to the evening, to tell her of his day, eager to make contact with home. The next morning he would escape the solitude of the hotel room and immerse himself in his surroundings but all too soon the silent evening life of the hotel would drag him back to solitude once more to nurse the heaviness in his chest as darkness fell. When they were together evenings were passed in a variety of ways, taking pleasure in each other's company, reading and conversing or watching bizarre foreign TV channels long into the night. She had enjoyed many trips with Ralph and she was forced to admit there was always a kind of melancholy about her when she was left at home. She could appreciate with renewed affection the qualities he possessed and reassess his importance to her. Usually he was away for just a week or two but this time the trip he was planning would be lengthy and she knew their need for each other would be strong. She had often decided during Ralph's absence that she would not see Edward again but as soon as their last meeting had taken place she found herself twisting time and commitments in order to meet him once more.

If only Ralph had not mentioned going away. His trip now added to her crowded thoughts. There was so much to do before the final countdown to the wedding. She would have to argue with herself, weigh up the pros and cons and lie awake at night planning alternatives and consequences. Why was it that within their society it was not acceptable to share ones love? Jealous intervention and the notion of rivalry inevitably sent one down the path of secrets and lies. How would she feel if she discovered Ralph had a female equivalent to Edward? She knew she would be devastated but why should she if his love for her were as strong as her love for him? There was no way out of her dilemma. She was held captive by her own emotions. Rarely, on the radio or television, documentaries were made about families or couples who successfully maintained relationships with more than one partner. Were they individuals who possessed some rare ability to eliminate jealousy from their emotional agenda? Even in relationships when all passion was spent, something in the human psyche demands the right to hold the prime position, to be the favoured one. All those years ago she and Edward could not have foreseen how entangled their lives would become. With Ralph, her life had been built on solid ground, safe and secure but the reunion of Edward had placed sand beneath her foundations. She knew that one unguarded move could shake all they had built into a rubble of crumbling bricks. Being aware of this she ought, she supposed, be wrestling with guilt. Inexplicably she was able to dispel this emotion for most of the time for whoever she was with aroused feelings of such love and affection she could not accept she was doing anything wrong. It was only during the darker moments of night it rose to take its place in the foremost regions of her thoughts and she was left to lie awake to wrestle with her conscience. Judith looked across at Ralph, noting the curve of his mouth and the distinctive outline of his chin. As a young man he had been extremely tactile and still, today, there was a physical attraction felt by her whenever she saw him.

"Keep an eye open for a large blue sign. Kate says it is first left immediately after." Judith was pulled back into the moment. She must now concentrate on immediate needs and ensure they carried out their mission with no errors. The wedding was to take priority and everything must be just right on the day.

Douglas lay on his back on the small bed in his narrow white room. His feet hung unsupported, something to which he had been forced to accustom himself once his height had reached its peak. He had just returned from the airport having taken Polly to catch her plane for London. She had spent the last two days with him and he was basking in the sea of memories she had left behind. It had been difficult for her to find time to return to Spain after her last visit but she had been determined to do so. He had wanted to spend every minute with her but she made a point of spending some time at the boutique overseeing the work. The majority of time they had spent together in the harbour flat learning about each other and making love.

His life had been completely overtaken by her. She was everywhere in his thoughts. Flashes of her face would materialize as he walked in the street, even as he talked to others. He could still not quite believe she cared for him even though she had assured him many times. She had been totally his this time and they had made love numerous times, each time, for him, plunging him deeper into another aspect of their relationship. She made him feel powerful, and yet, at times, he felt completely subservient. He was intrigued by her mannerisms and actions. She had a strange habit of recapping their activities and conversations as though storing the facts for a future "write up". It was slightly unnerving for Douglas. How could he forget any of the time they spent together when he could so readily replay every scene in his head at any given moment? This was, indeed, a strange kind of love. It was obsessive and possessive.

Here, in Spain, it was easy to be with her. Patrick by now knew how involved he had become but going back to England would be difficult. He was uncertain as to how Polly would want to play the relationship. He knew she would not want Edward to know, or anybody else for that matter. This sent a dull ache through him as he thought of clandestine meetings and hidden plans. He frequently chastised himself for having got into such a situation. There had been many beautiful young Spanish girls of his age who were ready and willing to form a relationship but the power of Polly was too great. They could only pale into insignificance when he looked at her. How had it happened? She was now such an enormous part of his life he barely had time for other thoughts or other people. She had consumed him. Was this the love writers so often described? If so, he understood their need to translate it into words. He wished he had the ability to write Polly a poem. Perhaps he could make her a beautiful piece of furniture.

He pictured her leaving for the hundredth time remembering with some disquiet she had not mentioned their next meeting. He had kissed her passionately before she left the flat and she had insisted he did not take her to the airport. He had overridden her wish wanting only to delay the moment of separation for he could not bear the thought of being in the same country without her. As she passed through the check in and into the passenger lounge he had been utterly dismayed by her failure to turn and wave. He had called to her but she had not heard. Their next meeting would be at Peter's wedding where he knew it would be extremely difficult to be close to her. How would she greet him? He recalled again for the hundredth time how she had clung to him that morning in the flat, kissing him tenderly, speaking his name. She might well have been attempting to imprint herself upon him, her behaviour being so fiercely possessive. Why then should he be feeling anxious because she did not turn to wave? Maybe, she was afraid somebody might recognise her. For his part he had no fear of recognition. Even if he did see somebody who knew him, he could introduce Polly without secrecy. His friends would not know who she was and would see her as a very attractive older woman, probably congratulating Douglas on his good taste.

The sun was now streaming through the window falling hotly across his face. It was midday. He had until three before resuming work. He and Patrick had worked so hard prior to the visit. It was comfortable working at evening time and they often continued into the early hours of the night. Douglas was constantly aware he was making each piece of furniture or fitting for Polly. He had given it his all. Most decidedly made for love. Patrick was a perfectionist anyway which made the end result of such high quality they decided to use photographs of it for their next brochure. This should bring in a lot of new clients both for the furniture side of the business and for their new shop fitment side. Douglas had tried hard not to leave Patrick with a greater proportion of the work but Polly had wanted him to spend the time with her and he was even more eager to comply. Just yesterday morning they stood together, looking out onto the sea. Her hair caught the sun as he watched her, increasing his desire to touch and feel her against him. They had stood silently for a while gathering their thoughts. The day would be another hot one. Douglas watched the boat people moving around the decks. There always appeared to be a chore requiring attention. He knew he should be working but Polly held him back, informing him there was time enough for work but little time for them to share. She had talked of the past describing incidents from his childhood and teen age years surprising him by the clarity of her recollections. She recalled times when, as a family, they had spent a few days with Polly and Edward. Douglas was a little ashamed to find his memories were not as clear and often different to those of Polly but he consoled himself by the thought that his pictures from the past were from a child's point of view. The importance of being allowed to do things considered rather grown up taking precedent in his memory bank. She liked to talk about his mother and certain places they had gone for their annual family holidays. She seemed particularly interested to discover if he could remember whether all of the family had remained together for the whole of their holidays or were there days when she was not there. Did Douglas remember her not being around for some of the time? Of course, he had not and had laughed at Polly's interrogations. Why would she want to know that, he had finally asked. She had laughed recklessly and told him she was interested in memory and how events, seen by different people, could alter and evolve. She had, she said, been on a fascinating course in psychology when she was at university. The subject matter was memory and perception. Ever since then it had interested her. A friend of hers was a magistrate and had talked of eye-witness accounts varying alarmingly. In a trial such evidence was obviously vital and witnesses were often adamant that what they had seen was what had taken place, often discovering this not to be the case. Eager to expand upon this, she asked Douglas to recall an afternoon, years ago, he must have been about ten or eleven, Hugh was still quite small. They had been staying in a holiday let quite close to where Polly and Edward were living at that time. He remembered the place. He and Peter had the top room that was decorated in a strange shade of mauve. They had all remarked upon it with wonder, incredulous that someone could have selected such a colour believing it suitable. It was a tall house, detached and not without charm from outside. It was on the edge of a village and about thirty minutes from the beach. There was a wood not too far away reached by a sloping path through fields of cows. They had been told badgers could be seen there late at night. He and Peter had taken their torches and sat nervously waiting in the dark for a sighting. The rustling and movements of the trees finally got to them and they returned rather defeated having seen nothing. Polly had asked him about their calling in to visit them half way through the holiday. Edward had recently returned from a trip to the Far East and had arrived bearing small gifts wrapped beautifully in oriental fashion. Polly thought this would provide a prop for his memory and she was right. They had all played cricket on the lawn, Douglas was bowled out after only a couple of bowls and had sat sulking beneath a tree. Later in the afternoon he and Peter had asked Polly to accompany them to see the camp they had made. It was near to the badger set and they were familiar with the route. His father had taken Hugh off in the push-chair, it was the best way to get him to sleep, and had waved to them as they crossed the field. Polly began to describe the path they had followed; she even remembered the old rusted tin bath once used to hold water for cattle. It had been thrown against the side of the fence and could be used as a target for their air gun pellets. They had continued down through the trees, Polly's presence gave them courage to penetrate deeper into the woods. They came across a large fallen tree trunk that they climbed excitedly. She had been very patient, leaving them to satiate their desire to climb higher and higher. Afterwards, they found a stream and paddled. Polly too. Douglas was amazed to discover he remembered her toe nails being painted an attractive shade of red and her feet tanned. It had been a great afternoon, both boys very appreciative of Polly's adult manner when she talked to them. She had been delighted by his sharp recall and edged him further on, providing the odd prompt when his memory failed. She had been most interested to learn what he remembered once they had returned. The house had been very quiet; there was no sign of his father or Hugh. They went looking for his mother and Edward but they too could not be found. Douglas was aware of a change in Polly. She had run into the house calling for Edward. He and Peter had exchanged glances wondering if they should feel alarmed. She returned to the garden asking where their mother and Edward might be. Were there any outbuildings, where did the lane lead? Peter reminded her that their father had taken Hugh along the lane and they had probably gone to meet him. There was a pub within walking distance. Maybe, they should make their way there? Her manner had changed. They were no longer the companions she had wooed so readily in the woods. She hurried them along the lane, barely speaking, obviously annoyed and yet he and Peter were unable to understand why. Reaching the pub, hot and tired, they asked for a lemonade but Polly, refusing their request, hurried them back along the lane. When they reached the house they found their father sitting in the garden with Hugh between his knees, reading him a book. He was quite relaxed and happy to see them. Polly, changing her voice, asked, casually, after Judith and Edward and learned they were at present making their way back from Polly's house having gone to fetch some rather special wine for the night's meal. They had taken the car about an hour ago. Polly, turning toward the house, said she would try to catch them on the phone; they had, she remembered, some delicious pate, which Edward might bring. Peter and Douglas made their way to the kitchen becoming engrossed in the manufacture of ice cream sundaes. Douglas remembered the thrill as large lumps of ice cream were dropped into the fizzy, clear lemonade, frothing and bubbling up the glass. It was a treat they had on hot summer days. Their mouths covered in creamy bubbles, tingled as they carried their prize into the corridor where, Douglas recalled in a sudden vivid flash, they found Polly, holding the phone, her face distorted and angry. As she turned, she caught his eye, forcing an unnatural smile and replaced the receiver. He felt uncomfortable with that part of the memory and did not relay it to Polly.

Douglas looked across at the clock. He had time still for a nap. He had been up very late last night. His feet were beginning to feel uncomfortable and he bent his knees to pull them back onto the bed. He was going to enjoy sleeping in his own bed when he returned. Polly had massaged his feet, her hands were so small and yet her fingers pressed firmly, finding places which hurt in a pleasurable way. He wished she were here now to do so again. He was aware of the cars passing outside, the lull between heavy with silence. There was a slight smell of dampness in the room. Until he had taken it over, it had been a storeroom for wine and olive oil. He could detect something of their aroma. He thought of his flat at home, empty now, awaiting his return. He had spent a lot of time choosing colours and furniture. His surroundings were important. He knew several of his friends were amused at him being so particular but small things made a difference to a room. A cornice, a fireplace, all affected the end product. He had made a piece of furniture for Peter and Kate. They knew nothing of its manufacture. He was excited to imagine the surprise and, he hoped, pleasure they would feel when he delivered it. It was a small kneehole desk. He had used oak but the style was modern. He felt it would suit. He always loved to make things. As a tiny child he was given a scaled down workbench by his grandfather complete with a vice and set of tools. His parents had provided a work corner for him, they had a video film of him sawing wood, placing it in the vice and turning until it held. He was not quite three. His parents always appreciated the pieces he made. One Christmas his mother was presented with a letter rack made at a Saturday morning class. She had it still. How enterprising of them to find such a class for him. Polly expressed amazement at the active role his mother had played. Her career was demanding and wasn't she away a lot, she had asked. Douglas did remember odd days when his father was in charge but his recollections of frequent absences were pretty much negative. As far as he was concerned, both parents were always there when he needed them and both were actively involved in their careers. He and Polly had spent a lot of time talking about his mother. She obviously admired her a lot.

    He thought of home and his stomach lurched a little. They had only briefly discussed the future. It was going to be different, he knew. Polly had hinted she did not want him to mention their relationship to anyone, at least not for a while. His mouth felt dry and he reached across to the small table for his bottle of Evian. His phone was within reach and the temptation to text Polly a message strong. She had asked him not to contact her she would contact him. It seemed a rather ridiculous arrangement right now. She had only been gone a few hours and already he was finding it impossible to remain without her. He did not even have a photograph. On his return he would trawl through the family album and take one. He knew there were several of Polly and Edward. Oh God. Edward. It was as though a bolt of lightning had struck Douglas. He raised himself from the bed and began to pace the room. How had this all happened? He had seen Polly on and off, albeit infrequently, for years. As a teenager he had found her arousing but then, as a teenager, everything was arousing. She never paid him the slightest attention, of course, she was friendly and interested in what he was doing, but she displayed the same amount of interest in Peter and certainly Hugh as the youngest. She often commented on how handsome they all were, but there was nothing, absolutely nothing, to give him the slightest hint that her interest in him was more than a family friend. Could she really care for him? She was returning to Edward. A sharp jealous pang chased through him. He did not want to think of any man making love to her other than himself. He pictured her naked, lying across the bed this morning, her tanned, smooth legs, crossed at the ankles. All the things they had done, would she do that with Edward? He did not want to imagine. He glanced at the clock. An hour or so remained before work but he could not bear to be in this room alone with such thoughts. He would ring Patrick; tell him he was going back to work earlier. There was still a lot to be done. Where was Polly now? Her plane had not been delayed but she would not be in London yet. He picked up his phone, held it for a few moments, then dialled her number, panicked and cut the connection. He did not want to incur her wrath. The situation called for calm. He would take a shower, get dressed and make his way to work. Polly would ring him he was sure.

The house was quiet. Here and there, half drained cups of coffee formed rings around the edges. The bathroom smelled heavily of perfume and aftershave lingering in the dampened air. Clothes were draped over beds or chairs, cupboard doors hung wide. Shoes, comfortable shoes, were left by bedsides and replaced today by smart, stiff, expensive pairs. Sheila, the Farrington's cleaner made her way through the house, picking up debris as she went. She had agreed to tidy the place while they were at the wedding. People may want to come back this evening, though Judith and Ralph hoped otherwise. Sheila had been invited but declined, preferring to be of use. She hated parties and functions if she herself were one of the guests. She loved the anonymity of passing round canapés, listening in to conversations, being invisible in her black dress and white apron. She had done a lot of silver service waiting in her youth but now preferred the relative calm in the role of family cleaner. Just the Farringtons and the Harriots. Now her children were married she and Ian did not need the money. She had grown fond of her families and coming in today was the least she could do.

Judith and Ralph were waiting in the hall. They had dispatched friends and relatives into their respective cars. Now they waited for their hired car to take them straight to the Barbican. They allowed plenty of time for traffic delays and were looking forward to the peace of the car interior. Judith wondered how Peter was feeling. He had stayed the night with them, leaving early to join his best man to check all was well. He looked dignified in his dark suit and wonderful bright tie. As he walked through the door he had kissed them both, thanking them for the years spent growing up under their guidance. Judith held him close, a lump gathering in her throat, unable to speak.

She loved him so dearly. His childhood over, he was now embarking on married life. Such a brief time ago he was a dear, gentle, little boy with aristocratic looks and an amazingly intelligent mind. They had been enthralled by his wide vocabulary and his involvement in such a variety of things. Really, she thought, one has them for such a brief time, by their early teens parental presence was important but they were expected to take the back seat. Now he was Kate's, as Ralph had become hers, and Kate would come first, as she should. She glanced in the hall mirror and checked her hair. She had not worn the hat bought for the occasion. Hats made her feel oppressed and uncomfortable. Mercifully, few people wore hats today and she would not look too out of place.

Ralph sat on the bottom stair, hands between his knees. He was wearing his "suit for smart occasions". In a suit he could almost become a different character and had she not known him she would place upon his personality a whole new range of traits. He projected a new kind of confidence she had not seen before which had the unnerving effect of making her almost shy of him. He glanced up and smiled at her. "You look good" he said and reached to squeeze her hand.

"Can time have passed so rapidly Ralph?" She asked. "How can it be so much of our past is now lost or reduced to a flash of photographic memory? These family events are like knots on a fathom rope, sinking deeper and deeper as the years pass. All our lives are reduced to moments and fragmented memories. If only these brilliant scientists who invent computer programmes and send men into space, could invent a way of going back into the past - just to look for a minute or two at a living replay of our children or parents, or friends. It's so easy to lose the ability to conjure a face and it's far easier to picture a room or place retrospectively"

Ralph stood, pulling down the back of his jacket. "What would you choose today?"

"I think I would like to see a ten month old Peter, followed by a three year old, then at seven - gaps in teeth - and then perhaps, a thirteen year old. He was such a beautiful child"

"He is rather a handsome young man. Takes after his Dad."

They laughed together and Ralph lent to kiss her cheek. It was a special moment for them both and a strong feeling of togetherness held them close. Ralph was reluctant to move away enjoying the smell of her perfume and the feel of her skin. Soon they would have time together and could forget about the wedding arrangements. He was excited by the thought of the two of them travelling along the eastern coast of America even though he would have to spend some of the time at the start on his own. It would be both relaxing and stimulating he knew.

The door- bell in the hall rang loudly wrenching them from their shared moment. "The car".

Judith took a last check look into the mirror. She felt incredibly nervous as though it were she who would be walking down the aisle. Her stomach rose and dipped with excitement and anxious anticipation. It would all be fine. Tonight she would be lying in her bed with a mind filled by the events of the day. Peter and Kate would be on the way to Turkey, Douglas and Hugh would probably be pleasantly drunk, she hoped somewhere safe. It was time to go and the day would take its course. "We are off now Sheila" she called.

Sheila appeared at the top of the stairs, her arms full of damp towels. "Give them both my love, won't you. I do hope it all goes well."

"Thank you" Ralph opened the door to greet the driver. "We are ready".

"You both look lovely" Sheila called as the door closed leaving her standing looking at the empty space. "God bless," she said.

Douglas looked across the room at his suit hanging from the door. He was rather pleased with it. Normally he would not think of adding such an item to his wardrobe but Peter's wedding had forced him to do something. Most chain stores could not accommodate his height and he had finally succumbed to bespoke. The last fitting had been slightly stressful, one of the sleeves had a kink in the lining, Douglas would not have noticed but the tailor was adamant it could not be left. Fortunately, there was time to see to it and Douglas had returned that same day for collection. Polly had helped him choose a tie in Spain. She suggested he go to a small shop close to hers, preparing the owner for his arrival. They had been very helpful and looking now at the tie as it lay across the chair, he was confident Polly would approve. He was longing to see her. His return to England was three days ago. He had left numerous messages on her mobile taking care to ensure they were work related but he had not received a reply, merely a very brief text message last night confirming she would see him today. He had replied immediately with an ambiguous text but she had not been drawn. At least it had seemed that way. He raised himself up on one arm and reached for his phone. Nothing. Surely, she could have sent something a little encouraging. He had lain awake for hours thinking of many things, all of them Polly related. Once his work was finished in Spain, they would have to find somewhere to spend time together. They could, of course, use his flat but Polly might have other plans. It was something they needed to talk through.

As Douglas pushed back the duvet and stood up he caught sight of himself in the mirror. This job had certainly toned his muscles. He had lost some weight too. Probably because this inner emotional turmoil had deadened both his appetite and his desire to join Patrick on his regular night- cap in the bar. He stood for a while flexing his muscles, aping the movements of body builders, then grabbing his dressing gown made his way to the kitchen.

Sitting at the table he stared into the street, his ears full of the sound of cereal crunching between his teeth. The weather looked good. How must Peter be feeling now, he wondered. He tried to imagine a picture of himself and Polly making their vows as Peter would be in a few hours' time and it evoked an extraordinary mix of feelings. Would he really want to spend the rest of his life with her? At present, he could think of nothing more wonderful, yet this euphoric sensation was swiftly followed by a deep sense of dismay as the rational side of him warned he was reaching for the unobtainable. Peter was lucky. He had fallen in love with the right person and here they were today preparing to marry. Kate was a terrific girl; she and Peter should be very well suited. When it was obvious Peter was falling in love with Kate, Douglas had worried she would affect his relationship with Peter but she had made it clear quite early on that Peter was free to spend time with Douglas or other friends without being greeted by a sulky Kate on his return. She was a great person. Douglas raised his coffee cup to the air and toasted her. They would have fun together. But could they? Again he felt sinking despair. Could they ever accept Polly? Could they go out as a foursome, spend holidays together? Would that happen? Oh God. The anxiety was there again. He put down his spoon and pushed the remaining cereal away. How could he eat? Taking a deep breath he sat for a moment and closed his eyes. Immediately Polly's face loomed into view, smiling at him, her extraordinary eyes lifted to his. How could he have known her for all those years and never notice how beautiful she was? He must ask her to go away with him. She had behaved so possessively during their last meeting, he was sure she would accept. If they had the chance to spend a really lengthy time together they could draw up plans for the future. Maybe, they should move to Spain. He would be able to pick up commissions now that people there had seen the quality and type of work he did. Maybe, Patrick would agree to set up the business there. Or, Patrick could keep the London branch and he take on the Spanish. Polly did not really need to be centred in London. She travelled around such a lot anyway. He felt better, elated even. There was a way out of this. Today he would enjoy the wedding. He would look for Polly and if the opportunity arose, he would tell her just how much he loved her.

Hugh sat between his grandmother and Beth, his mother's closest friend. Angie, another close friend of his mother sat in the front continually pulling down the sun shield to look in the mirror and adjust her hair or lipstick. The interior of the car was heavy with a mixture of perfumes and the aftershave he had stolen from his father's sponge bag. He was aware of the pressure from his grandmother to his left. She had trouble fastening her seat belt and positioned herself too far toward the central seat. Normally, Hugh loved to hold court but today he was enjoying listening. The conversation had included his birth, Peter's birth and Douglas's birth, quite dramatic and full of graphic detail which Beth contributed having been present at the time. From there, they had moved to his mother's birth, how Truby King ruled the actions of new mothers. Comparisons were made between

King and Dr. Spock, the guru of the sixties and seventies, it seemed. Hugh had scarcely taken note of the route but as he looked across Beth he saw they were still only half into the journey. He sat a little further back wondering what topic would follow as his grandmother reached for his hand.

"Well now Hugh, how is your love life?" He curled his fingers around her boney hand aware of her heavy rings pressing into his. She was a tiny woman, careful of her appearance. Her face held many of the features his father possessed. Hugh had inherited her cheerful, garrulous nature. Her bright eyes searched his with genuine interest.

"Pretty much non existent at the moment, Gran." He smiled broadly.

"I can't believe a lovely young man like you hasn't got somebody chasing after you". She was always keen to hear of the women in the lives of the three boys. Peter and Douglas had taken many girlfriends down for the weekend. Gran had plied them with food and drink. Her fridge was always full of the most unlikely food and she was still capable of rustling up something very appetising even when their arrival was unannounced.

"What about the girl who was over the other week?" Questioned Angie.

"Who?"

"The one with long brown hair, she couldn't take her eyes off you."
"Lucy? No, she is just a friend. I see her quite often." In truth he was seeing a good deal of her. They were beginning to rely on each other for company. He was aware of how much Lucy needed a friend right now but could not quite determine the route their friendship should take.

"Wasn't there something rather sad about her?" Angie was eager to learn more.

"Not her exactly. Her father was killed in a road accident early this year" It had been dreadful. Her father had gone away on a business trip and was knocked down by a motorcyclist. He was dead for twenty-four hours before the family were informed. Her mother had flown to India to bring back his body while the children waited numb with disbelief at their grandparent's house. Everyone was in a state of shock conscious of the dreadful gap his death left behind and the worrying realisation they had not had the chance to say a proper farewell. Lucy agonized over the fact she had been very uncooperative on the day he left for India and was still badly troubled by the repetitive sound of her own voice shouting angrily across the room at her father. Hugh wished he could do more to alleviate her feelings of guilt. Her father's death was so finite there was little he could do except be there. Lucy had relived that last day many times hoping to dredge something positive from the muddy depths. It was impossible for her to have known what was to follow. It was only after the event she realised the powerful strength of feeling she had for her father that now could never be revealed.

Hugh's announcement caused a momentary pause in the conversation as the three women silently re lived their own dreadful moments when they too had been left widowed and alone. His grandmother was the first to recall her story and as Angie and Beth sensed a willing and captive audience they too allowed their guard to drop and shared their grief. Hugh was aware of how lucky he was to have his family about him. His childhood had been so happy and secure. He knew he had benefited from being the youngest and was positively cosseted in love. He got on well with both parents and had just about forgiven Peter and Douglas for the rough justice they administered when he was a small boy. Now, it was great. He could go out with them and be treated as an adult. His parents had never been the type to shout and argue and his friends envied the relationship they had as so many of them had parents who were divorced or remarried to people they could not care for. He was so looking forward to this wedding, not just because he could drink, but he wanted to see what it was like to go through a marriage ceremony. He would watch Peter's face like a hawk. Would he change once he took the role of a married man? Might he see less of them? Kate had already stolen Hugh's affections and she had been so supportive when he could not make up his mind about staying on in the sixth form. He really did value her opinion. He would like to continue to call on them as he did now. He was thrilled to have a sister at last and he knew how delighted his mother and father were to finally have a daughter in law. They were such a great pair, his mother and father; he really should make a point of telling them so.

Peter had been awake since five thirty that morning. He lay in his old bedroom looking at the familiar shadows and shapes aware of the fact this was the last time he would be as he had always been. He was, of course, still Peter, the son, the brother in the family, but from today he would follow a different path, one that would lead him toward a family of his own. Many of his friends had decided against marriage, preferring to live together with their partners. He and Kate were only the second couple in their circle of friends who had chosen to marry. They felt it important to commit. Peter was sure marriage would provide him with a real sense of purpose. Once settled inside marriage they would be free to direct their lives and the thought excited him. It was like standing at the starting line looking toward the tracks, but tracks that turned left and right. At any given moment they might be forced to make a choice but the decision would be theirs. The thought that he may lose some of his independence did not worry him. He was not fearful of losing his identity as one of his friends had suggested he might when he had first announced his intentions. The future held no fears but today brought with it a nervous anxiety that everything should run smoothly, the timing, the food and his speech. The ceremony itself would take place upstairs, the food and reception below leading onto the beautiful tropical garden. It seemed an age ago he and Kate had agreed on the Barbican. It was beginning to worry him they would never find anywhere suitable when she had come home with the idea of holding it there and he willingly agreed. If he were honest he would have settled for his own house or the local offices, but Kate had been persistent. She was right. It was a great venue. Today would be rather a unique experience being centre stage and, apart from a few of Kate's distant relatives, he would know every person in the room. He hoped his speech would be right. He and Maurice, his best man, had spent a long time together exchanging ideas and jokes. He would try to find a moment to read it through later. He hoped it would not rain. People would be inside, but arriving wet wasn't good. He sat up and turned on the bedside light. It was still dark outside. He pushed back the duvet and made his way toward the window. Cupping his hands around his face he peered into the orange darkness of London. No rain. He let his eyes grow accustomed to the glow, taking in the silhouettes of roof-tops, the horizon line broken by chimneys. He had grown to know this view so well. He could see the house where Maurice once lived. They had met one-day riding bikes around the block. Their back gardens were almost backing and had become the main route home when they stayed late. That fence had taken a battering as they heaved themselves over it time and time again. Their parents had become friends through their friendship and Maurice had become a very important part of his life.

Peter stood back and adjusted the curtains. He checked his clothes on the hanger and readjusted the trousers. The house was quiet. Should he go downstairs and make a drink? The idea passed and he made his way back to bed. Lying on his side he noticed something written on the wall, almost hidden by the bedclothes. A smile broke across his face as he remembered. He read, "We love Judith and Ralph" "Judith and Ralph are great" Sally Freeman had written it. He was about nineteen at the time. Sally was fun and at times reckless. That evening his group of friends had gone to a particularly noisy place in Covent Garden and come back drunk. There must have been at least eight of them all creeping upstairs to his bedroom trying, without success, to make no noise. His mother had appeared from her bedroom, dulled by sleep, whispering loudly to them to keep the noise down. They had all began to shush each other and then to giggle. Suddenly in a great rush his father had run out of the bedroom shouting at them that it was two o-clock in the morning forgetting he wore no nightclothes. They had all found the situation hilariously funny. Amazingly so had his parents, their anger defused. Just before Sally had fallen asleep she had written on the wall. Peter thought of them now, both asleep downstairs. They were such good role models. It could not have been easy when he and Douglas were going through their teens and now, with Hugh, it was all regenerating. He referred to them a lot in his speech illustrating how their relationship had helped him arrive at the decision to marry. He wanted what they had. The notion of being with Kate for years held no worries. In fact it was an immensely comforting thought. He had heard of several couples that, following enormously expensive and lavish weddings, had separated before the year was out. He was not foolish enough to believe they would walk into the sunset to live happily ever after but he loved Kate so deeply it was impossible to imagine they could not be compatible.

The door along the hallway opened. Peter could hear somebody making his or her way toward the bathroom. Another early riser. Perhaps it was his father, always the first. When they were all small he would give them their breakfast before Judith came down. Those mornings were often chaotic, particularly when they all had different places to go, at different times. On occasion, Peter would have time alone with his father before the others were up. Sometimes they did not speak enjoying the peaceful start to the day, or over a bowl of porridge, they would discuss all manner of subjects. His father had always treated them in a mature fashion, recognising their needs and interests. Peter owed his ability to debate a point to those early mornings. His father had such a good sense of humour too. Some mornings Douglas would interrupt them wanting to know what they were laughing at or the topic of their discussion. Peter resented his intrusion at times but his father would always include Douglas and together the three of them would continue. When Hugh was born and able to sit, they would place him on the kitchen table to bang spoons or play with plastic cups while they talked. That is probably why Hugh was so verbal. Peter smiled thinking of Hugh and his capacity to talk. He was always so full of enthusiasm. Kate's family took to him immediately. Kate herself was engineering a situation for romance between him and her young sister. Peter thought him a little too young for long term affairs. Whoever had gone to the bathroom was now returning. Peter wondered if he should get up now and shower before everybody woke. His mother had said she would bring him breakfast in bed as a final maternal act. Peter was sure she would not mind forfeiting this treat. In fact, he could make them all breakfast - well, just the three of them and take it into his parents' room. They could enjoy a last morning together before events of the day took over.

The guests, meeting for the first time in the lifts either shrieked in pleasurable recognition or eyed each other warily wondering from which side of the family they came. Their smart clothes singled them out from the general public there to buy tickets for future concerts or plays. Everyone had made an effort to look their best, hoping the hours spent deliberating on the outfit would be rewarding in some way. For the young, the possibility of romance, for the old a new confidence in their appearance after months of comfortable trousers and loose tops. The air was heavy with excitement. Everyone was happy for the couple, pleased to be able to share this day. Hugh, having arrived a little early, had accompanied the ladies to their seats upstairs and then taken the opportunity to slip downstairs again for an illicit cigarette. His parents, he hoped, were still unaware of his recent smoking habit. Perhaps today he would allow himself to be seen. They would both be on a high and certainly could not make a fuss in front of all the guests.

As he passed people making their way upstairs he smiled at the faces which were familiar but as yet, nameless, probably friends of his parents or Peter and Kate's. He rather hoped he would not meet anybody close to him. The idea of a quick smoke took preference. There were notices on each floor giving directions for the guests to make their way to the top. "The Farrington/Williams Wedding" boards a welcome relief for those unfamiliar with the Barbican and its lengthy corridors and numerous doors. Being the bride and groom made them celebrities for the day but it also gave a certain glamour and status to the guests which Hugh was enjoying to the full. Everyone would be looking at Peter, eyes reflecting affection and good will but they would also be looking at him as brother of the groom. He would be seated on the top table with a perfect opportunity to scan the room in search of unknown girls from Kate's side. Kate had placed him next to her sister and her grandfather. It should be fun, as he knew them both.

The Barbican had many rooms leading off from a centre corridor. Hugh looked for a suitable spot to smoke and was careful to respect any no smoking signs in the main entrances of each floor. He had been here a few times before to the theatre and a couple of times, as a child, with the school for special musical concerts. He checked his watch and gauged there was time to go down to the main entrance. He had descended the stairs somewhat hastily and looking for reassurance, felt in his pocket for his Ventolin inhaler. It was such a bind having to take it with him everywhere. Last year on the beach he had a bad attack. Fortunately, he was able to return to the youth hostel only metres away. As he came to the ground floor he caught his breath and paused for a while to consider the best advantage point for a forbidden smoke. He glanced along the corridor to his left and was surprised to see Douglas and Polly Ashton talking earnestly. They were positioned behind some glass doors leading off from the entrance, hardly visible, but Hugh had immediately recognised Douglas by his height. As he began to approach them something in their body language made him cautious. He stopped dead causing a gentleman behind to knock into him. Apologies were made on both parts and Hugh was obliged to move forward. His instinct told him not to reveal his presence and a nearby group of people provided him with the cover needed to continue observing the unlikely pair. Without really understanding why, he attempted to behave "naturally" and stood behind a woman in the group, glancing in the direction of the glass doors. At that moment Douglas could be seen leaning down and clasping Polly close to him, she then looked up into his eyes and placed her hand on his cheek. They remained in this position for what seemed to Hugh an age and then, to his horror and disbelief, kissed passionately. Hugh's breathing became wheezy. He reached for the Ventolin. Polly and Douglas! Polly was Mum's friend, Dad's friend. Douglas was working for Polly. Polly was married. Polly was old! What on earth was going on? Hugh turned and pushed his way toward the gents. He did not want to be seen. The racing of his heart registered a high degree of shock. What on earth would his parents think? He wished he had not been witness to such a scene. Only minutes ago he was charged with happiness, now he was burdened with knowledge he did not want. He sat for a while inside the cubicle staring at the graffiti. An unexpected surge of rage coursed through him. Why had they met and kissed like that here, today of all days? Supposing his parents had seen them? Oh, God, he could not possibly tell them what he had seen. He had so been looking forward to spending the day, in part, in the company of Douglas but knowing what he knew it would be difficult to behave naturally. He was fearful his face might give him away but knew he could not stay where he was any longer. He needed that cigarette now but there would not be time. He stood up and opened the door attempting to keep his face as expressionless as possible when a voice called excitedly. "Hugh, how are you!"

   He looked up to see his cousin, Sam, standing at the urinal. Hugh summoned a voice from within that would not betray his true feelings. "Sam, how you doin'?" He waited for Sam to finish and they both embraced Hugh took comfort in the warmth of Sam's body and his pleasure in seeing him here. The recent episode lay like a heavy rock inside his chest but there was genuine pleasure in seeing Sam who would help lighten the load as together they made their way to the wedding to take their respective places.

Later, Douglas arrived to sit beside him. Hugh gave an effusive greeting which he felt to be fake. From the corner of his eye he noticed Polly take her place beside an already seated Edward. As usual, she was expensively dressed and caught the attention of those gathered near. She did not look across at Douglas but settled herself comfortably to sit, straight backed, waiting expectantly for the ceremony to begin.

Now all the guests were seated. Many heads, particularly female, turned to the door waiting for Kate's arrival. Peter and Maurice, his best man, stood talking together quietly, glancing every so often at the seated crowd to smile or, discreetly wave a greeting. The centre table was covered with white linen and a delicately coloured array of flowers was placed on either side in an altar like fashion. Two officials stood ready checking documents. Behind their heads the tops of the exotic plants from the central atrium stretched into view, large palm fronds and delicate bamboo broken at irregular intervals by lanterns. Lanterns that would provide subdued lighting that evening when the party was underway. The murmur from the gathering was gentle but expectant, the odd ripple of laughter breaking out from groups reunited by this event. Those of the women who wore hats wore them proudly unabashed by size or shape. Amongst the young a predominance of black, amongst the older generation, colours to suit their mood or complexion. All the men were suited, the generations distinguished by the cut or boldness of a tie. Each guest held a small plastic bottle filled with soapy, scented water that had been placed on the seats in readiness. At the given moment they had been instructed to blow bubbles as confetti to wish the couple well.

At last, the double doors opened and Kate, holding her father's arm on one side and an exquisitely beautiful bouquet of flowers on the other, entered the hall. She looked young and small. Peter caught her eye and they both smiled broadly. Everybody rose to their feet, the shortest amongst them raising themselves on tiptoe to watch the procession make its way across the back and down the central aisle; Peter and Maurice paused to allow the two bridesmaids to take their place behind Kate The string quartet, all friends of the bride and groom, accompanied them with music as aesthetically pleasing as the visual scene before them.

Arriving at the designated spot the bride -groom, best man, father and brides maids positioned themselves as rehearsed, their eyes now riveted on the officials. The music ceased and guests were requested to sit. Some people took this as their final opportunity to cough while others moved in their seats to gain a more comfortable viewing position. There was a sense of relief at finding themselves in the right place and on time with nothing before them but the chance to witness this wedding and enjoy the day.

Throughout the ceremony, broken several times by readings of poetry and prose, those present could not hold back the intrusion of their own thoughts as they listened to the words. For some they evoked sad memories of a marriage failed, for others the joy of their own wedding day. Several of the young women nursed a secret wish that they too might soon be standing as a bride in front of their own group of guests. The young men hoped to meet a woman with Kate's qualities strong enough to help them throw caution to the wind and commit. But whatever their own particular desires they were all united in the wish for these two people to remain happy and together for many years to come.

Hugh tried to listen carefully but he could not dismiss the vision of Douglas kissing Polly. They must have started their relationship in Spain, he supposed where they would have been unobserved. Patrick must have known and colluded with them. . Douglas had girlfriends here, terrific girls in fact, why would he want Polly? She was attractive but the age difference was huge. She was almost the same age as his Mum! Imagine kissing somebody of that age! He looked across at Polly. She was just in his eye line, sitting, listening intently, her hands resting together on her lap. Edward, sensing his scrutiny, turned towards him and catching his eye, smiled warmly. You poor sod, Hugh thought, you haven't an inkling of what is going on. Somewhat guiltily he returned a smile he hoped conveyed sympathetic warmth towards a man whose wife was practising deception. He would not want to talk to her at the reception, or Edward. He would hate to think Edward might believe he was involved in any part of this liaison and he focussed his eyes firmly on the back of Peter's suit. Would his face reveal the presence of this unwanted knowledge he wondered, would Douglas sense that he, Hugh, knew his secret? He turned to Douglas in verification but was relieved to become the recipient of a brotherly smile. Hopefully this relationship was what was commonly known as a "little fling", a few stolen kisses and nothing more. Yet something in Douglas's behaviour and facial expression had conveyed a different story. It was more than that. Why did this fact disturb him so deeply? Why was he sitting here now, unable to involve himself in the ceremony? He had looked forward to this day for months and wanted to watch and share with Peter his reactions but he was hardly aware of anything. The guests suddenly laughed at something the reader had said. He had heard none of it. His father, seated on the other side, gave him a gentle nudge wishing to share the humorous moment. Again, a sense of rage against Douglas for spoiling his day arose in his chest. He wanted to punch him and at the same time he wanted to protect him. Why?

Judith was enjoying every moment of the day. It had started so well with the surprise breakfast tray and Peter's company. He had sat on their bed and all three had a liberal dose of good, old fashioned, reminisce. Highlights of his life, small incidents, both good and bad, she had never realised how upset he was by their insistence he continue with the violin! She had asked him if her working, often late into the evenings, had affected his upbringing. He was proud oh her professional career and would not want it otherwise but admitted to occasional dreams of arriving home to the smell of cakes cooking and her presence in the house.

As the doors open Judith saw Kate and was enchanted by her appearance. She really did look stunning. Today was the first time she had seen the wedding dress. Although this was not a religious ceremony Kate had chosen white. It was very simple, long, short sleeves and extremely elegant. Judith had found her own outfit after a good deal of searching, in a small shop in Kensington. It was comfortable and gave her a new feeling about herself. It was silly in a way to be changed by pieces of material, but this jacket, this skirt, these shoes, all contributed greatly to her sense of well being and confidence. She had taken particular note of Polly's dress and jacket, obviously a designer piece, beautifully cut. She looked wonderful and had about her an air of both mystery and expectation. But today Judith felt well matched and equally elegant as she brought Edward into her visual range. He looked striking, his shirt cuffs just showing at the wrists revealed the cufflinks she had given him years ago. Seeing them caused her heart to jump. Would she always react in this adolescent manner? Already now in her fifties she could relate her feelings to those of her teenage years and was sure they were very much the same. Was this the secret of enduring love? Was the fact of their meetings being so infrequent a reason? Could they only experience the highs when time was short?

She was gratified they had both been able to share this day and the pressures of work had been relegated to a position of unimportance. He could share this family event with them as they had all hoped he would. Peter had known him for most of his life and having him there together with everyone who meant anything to her made Judith immensely happy.

Douglas held his hands in his lap. His whole body was wracked with an overwhelming sense of dismay. He had finally managed to make contact with Polly, catching her on her way up to the wedding, by feigning a need to discuss a last minute important business matter. Edward had excused himself and continued upstairs leaving them both to find somewhere discreet beyond the glass doors and out of sight. He had behaved stupidly complaining of her negligence since her return from Spain. Why no messages? Why had they not been able to meet? Why had she prevented him from seeing her? His tone of voice was wrong, he knew, a whine creeping in, childlike and petulant. He had hated himself for it but was compelled to continue. He was so sure he had everything under control just days ago and here he was embarrassing himself and her. His constant questioning, he knew, although she had denied it and refused to look him in the eye, irritated Polly. She had no idea the turmoil he was experiencing. Seeing her in the outfit he had helped choose he was overcome with desire and could not prevent his mind flashing back to the bedroom in Spain to summon forth the image of her naked body and the feel of their embrace. It was difficult to think of anything but the next opportunity to make love to her. He had recklessly kissed her there in the corridor and was compensated somewhat by the responsiveness of her lips and a promise of a meeting very soon. He had agreed to leave her alone until she elected to find him. Then and only then would they spend time together. When the opportunity arose, she would seek him out.

Douglas sensed Hugh looking at him and turned to smile hoping the smile was normal He really did not want today to be spoiled by anything and he had promised Hugh he would spend time with him. It was good to be here with his family. Suddenly, everybody laughed and his reflexes caused him to laugh too. He was unable to gauge the amount of time his thoughts had been distracted and, returning to reality he realised a friend of Peter's was reading something to the guests and that this was the source of the hilarity. So far, he had missed it all. Consumed with guilt he steered his attention back to the words determined, for the moment at least, to be an active participant.

Ralph was aware of tightness in his left shoe. Having a high instep made shoe buying a nightmare. He hoped it would not get any worse and cloud an otherwise perfect day. Being family they were placed at the front which made it difficult for him to make the necessary adjustment He glanced at the back of Kate's neck, marvelling at the smoothness of her skin and the small strands of hair that had escaped to curl around her top vertebrae. It was so sad that the majority of young people always found fault with their bodies or appearance. It was only on reaching middle age one could appreciate how lovely they were. He had agonised about his height for several years only beginning to grow rapidly in his later teens and early twenties to reach a very acceptable six feet. What must it have been like for Douglas during those growing years when he appeared to be racing upwards every week? He had towered above them all at sixteen.

Ralph turned his mind to the ceremony. They had all been asked if they knew of any lawful impediment why Kate and Peter should not be joined in matrimony. At their wedding they had all stifled laughter at this point. The Registrar had an extraordinary accent pronouncing lawful as lafful. Ever since they had mimicked him when the word entered their vocabulary. One only ever heard or saw people objecting in plays or films but nevertheless, there was always a slight frisson of apprehension when the question was offered. One of Peter's friends made his way to the front. It was Tom Weldon. Ralph had not seen him for quite a while and he was certainly a very handsome chap now. As a boy he had been incredibly thin. Unexpectedly, he had chosen the Air Force as his career and was now a fighter pilot. Obviously, the regime of service life agreed with him. He looked immensely fit. The reading was taken from "Captain Corelli's Mandolin". It was very fitting. As Tom came to the lines comparing lust to love many people laughed. Ralph turned to Hugh and gave him a nudge; take a note of this he wanted to say, these are good words of advice. Hugh jumped a little, probably had not been listening. Soon they would be coming to the close. The Registrar had been extremely good. A Civil wedding could be rather empty and without soul but they had taken their time breaking every so often for readings of prose and poetry to provide focus and depth. Young people now were fortunate in being able to choose the location for their weddings. It had taken far too long for the practice to be adopted. Peter was looking intently at Kate. It was a mannerism Judith and Ralph noticed him adopt when he was nervous. He would fix his eyes upon Kate, it used to be Judith, and address his comments to her alone, his eyes never straying from hers. He would not relish the thought of being centre stage all day, Ralph suspected, though now his confidence had grown enormously. The sentence for which they had all been waiting was finally spoken. Kate and Peter had been pronounced man and wife. Tears prickled behind Ralph's eyes. It was an emotional moment. How he wished them a happy life together. It was a gift one could not give. Whatever happened now was very much up to them. Living one's life with another person was a situation to which one adapted imperceptibly. As years passed small mannerisms, odd behaviour, were absorbed into the fabric of the relationship. For some they caused an irritant or friction, for others they became a kind of matted felt, soft to the touch, receiving. The joy of shared silence was perhaps one of the finest things Ralph appreciated in his long marriage. He was under no pressure whatsoever to speak; he could be totally at ease with Judith.

Taking his small bottle of soapy water Ralph joined the guests in their bubble blowing. The aperture through which the filmy liquid passed was heart shaped yet the bubbles were round. As Peter kissed his bride the room was filled with gently floating bubbles which, after an initial rush to break free, caught the light to make their way towards a passing shoulder or head or simply to burst upon the air in a tiny joyous explosion. People became reckless in their blowing, shouting congratulations. Everybody laughed, pleased to be present on such an occasion. Ralph moved forward with Judith to kiss the bride, his daughter in law, and Peter. Ralph clasped Peter to him as he spoke emotionally "Congratulations Peter, I wish you years of happiness together"

"Thanks, Dad. I hope we last as long as you two" Peter stood back looking at both his parents affectionately and moving towards his mother held her close. Ralph in turn took Kate into his arms feeling a sense of privilege to be sharing her now with Peter. Suddenly everybody was crowding round them.

Maurice, the best man, took control and began to direct everybody downstairs where he promised they would have the chance to congratulate the pair before being seated for the "wedding breakfast". Few people took notice of his wishes and he was forced to raise his voice and block their way, cheerfully shouting directions and insisting they followed his instructions. Ralph took Judith's hand and guided her through.

"Perhaps if we make a show of where to go, others will follow" He cleared a path for Peter and Kate who swept in their wake a gathering of young people. Gradually the crowd began to thin to form a corridor through which they passed, the remaining guests following like a human train behind Kate in her wedding dress.

Ralph caught sight of Polly and Edward. Catching Polly's eye he raised his eyebrows in recognition and was somewhat unnerved by her response. She did not call hallo or break into a reciprocal smile but began to mouth something at him that he could only interpret as "Another farce". What did she mean? He must have misinterpreted. But what other two words were similar in their formation? He raised himself to look for her again but by now everyone was eager to be downstairs and she was lost from sight. Judith was squashed against him and there was no way he could inform her of Polly's extraordinary statement without making it public. He could not believe it had happened. "Another farce?" The words rang in his head and the outline of her red mouth against the whiteness of her teeth as she formed them had imprinted itself so clearly in his visual recall he could not pretend she had meant otherwise. Perhaps he had missed an incident she believed him to have witnessed. This thought seemed a reasonable one and he felt slightly less agitated, that must be it. Somebody had done something or said something. It would all be made clear once he had a chance to speak to her when all the formalities were over.

Downstairs the newly married couple positioned themselves centre of the topical plants. Each guest filed through to receive a glass of champagne from a lively group of young waiters and waitresses. One, dressed in her official black dress and small white apron wore, upon her beautiful face, an assortment of metal piercing. Across her eyebrows ran small bobbles, the side of her nose displayed a raised jewel while beneath her lip a bright silver stud provided something on which she repeatedly tagged and pulled. On occasion she darted out her tongue to reveal a ball of metal that sat full centre. They greeted the guests graciously thinking of the sum of money promised at the end of the day. Peter was shaking the hands of newly formed, distant relatives and kissing the cheeks of others. Everyone affectionately hugged Kate, her face now pink with the residue of lipstick left by friends and family. The queue was long and there were many waiting to exchange a personal good will message. The noise of many people talking simultaneously rose to almost obliterate the music of the small quartet who continued to play with gusto, sipping their champagne when a break in the music arose.

Hugh had managed to extricate himself from the family and was standing further back with Sam and his two sisters, Rachel and Eva. They were a very extrovert trio, talking loudly, laughing loudly. He was glad to be at the epicentre. It made talking to Douglas impossible. He could see him now at the front end of the queue waiting to speak to Peter and Kate. He was with Judith and Ralph, engaged in conversation but Hugh noticed his head moving, eyes raking the crowds, almost certainly trying to see Polly. His stomach dropped and a feeling of sadness crossed his chest.

"We had a brilliant time in Thailand" Eva was saying. "Do you think you will have a Gap Year Hugh?"

They had all talked of recent travels. Sam and Hugh were almost identical in age and still at school. The two girls were now at university leading independent lives. Hugh was a little in awe of Eva who seemed to possess an abundance of confidence and good looks. Rachel was fun with a great sense of humour. They had all grown up together and although their houses were distant each year the families would meet for a holiday together. He continued to discuss the pros and cons of gap years, his eyes constantly on Douglas to keep him in sight. He felt that by doing this he would be able in some way to contain the situation but, of course, he knew this was nonsense. As Sam began to talk, Hugh looked further into the surrounding guests for Polly and Edward. As his eyes followed the line of people intervening guests who waved or smiled or raised glasses believing he was searching for them blocked his gaze. He thought he could see Edward's head some way in the middle and had determined to avoid them both for as long as possible. Soon they would all be seated in their allotted places and he would be cushioned by protocol. After the meal, there would be speeches imprisoning him for a while longer. Following that, there were so many people whose company he could seek, it might just be possible to string out the day with avoidance. An apology at a later date would be acceptable.

The lump in her throat did not surprise Judith. It had risen during the ceremony and was only just becoming controllable. She could not see Peter or Kate's full expressions as they faced the Registrar. A marriage was always filled with hope, change and, conversely for some, bereavement. Parents of the bride had less to lose for Judith had noticed that parents of girls could expect frequent phone calls and visits even after marriage but sons were less aware of their parents emotional needs. She could not help repeating the phrase "A daughter is a daughter for all of her life, but a son is a son till he gets him a wife". Normally she would dismiss this expression but for a moment, today, she was aware of a kind of loss. She was not really sad, the tears that prickled in her eyes rose from some inner instinctual emotion. She had felt great happiness only moments before and this roller coaster of feelings was new to her. She broke from her self-indulgent thoughts to look at Peter and Kate. What a splendid pair they made. How enormously fortunate they were to have Kate now as a daughter in law. One or two of Peter's earlier relationships had been with girls who made them awkward in their company. It had distanced them from Peter a little as they were unable to express their genuine opinion of them for fear of hurting him. They had loved Kate as soon as they saw her and had many years ahead to enjoy her company. Now they were a married couple and she could only wish for them a future together that would be happy and fulfilling.

Judith and Ralph found themselves in the centre of a group of Ralph's relatives; His sisters and husbands were delighted to have the pleasure of their company and being reunited for a while. Ralph's mother was busy talking to Tessa who had left the farm with Tom and the children very early that day. Anne and Richard had almost to cancel at the last minute as Anne had found it difficult to locate a locum doctor to take surgery. She looked a little tired and no wonder. Judith marvelled at the way she had organized her life around the family and patients.

Somebody squeezing her arm caused Judith to turn. Edward and Polly stood behind them.

"Hallo!" Judith exclaimed with pleasure. "Wasn't it a delightful ceremony?"

"Delightful" said Edward leaning forward to kiss her cheek. Polly made no move towards Judith but turned instead to Ralph and kissed the air somewhere in the proximity of his face.

"All these months of preparation suddenly seem worthwhile. Ralph and I are amazed at the calm manner in which Peter and Kate have organized everything". Judith nursed Polly's snub wondering on it's intent. She could move forward and force a kiss upon her but the fear of a second rebuff restrained her.

"They appeared to be enjoying every minute." Ralph's eyes searched Polly's face for a clue that might reveal the reason for her earlier exchange mouthed from across the room.

"Did it bring back any memories of your own wedding?" asked Polly staring hard at Ralph.

"As a matter of fact it did," answered Ralph. His tone was defensive though he knew there was no reason to be. Before he could elaborate Polly interjected.

"It was interesting to hear the commitment we all made again. The words haven't altered as I recall. One wonders what percentage of people go on to divorce." Polly's voice was rather flat as she directed her thoughts to Judith.

"Good heavens, Polly" exclaimed Edward "that's a statistic we can do without today!" He smiled warmly at Ralph and then Judith. Raising his glass he said, "Let's all wish them every happiness for a long and enjoyable relationship".

Ralph noticed Polly did not lift her glass and his earlier sense of disquiet returned. "Well, we are still together" he replied putting his arm around Judith.

"Are we?" said Polly and turned to Edward. A bemused expression spread across his face and he threw a questioning glance at Ralph. They were left for a brief moment to share their embarrassment before a welcome interruption intervened.

"Here you both are!" It was Maurice. "Everybody has been searching for you. The photographer is about to take the family groups. Hugh and Douglas are making their way. Can you see the far corner? There is a small kind of river with a bridge. Well, that's where he has set things up." He turned to Polly and Edward. "Sorry to interrupt so rudely, but everything today has to run to time."

Edward shrugged. "We quite understand. It is a very responsible position being the best man." He wished Polly would not behave in this unpredictable way. She had been off hand all morning and hardly exchanged a word to him in the taxi. He was grateful young Douglas had turned up to take her off his hands for a while. He wanted to enjoy the day. It was rare for the pair of them to be anywhere together recently and they should at least try to be sociable.

"And how!" Maurice looked around. "I have got to find Kate's sister now. We should have organized a microphone in this section but don't worry I'll be back to herd everyone into the dining area as soon as the photographer has finished. I expect you're all hungry." He returned to Polly and Edward." Do your drinks need refreshing? The waiter is coming round. We want to keep everyone happy."

"I am very happy, thank you," said Polly, again the strange tone in her voice caused Edward to look curiously at her but she merely turned away focusing into the distance.

The photographer was very innovative. No straight "groups", everyone carefully positioned to make the most of the luscious plants and water features in the background. While he concentrated on the bride, groom, and immediate family, his partner mingled with the guests compiling a signed portfolio of Polaroid portraits. By the end of the day they would have a record on film with accompanying comments on the day from each person to provide an interesting collection of memorabilia for the future. Some of the more literary guests dashed off amusing comments or quotes spontaneously, while others pondered at length, afraid of committing themselves to something so traceable. Weeks later they would recall the comment to raise a flush of embarrassment and regret.

The appearance of the dining room had a calming effect on the ebullient crowd. The atmosphere was calm and serene. Large round tables were laid with pristine white linen and heavy silver cutlery. Each place label had been beautifully designed to compliment the floral arrangements that stood in the centre. Beside each place setting was a small folded box inside which were little heart shaped sparklers, fortune cookies and a tiny flower. Voices were automatically lowered as searches were made to find the correct seating. For those who were unacquainted introductions followed and questions were put in the hope of discovering a distant family connection or friends in common. The fleet of waiters and waitresses stood ready eying the tables for which they were responsible, hoping their group would be responsive and undemanding. They had been groomed to do their best, be polite, to make this occasion a happy one. There were to be no repercussions, no calls for complaint and although the majority of the staff had other occupations, or were following a course of study, each and everyone of them felt proud of the room and tables. They had tried their best. The reactions of the guests pleased them. It did indeed look spectacular. Everyone in place, they stood hands gripping the backs of chairs, waiting as though at school, for permission to sit. Maurice stepped forward graciously to request they do so and within seconds the room was filled with conversation and noise. Cameras flashed to record the room and people before the waiters arrived with the wine. It was now nearly three o'clock. Everyone was hungry and eager to appease the call of his or her stomach. Food followed swiftly on the wine. It was time now to concentrate.

Judith, from her position at the table, could just see Edward and Polly through the adjacent shoulders of Kate's mother and father. They had been placed close to the family at the table immediately in front. Edward was talking animatedly to Anne. Over the years they had met at different family functions and enjoyed each other's company. Polly was seated beside Tom. He would, no doubt, bring the conversation round to farming and the government. Polly enjoyed discussions. With her new knowledge of Spain, she might well introduce the EU. She looked serious. Perhaps she had already done so! Judith could not help being amused by this thought. She had drunk several glasses of wine and champagne and having eaten little since early morning felt light -headed. Edward looked up at that moment, catching Judith's smile and held her gaze. They had managed a brief meeting just prior to entering the dining room. As the guests moved slowly forward, the crowd narrowing by the door had pressed them close. He took her hand, placing his palm against hers. Simultaneously, he bent his head to hers and kissed her back of neck. A lighting bolt of surprise shot through her and she returned the pressure of his hand in acknowledgement.

"We must talk later" he whispered. "I need to know your reactions to the decision I have to take".

They were through the door, the crowd thinning as they made their way to the tables. Judith had not had time to reply. She knew he was referring to Australia. She knew she did not want him to go. It was too far away and any journey back or forth would be inordinately lengthy and difficult. Thankfully her thoughts were interrupted by Kate's father's voice asking her opinion on the quality of the wine, hoping, she found it as delightful as did he. They fell into easy conversation as the meal progressed, confirming Judith's opinion on the merits of Kate and her family.

The noise in the dining room grew with the courses. Wine glasses were constantly topped and a feeling of warm contentment wrapped itself around them all. Everybody's fears had been quelled. Their outfits were well received; they had talked amiably and interestingly to the new acquaintances of the day. Now they were happily seated besides cordial people, eating a very agreeable meal accompanied by plenty of good wine. Little would be asked of them now other than they did not become inebriated and objectionable. They could remain seated, listen to the speeches that were to come and then circulate around the room to reunite with friends or relatives whom they had not seen for a while.

Douglas was beginning to feel the effects of the drink. He should be cautious, he did not want to loose control today of all days. Everybody around him was talking and he had been engaged in an interesting discussion earlier with Kate's father on a recent article in the newspaper encouraging people to help replant the forests of England. This had led to wider issues and both had been satisfied to find they were in accord. From his position, he could not see the guests. His back was to them. Apart from signalling the waiter, he had no cause to turn. He was aware of Polly's presence behind him. He had seen where she was seated, cursing the fact of the impossibility to observe her. There was a physical sensation running down his back reminding him of her proximity. Later, he would leave the table and go across. He knew she had told him to wait but what possible harm could there be in his desire to make contact with Polly and Edward? Nobody would read anything out of the norm in that. He noticed Hugh's voice becoming rather loud as he conversed with Kate's sister. One forgot he was only seventeen. He must have downed a fair amount of alcohol so far. Douglas felt responsible for him. He must remember to keep an eye on him, make sure he didn't overstep the mark and embarrass them all.

Peter sensed it was almost time for the speeches. They had agreed he would read his after Kate's father and his best man. He felt buoyed by the champagne and wine and very happy. All the preparations for this day now seemed worthwhile. At times he had wondered and occasionally dreamed of a simple ceremony somewhere, two witnesses and away. The whole thing had snowballed so quickly and by then it was far too late to make changes of any kind. Kate's family and his had been generous, but a lot of the financing had been theirs. There were plenty of other ways to spend money but today he realised it was the best way to have spent it. All these people, all the connections between family and friends formed a warm cocoon around them. After today it was up to them to make their own success of life. His parents had so many years of marriage behind them and he was anxious to follow their example. The institution of marriage was not dying as so many of his less committed friends had told him. He was more than happy to join the ranks and support the institution.

Kate's father was rising to his feet, hands folding and re folding the notes from which he would read. He was an impressive man with thick, white, wavy hair. His large nose supported a pair of half rimmed spectacles above, which his eyes glanced around the room hoping to convey the need for silence. People shifted in their seats or moved their chairs for a better view and he settled back on his heels, peered around at the guests one last time and opened fully his sheet of paper. He looked affectionately at Kate and began with several amusing anecdotes of her childhood while the audience, sensing his ability to tell a good tale, allowed their shoulders to fall and relax.

Hugh was beginning to resent the way Douglas was vetoing his drinking. Quite honestly he was hoping to get drunk. It might help in some way to quell this constant tightness in his stomach. Douglas was behaving as though he had nothing to hide being charming to Kate's relatives, collaborating with the waitresses to ensure, he, Hugh, did not receive a full glass. It was annoying. He almost felt like telling him what he had seen. Another wave of rage surged through him and he drained the last of the wine. They would have to refill his glass for the toasts. Douglas could not object to that. Hugh caught the eye of a passing waiter and lifted his empty champagne glass. Before Douglas could intervene it was full and bubbling, the surface jumping, sending tiny explosions into the air. Raising his eyes he was disturbed to find himself looking straight into the eyes of Polly. She had turned her seat for a better view of Kate's father and was now visible. He got the weirdest notion from that brief glance, he had looked away immediately, that she was smirking at him. Perhaps she noticed his manoeuvre to gain an extra glass of champagne. It could be, but something kept him from accepting such a conclusion. Hugh looked at Kate's father and feigned deep interest in what was being said but his head, as though being pulled by puppet strings, strayed to Polly. She was still staring at him. This time he nodded and forced his lips into a tight smile. She raised her eyebrows but did not return the smile. Perhaps she knew he had seen them.

The room was filled with noise as chairs were scraped upon the floor and glasses raised to the bride and groom. As soon as the guests were re seated Maurice, still standing, began his speech. He was by nature a witty man and took pride in his ability to entertain. He had spent time on this speech wanting to make it memorable. He remembered to check the pace and to keep his voice clear and loud enough for those way back by the door. He was looking forward to delivering the jokes he had placed strategically into the speech. As he warmed to his audience, they, in turn, warmed to him. It had been well worth the effort. Everybody seemed to be laughing at the right moments, even wriggling on their seats a little and clapping enthusiastically. It was slightly intoxicating having all eyes upon him. He felt bold and excited. This was turning out to be a great wedding.

As he thanked the brides' maids and delivered their gifts he felt a sense of disappointment that his moment of fame was coming to a close. One more joke to go before the final call to be upstanding for the bride and groom. It went well he knew and as he returned to his seat Peter came forward to embrace him. Maurice had not let him down.

Peter allowed the applause to die before making his thank you introduction. He was pleased to find how buoyant he felt. The atmosphere in the room was terrific and the ceremony, in terms of official things to be executed, was virtually complete. He and Kate were now just a few hours away from departure. They then had two full weeks alone. It would be fantastic. He recognised this moment of true happiness. No more loneliness, no more searching for someone. He could move on and begin his life. He took a deep breath, swept his eyes across the expectant guests and began "There were several ambiguities in that speech Maurice, I'm not sure I should give unequivocal thanks". Everyone laughed remembering the anecdote that had caused most amusement. "But I would like to thank you for being such a fantastic support today and during the past fifteen or so years since we met. My school days would never have been the same without you". Peter listened to his own voice as he ran through the, well rehearsed, opening of his speech, careful not to omit anyone. "But, of course, the people to whom I owe the greatest thanks are my parents for giving me their love and support and Kate's parents for welcoming me so warmly into their family. Thinking of what I should say today led me back into my past. Many snap shots of my childhood came flooding in and as I tried to put them in order I realised just how much I owed to my parents who were always there, always supportive and instilled in me such a positive outlook on life. Douglas and Hugh will, I know, second me in this. We have been lucky to be brought up by two people who display such respect and affection for each other. They are the best of friends. Looking at them I hope Kate and I can achieve what they have achieved and if we, after twenty-six years of marriage, can say that of ourselves we will be more than content. Finally, on behalf of my wife Kate" Peter was aware of the novelty these two words as he raised his glass "thank you all for contributing towards this wonderful day." The guest's half rose then stood to participate in a chorus of toasts, their glasses finally drained. Peter could now relax. He had played his part and it was time to mingle with the guests for a while before he and Kate could escape.

The room fractured as people rose to cross from table to table. Relatives opened handbags to show off their children or grandchildren. Older guests hurried to the lavatories while younger guests made their way to the bar. The immediate family remained seated for a while, staring out into the crowd, searching for those with whom they hoped to make contact. Hugh was the first to rise, kissed his mother before kissing Kate and made his way hurriedly toward his cousins at the far table. A pianist took up his position at the large grand piano and began to play, his fingers pressing gently on the keys. He was aware of his purpose there to provide entertaining but unobtrusive background noise and was grateful for the chance to practice and receive payment. Later when people began to thin out, someone or even a small group would end up standing around the piano to make their requests. He could reproduce many tunes off the cuff but for now he would stick to the promised programme.

Kate's family were besieged by well wishing relatives. Ralph shook hands with several and catching Judith's eye, signalled retreat. They wove their way through people, exchanging smiles with each eye contact and as they came to a relatively quiet area of the room were met by Polly flanked on either side by Edward and Douglas. Edward exchanged a rapid quizzical look with Judith. "Polly has gathered us both together, she appears to have some kind of mission" He raised his eyebrows again and looked back at Polly.

Ralph noticed Polly was holding Douglas's hand. She probably wanted to tell them how thrilled she was with the work he and Patrick had been doing in Spain. But was forced to concede this could not be the case as he noticed Douglas's face was registering alarm and avoiding his gaze. Was Polly disappointed, surely she would not tell him here today in front of them?

No one could imagine the panic Douglas was experiencing. Polly had approached him as soon as the toasts were complete. The family table numbers had swelled with advancing guests, and then began to thin as people fanned out into the crowd. Hugh, he thought, had left rather too promptly and he was just beginning to plan his own exit when he felt Polly's fingers pressing into his shoulder, her long nails digging into his flesh. He knew instantly it was her and sensed his neck and face reddening. She had come for him! The thunderous noise of his heart as she spoke his name reached his eardrums with a deafening pitch. His facial expression changed however as he stood to face her for there, by her side, was Edward. They exchanged greetings somewhat formally and Polly began to purposefully lead them through the noisy groups until they came upon his mother and father. He had been unable to detect what she had said to him as they progressed across the room but the tone of her voice chilled him and made him very uneasy. As they came across his parents he looked beyond his father not wanting their eyes to meet. He knew his mother too was directing her gaze at him but something internal and instinctive would not permit him to reveal anything of himself.

Judith was about to say something about the day, how excited she was, how particularly glad she was to see so many people, many of whom she had not seen for such a long time but something in Polly's manner prompted her to remain silent. Edward still looked bemused. For some extraordinary, unexplainable reason, her joy, her total delight, her pleasure was draining away, leaving her with one sensation, her own heart beat. Searching for relief she turned to Douglas but he was looking elsewhere.

"I believe there is a small room behind this door" said Polly looking hard at Judith "I would like us to go there because there is something I think you should know."

Douglas was positively panic struck. "Polly" he began "perhaps this isn't the time." He bent towards her removing his hand from her grasp but she reached out and retrieved it firmly.

Judith looked from Polly to Ralph and then to Edward. Their faces revealed a shared expression of intrigue and surprise.

"I think it is" she replied. Again the hard stare was on Judith.

Judith was still on a high, the taste of champagne lingering in her mouth. She had always respected Polly, admired her for the successful business venture she and Rebecca had built together. They were good friends, not as intimate as she, Beth and Angie, but sufficiently so to exchange confidences. This look Polly now gave her was not the warm exchange with which she was familiar. It was filled with loathing! The excitement of the day drained away to leave her sober.

They had all picked up on the atmosphere Polly was creating. The surrounding noise of guests, of music, of cutlery and dishes being cleared, all transformed into a claustrophobic hum. Everyone moving in slow motion, their faces showing a hazy swathe of white as mouths were stretched in speech. They wove their way between them catching as they did the odd shoulder or elbow in passing.

"What on earth is this about, Polly?" demanded Edward harshly. He too was gripped by sensations of both irritation and unease. The tightness of her hand merely increased as she pulled him like some reluctant toddler. "Polly?" he repeated, angered by her refusal to respond.

She merely strode ahead, pushed open the door and they, drawn by this as yet unexplainable behaviour, followed.

The room was small with a large wooden table placed in the centre. Judith noticed one of the curtains was caught in the window frame. Somewhat irrationally, she felt a strong urge to straighten it out. Instead she sat down on the nearest chair, grateful for the proximity, as her legs by now felt slightly shaky.

There was a strange, clean, smell in the room as though earlier someone had sprayed a perfume deodorizer. It was slightly sweet and clawing. The chairs were upholstered in pale grey with arms bowed to mimic those of Chippendale. It was obviously used for parties or conference meetings. The bowl of flowers centrally placed was disappointingly fake, their silk petals falling in pre-determined positions. On the walls were reproduction prints of foreign cities, most of which Judith recognised. How she wished she could predict the reasons for this meeting to prepare her in some way. It was the behaviour Douglas displayed that she found so unnerving. She had never seen him look so anxious, even fearful, since he was a small boy. Could he have done something terribly wrong in Spain? Surely not. He had been so happy on his return informing them of his work there and how well it was going.

Ralph, whose nerves were on high alert, began to feel rage rising. Why were they coming here when beyond the door all their friends and family were waiting to link up with them? It really was insensitive of Polly to drag them in here like this. What could she be up to? He also felt a little drunk having had by now several glasses. He moved to take up a position besides Douglas. There was an instinctual feeling he may be in need of support though for what, Ralph could not imagine.

Polly finally released the hand of Douglas, taking a chair immediately opposite Judith. As though by silent command everybody sat, eyes firmly on Polly as she began to speak.

She settled on the edge of her chair placing her hands uppermost. Her elegant fingers, carefully manicured, playing with the large diamond ring of her wedding finger. She had all the confidence of a chairperson revealing nothing as to the direction this gathering was to take. She took her time composing her thoughts, waiting for the chairs to cease moving and for everyone in the room to be called to order. Her eyes ran slowly round the table looking at them all defiantly, daring anyone to object to the proceedings. There were several seconds of total silence before she began.

"This is a meeting I have longed to organize for quite some time but it's always been impossible to gather everybody together. Edward is away so much, Judith busy with her work, Ralph involved in his latest book, but today I knew we'd all be here. This wedding has given me a perfect opportunity to deliver my own rather special gift to all of you, a sort of "icing on the cake " so to speak, rather appropriate considering our reason for being here". She beamed at Douglas. "I first conceived this idea some time ago so the planning of its execution has taken several months. Douglas is still unaware of the role he has played," She looked around at their astonished faces as Douglas half rose in his seat and she abruptly motioned him to sit down." Without his cooperation I may not have found the courage but once the idea had taken hold I was determined to carry it through to the bitter end; for my own peace of mind, if nothing else." She paused as though she had the leading role in some West-End production. She moved her body closer to the table laying her fingers flatly upon its surface." It's my greatest hope that after today I 'll be able to get on with my life free from the burden I have ......"

"Polly, what is all this?" demanded Edward once more, his voice now heavy with exasperation and confusion.

"Be quiet, Edward" she replied curtly. "I've just sat through a series of speeches heavily laced with self congratulatory comments watching all of you wreathed in smiles of self satisfaction. "Hasn't it all gone well, don't they make a happy couple, aren't we a wonderful family". Well now it is my turn to make a speech but sadly, I don't think your faces will reflect the same pleasure because what I have to say won't bring about any backslapping or congratulations. All of you smugly present such a united front, so pleased with yourselves and your family, giving the impression of love, of harmony, of family togetherness and pride." Her voice took on a mocking tone. "Three wonderful sons, a long, fulfilled marriage, ambitions realized. As I sat there listening I found it more and more obnoxious and difficult to stomach. I did have the courtesy to remain silent but there were so many moments when I longed to spring to my feet, turn to the crowd and shout, "Don't be taken in by these people. The whole thing is a sham, a farce."

Ralph's mind flashed to that moment by the door when she had mouthed those very words. He was not mistaken. Before he could demand an explanation Judith spoke.

"Whatever do you mean?" Judith lent forward challenging a reply yet aware of the fact she was suddenly gripped by a dreadful feeling of unease. She looked around the table hardly able to believe they were sitting there in the middle of Peter's wedding holding what seemed to be a kind of meeting. She was conscious of the odd burst of laughter and music from outside that contrasted with the atmosphere building in the room. Were people looking for them? Shouldn't she just get up and go back to the guests? Polly's actions were becoming more baffling and uncomfortable by the minute. Judith did not like being there and began to stand.

"Sit down Judith. I want to answer your question." Her voice was so commanding Judith lowered herself back into her chair. "I found it a farce because I know things not to be as they seem." Polly lent back in her seat knowing she now held the reins. Judith felt her palms begin to sweat and a wave of nausea pass through her.

"What could you possibly know?" demanded Ralph. He could not help looking at Douglas whose face was contorted with anxiety, his eyes moving jerkily from Polly, to Edward, to Judith. Was this some kind of complaint against Douglas? What could he have done? Surely this wasn't the time or place for her to be accusing Douglas.? But then she kept on about the family. Why? When would she get to the point? Her behaviour was unnerving but the expression on Douglas' face was even more so. How could he have colluded in this? He was looking guilty about something, what could possibly have happened in Spain?

"Oh, Ralph, poor Ralph" she sighed and once again lent toward Douglas taking his hand. He looked helplessly at her and then across to his mother not knowing what Polly would say next. He felt the familiar pressure of her hand as she reached across but now there was a difference, now he wanted to pull it away and escape. He had never seen such a venomous expression on Polly's face and it frightened him. If she was about to reveal their relationship why did she need to insult his family? It had been his intention to speak to his parents alone and gently introduce the idea that he and Polly had become an item and what she meant to him. It would have been a shock he well knew but nowhere near as catastrophic as this might turn out to be. Why though, should their relationship affect the way his family had behaved together? They were all very close; they did all love each other. What was wrong with that?

Ralph hated the sympathetic way she had used his name. The pity in her eyes as she looked across at him struck coldly. What on earth was happening? The wedding ceremony seemed hours ago, in another time, a time when they were all untroubled by this new Polly so full of anger and animosity. What did she know? How could she know things that they did not? He and Judith always told each other everything.

"First thing first, I think" she continued. "It's true, I admit, you do have three wonderful sons. All three have something special and all three are very attractive young men. One of them, I found to be so attractive that I just couldn't resist going to bed with him." She looked around triumphantly waiting for their reaction.

"Polly!" Edward exclaimed in disbelief. He shot an angry glance across at her that was retuned with a look of cold, hard, hate.

Judith laughed a tight, frightened laugh. "With Douglas? You? But he is so young!" Her stomach clamped hard against her diaphragm pushing air rapidly through her mouth. The idea of Polly and Douglas in bed together seemed incestuous. She had been there at his christening, for his early birthday parties. She was, for all intents and purposes, his aunt, for God's sake. Aunts did not go to bed with their nephews. How could Douglas be so taken in?

Polly was savouring the moment, aware of greater things to come. Her cheeks were flushed her eyes sparkled. Edward was dumbfounded. She revelled in his surprise and felt giddy with power. He had no idea what was to follow. She could crack the whip and hold them all in her power by fear and anticipation. Today would not to be their day as planned, today would be hers. A day they would all remember but for different reasons than those expected. She drew in her breath and gave a sickly false smile revealing her white, even teeth. Now she would go for the kill.

"It's suddenly occurred to me, we really ought to pool our resources. There you were Judith, at the receiving end of a wealth of emotional goodies whilst I felt somewhat lacking and deprived. Why should all that love go into your coffers? Why shouldn't I have a share?" Polly was revelling in the reaction her words caused. She remained amazingly calm holding her body still and erect as her breath was expelled in an even regular rhythm. Her face registered distain for them all.

"But Polly, we have always sympathized with your inability to have children. Our own boys have always cared for you." interjected Ralph. For God's sake, was she using their valuable time on Peter's wedding day to rustle up sympathy for her inability to conceive? Had she gone completely mad? What on earth did she expect them to do? Did she hope Douglas might make her pregnant? Maybe the fault had been with Edward all these years. They couldn't know that and anyway there was little to be done now as Polly was well beyond childbearing age. Ralph felt disgusted by the idea of Polly taking Douglas to bed. Not because of their age difference, she was after all a very presentable woman, not without sexual appeal, but that he had grown up with her. They were not related but they might just as well be. He didn't want Polly to take his son, destroy his chances of children, possibly to break his heart when she grew tired of him. A woman of her sophistication could surely not adapt to his life style. She was used to luxury and wealth. Douglas could never give her that. She might use him as a "Toy boy" for a while and then? He looked questioningly at Polly.

"I'm sure you have Ralph, but sympathy is something I don't and did not need. I might accept I could share family celebrations with you and your children but what I couldn't accept was I should be expected to share my husband".

There was a rush of indrawn breath as Judith, Ralph, Edward and Douglas registered these final words. Polly knew she now held them captive and continued. "I have had my suspicions for a long time but there was never any concrete evidence. Then several months ago a friend of mine happened to be at a conference in Florence. She recognised Edward and thought she'd introduce herself but as she approached she saw you Judith and picked up something from your body language that warned her off. Being a good friend she kept herself hidden and watched. There's no use pretending it was all very platonic because she was witness to your sharing a room that night and the following night. When she got back she told me and I've had Edward watched ever since. You can imagine this set me thinking and I began to piece together the past and came to the conclusion that this affair must have been going on for quite some time. The scales were so unbalanced don't you agree Ralph? So, I thought, as Judith had taken such a very large share of my family, it was time for me to take part of yours." She looked at Douglas.

Ralph seemed to be stepping into an entirely different and unknown environment. One that was rapidly filling with pain. He was always aware of how Edward and Judith felt great affection for each other but had never thought, never believed it to be sexual, never. Could this really be true? If so, their married life was based on lies? When Judith had said she loved him did she really love Edward? Edward? When Ralph believed her to be thinking of him were her thoughts with Edward? A lightening flash of rage ran over him as he looked at Judith and saw without doubt her facial expression signified guilt. How unbelievably cruel of her and how very cruel of Polly to choose his son's wedding for this revelation. Molten anger surged through him rising in uncontrollable bursts to blur his vision and crowd his thoughts. Not only had Polly destroyed him today but also by using

Douglas in such a despicable way, she must inevitably destroy the boy. His heart raced as he thought of further destruction. Peter and Kate must not learn of this. Not today of all days. For the moment his thoughts on Judith, on Edward and Douglas were totally superseded by his desire to keep this from them.

Suddenly, the door was thrown open and a young couple, both very much under the influence of the alcohol they had consumed, burst in. Their arms were intertwined, hands balancing glasses of red wine, one of which had already spilled across the front of the young woman's jacket. They stared, somewhat shocked, at the group of seated people and for a few seconds the room was eerily silent. Now that the door was open, others nearby looked in and began calling to Douglas and the heavy oppressive atmosphere was altered by their intrusion.

"Hey, Douggie, come and have a drink with us" called an attractive young woman. Her surrounding colleagues waved their glasses in the air.

Douglas was falling. He clasped the side of his chair hoping to keep hold of something concrete. He remembered Polly's words "I will be your Delilah". She had not cut off his hair but she had taken his strength. Was that how she had seen him for these past months, merely as merchandise to balance her scales? Used him to reap revenge on Edward? He glanced across noting Edward's registered surprise and unguarded embarrassment. His mother sat motionless. How could she? How could she betray his father? A rush of protective love flowed from him to Ralph. For the moment he did not want to look across his mother. She had become a different person and he did not like that person. His thoughts were in turmoil, trying to assimilate this news, trying to accept the reality of Polly's feelings for him. The same thoughts looped around his mind like the fragments of a tune.

The group by the door called again for Douglas. Ralph rose to greet them placing his arms gently around them and moving them back beyond the door. "We're just having a few quiet moments. Douglas will be out in a minute." He smiled and they raised their glasses to him. Their laughter and obvious enjoyment of the moment contrasted strongly with the feelings he held in check. As they retreated into the dining room Ralph closed the door and made his way toward Polly. He was still reeling from the revelations she had made and yet his parental instinct to protect his children overrode all else. He was determined to get them all out of here. The air had become fetid. He needed a drink. "Whatever happens, Polly, you are not going to destroy this day for Peter and Kate. I shall make sure they leave for their honeymoon without knowing any of this."

Polly gave him a petulant look. Dissatisfaction displayed on her face as she sensed Ralph's rising prominence in the order of things and her power over them all beginning to ebb. This look provided Ralph with the fuel he needed to take control. He was surprised and buoyed by his rising confidence and felt his ability to take control rising. Probably the state of shock had clicked in but he did not have time to consider this. The uppermost thought in his mind was that this encounter, this revelation, remained within the four walls of this now repellent room. He was very aware of the noise from the young people outside and sensed they would return. He could not bear to look at Polly and as he saw Edward's pale face the desire to punch him was so great that before he could check his own actions he had thrown his fist against his chin and sent him reeling backwards. Judith cried out for him to stop as he drew back for a second blow. He turned to face her and she stood shakily her eyes pleading. He was no longer her champion. Was he no longer her husband? He wanted them all to be gone. He had to get rid of Edward and Polly before Peter and

Kate came upon them. There was to be no opportunity whatsoever for them to meet.

Edward slowly raised himself from the floor to face Ralph. He could think of nothing to say other than "I'm sorry. I really am sorry." Turning to Douglas he repeated the words although he knew they could carry no weight. He was trapped by his own guilt and could say little in his own defence.

Douglas scraped back his chair and stood. He could not believe what had taken place or comprehend Polly's behaviour. Had she really set out to use him as the catalyst to set all this in motion? Had she never really cared for him? She had intended to destroy them all and knew the news of his mother's adultery would be twice as shocking if it was heralded by their liaison. A large ball of pain and grief invaded his body. How could he leave this room and face anyone? He had to get away. Edward's feeble attempt to apologise only served to make things worse. He did not want to speak to any of them. Not here. There was still too much to be resolved.

Douglas was pulled back to the present as he heard his name being called as the door was once more thrown wide. The music and gaiety of the outside party mood poured into the room to weaken the concentrated atmosphere of enmity. Stephanie, an ex girl friend, left the group and made her way to his side totally unaware of the extraordinary revelations made to Douglas just minutes earlier. "Come and dance with me, you lovely man," she cooed, grabbing his arm and pulling him towards her." She turned to Ralph and swayed slightly on her feet. "Can I take him now please Ralph he owes me a dance?"

Ralph feigned pleasure at their intrusion and forced a laugh. "Yes, Steph, take him away. We were just enjoying a sneaky minute or two's respite from the crowd." As he helped direct them to the door he managed a whispered message "We mustn't' spoil Peter and Kate's day. Try to keep going".

As Douglas departed Ralph moved toward Judith. She was sitting very still, her eyes, now filled with tears, were staring into the distance. His rage was ebbing away and an overwhelming sense of despair taking its place. It was all he could do to stop himself releasing huge, loud sobs of misery. The pain inside his chest was growing and he took a gulp of air to hold it inside his body. The acute desire to go pressed hard upon him. They must get out of this room at all cost before Peter or Hugh came to find them.

"Judith?" He called her back from her thoughts "We have to go and entertain our guests." He could not look her in the eyes and turned to Polly his voice masking his wretchedness by rising in volume

"Polly. I want you to leave. Edward, would you take your wife home?" He forced himself to face Edward who stepped forward about to speak. "No, Edward, I don't want you to say anything. Polly has said enough. All I want now is to ensure my son's wedding is not tainted or ruined. Just get out of here" His face became contorted as he forced the words from his mouth. In spite of his grief he was determined to remain strong. His emotions were changing by the minute and he was amazed to have found an inner strength he did not know he possessed. Everyone looked to him to take command and he would. It was imperative he remove Polly from the scene. Her behaviour was unpredictable and she might be driven by her quest for revenge to do anything.

Edward, his chin now smarting and red, took hold of Polly firmly be the arm and began to escort her from the room. She shook it free with disgust. "I'll leave because you, Ralph, have asked me to. I have no grudge against you but you must understand this, I was not prepared to harbour deceit and lie any longer even if it meant the destruction of your family. There's still so much I would like to say to your wife but at least now you know the truth. Your life Ralph, like mine, will be radically altered and you'll have to decide what path you want to take. I've already decided but you may find it more difficult. You can be certain of one thing, things can never return to how they were, can they?"

She walked to the door with Edward in tow. As they entered the dining room the pianist was playing the tune "I can see clearly now the rain has gone" The irony did not escape Polly as she pushed her way through the groups of people. Now that she had executed her plan she could not bear to be among such a happy crowd a moment longer. Holding her head high she strode quickly across the room, her eyes straight ahead until reaching the exit she allowed the doors to swing back heavily against Edward to form a barrier between them.

PART THREE

THE PRESENT — RALPH

The room in which Ralph sat was somewhat bare. He had determined to rid himself of clutter. No ornaments, just bookshelves and paintings; even those he dramatically culled on moving here had been left in the cardboard boxes and stored. The view itself was sufficient. From where he sat he could see the Thames curving away in the distance. Small river craft moved to and fro with the occasional excitement of a large, ocean going liner or a wonderful old sailing ship in full sail. The river police kept a regular watch but in the four years Ralph had lived in the apartment he had never witnessed any incident that could be crime related. As evening fell the lights along the water's edge sent amazing reflections into the once, grey, green water. Patterns emerged to break the colours into a kaleidoscopic surface. From his small balcony the movement would mesmerize Ralph. There was space outside for a small table and two chairs. The master bedroom also looked onto the river allowing Ralph to enjoy the activities of the waterfront from his bed. Hugh had occupied the smaller bedroom at the back for a while then an apartment had become vacant and he had moved into the same block earlier this year. It pleased him enormously to have Hugh so close. He was rather anxious initially; afraid of calling too frequently and becoming a nuisance, but they had fallen into an easy pattern of socialising. If they were both free they might go for a meal or the cinema, but mostly it was pleasant to sit facing the river and share a bottle. He checked the time on his wristwatch. In an hour or two David and Carol would be arriving from Wales. He had prepared a meal for them, tomorrow they would go out.

Sitting quietly as he waited Ralph's thoughts returned to their house in the small Welsh village where he had spent many months writing, trying to block the tide of emotion he felt after his life had been so fractured. The intervening years did little to soften the enormity of those early days but now he was perfectly able to ride them and, if he were truly honest with himself, enjoy the sensations he could summon at will. He could switch on and switch off, immersing himself in particular periods of his married life without the fear of breaking down. There were still moments of sadness but these could be replaced with plans for his present life, which provided him with a new kind of excitement. His future was now unchartered and foreign but contained no sense of fear. In the past he would never have believed he could be living, as he did now, a contented and slightly selfish bachelor's life. This morning he smiled to himself as he tidied things away. Years ago he would not have given the slightest thought to the idea of order in his environment but now it took on a new importance. The responsibility of the flat was his alone, he had selected every piece of furniture and the final lay out had taken many days to decide. He was flattered by the reaction he received from people who came to call. Looking at the paintings on his wall Ralph was grateful he and Judith had not fought over their possessions. He had been able to select the pictures he favoured most and now, with time to enjoy and appreciate them, he was discovering greater depths almost as though he saw them for the first time.

He rose to change the CD. He had bought it for himself yesterday. His eyes raked the CD shelves for something else. When he was in Wales he played Mozart, particularly the opus 21 piano concerto. It provided the right emotional support he needed then. He had not given it much thought for quite a while. Pulling out the disc he held it between his fingers and thumb staring into the middle distance recalling the hours he and Judith had sat talking. Hoping, he supposed, that words would provide a solution. They had gone round and round in circles sometimes able to discuss things rationally and other times screaming at each other. Judith had no grounds for defence as far as he was concerned and as the talk was replaced with silence a sort of resolve set in and one evening, quite inexplicably he had made the decision they should separate. He could no longer love her in the same way. He was somehow able to look upon her with a form of affection, affection for having his children but there was no real depth in it any more, not now, not when all trust had gone. He could not accept that Judith loved them both any more than he could accept that his life in had not been utterly tainted. The pre Edward years were dear to him as they were uniquely his but after that period he could rely on nothing. He could hardly allow his mind to think of certain times they had spent together, days when he had felt so happy to be with her, days when he felt so fortunate to have her. And all that time, all that time, she had been scheming to see Edward or sitting there opposite him with Edward in her thoughts. He felt such loathing for Edward and an even greater loathing for Polly. He had not seen her since that day. Whenever he thought of her he saw her hands placed upon the table, her fingers twisting her wedding ring as though the gold were molten hot and searing through her skin. When he tried to think rationally and give meaning to her behaviour he had to concede to a tiny fraction of sympathy in her direction but it's course was inevitably rerouted when he thought of Douglas and the way she had almost destroyed him. He knew nothing of her whereabouts and shrank at the idea of meeting her unexpectedly one day. Her name was never mentioned by any of them. In Ralph's view it was Edward who had, in the early days that followed, appeared to emerge from the disaster unscathed. He had obtained his goal. He found it hard to believe that Edward would have deliberately wanted to destroy his marriage but he couldn't help feeling it may have been his eventual aim. Ralph often wondered if Judith would have left him had Polly not intervened to bring everything into the open or would she have continued her clandestine meetings when circumstances allowed? Edward's secondment to Australia may have altered things he supposed but he wondered if Judith would have said goodbye to Edward or goodbye to him. He had once been a little in awe of Edward but at the wedding things had changed. He had experienced what might be called 'he supposed,' his road to Damascus. He had suddenly felt himself growing in courage and resolution and as he grew so Edward shrunk. Even though his pride was hurt and his family shattered he became aware of an emerging toughness he had not known he possessed that held him together and steered him in the right direction. When he was with Judith it had lain dormant for all those years. It had been a life without crisis, one in which he had never been called upon to fight but when the bugle blew he had been ready. He had not been found wanting when it came to the crunch. Ralph understood from Hugh that Judith and Edward lived in some style in Australia, money being no object. He felt no envy, his own finances were sound and allowed him, more or less, to go where he liked and do what he liked. The bitterness he felt over his betrayal had taken far longer to dispel than petty worries over finance. Over the last few years he and Judith had met several times on family occasions and now could fall, to his relief, into easy conversation. When he saw her, he did not want her back. It was rather a strange feeling to stand besides her knowing she was now Edward's wife and to know they wouldn't be returning home together that evening. It had take a while to reconcile himself and accept they had lived their period of life together and moved on. He supposed he should be grateful that all the years they had spent together had been amicable but his gratitude was that he had been left with the unshakeable support of his sons whereas Judith had had to work heard to regain just a portion of it. He was thankful the boys were all adult at the time of their separation, though poor Hugh was still on the cusp. The memory of Hugh's grief could still move him to anger. Edward had been aware from the start that Judith was married and yet he had carried on the relationship befriending the boys and Ralph in the process. He must have known what he had put them through. At least he had not been forced into the agony of going to court to seek custody or of being placed in the role of a "Saturday father". They were thankfully all too old for that.

Ralph returned to the present and placed the CD into the player. Within seconds he was back in Wales. The cottage overlooked the hills and from the kitchen window one could see a small stone bridge. The bridge had taken on a significance, to cross or to remain this side. David had been a great companion offering advice only on request, listening for hours into the night, never complaining of lack of sleep when he rose at the crack of dawn to milk the cows. One morning Ralph had come down to breakfast to find his laptop and a pack of A4 paper on the kitchen table. David had switched it on typing in the words "use me" across the screen. It had jolted him back. He was drained of emotion. It had all gone to his sons and their needs. He had escaped for a while and could think of nothing other than shutting himself away and trying to escape. Seeing those words sent shock waves through him as though David had slapped him hard.

For the first time in months he felt a different kind of emotion and realised how long he had been smothered by the outcome of Polly's words. She had been controlling him, controlling them all. It was time he took the reins and sent the harnessed grief galloping away to leave him free once more to get on with his life. At that moment it suddenly occurred to him that the right thing to do would be to write about his experience and use Polly's "coming out" as a central plot and weave a story around it. It would be a different approach for him but it could just work. That morning he had made himself a coffee and, seated at the kitchen table, with the bridge in sight, began to type. By the time David returned later in the day Ralph had drafted out the plot and completed the first chapter. Carol had silently brought him food and drink throughout the day and disappeared leaving his thoughts unbroken. The book had sold well. With the proceeds of the sale of their house and the book, he had become relatively well off. Judith had insisted he keep all the money from the house and use it to help the boys as well as him .He was grateful for that even though he knew it was her sense of guilt that prompted the offer. He was still smarting sufficiently to accept it. Peter and Kate were able to move to a bigger place earlier than planned, Douglas had injected the money into his business. Four years ago with his savings still intact he had bought this apartment and later, given Hugh the deposit to buy his. He smiled affectionately as he thought of Hugh and his face softened. They had been a great comfort to each other on the trip to America. At first, Ralph thought it better to cancel but the idea of escape appealed to them both. The weather had been rough and wild, the snow falling in great white sheets. They had travelled the length of the eastern coast stopping in Band B's or small hotels enjoying the hospitality of the patrons. Even though Hugh could not drink in the bars they would share a bottle of wine or a glass of beer in their room talking long into the night. They became each other's counsellor and by the time they returned home felt a good deal stronger than when they had left. They had become very close since then. He had Polly to thank for that, he supposed. Hugh had great natural resources and had gradually come to accept all that had past. There were still times when Ralph caught him unawares and recognised the brooding expression he adopted when his thoughts returned to the past. Hugh and Judith had a relationship now and Ralph was grateful for that for initially it seemed as though Hugh would never be able to speak to his mother again. He had spent many hours trying to comfort him and to help him evaluate her actions until finally he had agreed to see her. He knew how much Hugh was missing her though he would never admit it and although he could empathise with his reticence to renew their acquaintance he knew it was the only right way to proceed. They had to take a stand and finally move on. Ralph had found his own reward in providing overwhelming support for all three of his sons and they, in turn, had formed a wall around him, making every effort to buffer any hurt, which might come his way even though they themselves were smarting.

The light was beginning to fade. Looking round Ralph felt he was happy with his lot. His life had been forced in a different direction that had brought about change and bizarrely, greater success. He found a renewed vigour in his step and could confront the notion that he was ready to begin again with someone else. The sense of failure to sustain his marriage, which bugged him for several years after the divorce, had dissipated. The thought of falling in love made him smile but it was not impossibility. Many of his friends had remarried; several of them even starting second families but he shied from that idea. He was enjoying order and silences too much these days but he could not deny that with the rush of love comes madness. He was not too long in the tooth to remember how falling in love with someone could take total control of ones normal behaviour. It was possible to be "madly in love" even in ones sixties. He had his hair, his own teeth and a waistline that could still accommodate the same size of trousers he wore in his thirties. It would be wonderful to make love again with feeling. He did miss that. He would like to share his bed as well as his life if the right person came along. It was deliciously intoxicating to have one's future totally unmapped. The predictability of life had disappeared along with his past and now he was awakened to the possibilities ahead. He had come to accept that Judith's in fidelity had been the catalyst to change his life and he was glad. Few things worried him now. He could look after himself and was happy to spend time alone. He felt strong and in command of his own destiny. He walked to the source of music, ejected the Mozart CD, carried it to the balcony and threw it in a Frisbee like fashion into the Thames. For the next ten minutes he watched it float, as the lights caught in its reflection, further and further along the river until eventually he could see it no more.

Peter made his way upstairs to the girl's bedroom. It was time to settle them down and read a story. The hall was finished at last and they could reclaim the property. The builders had been around for what seemed like years but tomorrow they collected their gear and were off. Kate had born the brunt of it being home all day but they were a very likeable bunch and worked hard. It was the mess that had finally worn them down. The house was an unusual shape, on three floors and it had been difficult to avoid each other but in every other respect they were lucky to have so much space. It was a wonderful feeling to be home. He had just returned from a business trip to China and was feeling the effect of jet lag. He had not seen the children for ten days and, despite his fatigue, he was determined to spend as much time with them as possible. He could hear his daughters talking and slowed his pace. It excited him to think they were now old enough to converse with each other. Their childish minds were intriguing and he loved to hear them play and watch them mimic. When Tilly was just two she would hold the telephone to her ear and walk up and down making indecipherable sounds. She was very like Kate in many respects and Amy was like her father. Tilly had just begun Nursery school and Amy was asking her what she had done. It was the same Nursery that Amy had attended at that age and she was feeling rather superior now she herself attended the "Big School".

As Peter entered the room they both looked up to greet him.

"Daddy, daddy, sit here" demanded Amy patting her bed.

"No, by me, by me." Ordered Tilly.

"Why don't we all squeeze together?" He said as he lifted Tilly from her bed and brought her wriggling and laughing across to Amy's. Amy moved over giving him space. He climbed inside the duvet and covered them all tightly, kissing their cheeks and holding them close. Within seconds Tilly had manoeuvred herself into his arms and reached to hold the lobe of his ear, her thumb firmly wedged between her lips

"What have you girls been doing today/" he asked.

"Mrs Partington let me put away the art brushes," said Amy proudly.

"I did do a painting," said Tilly not wishing to be outdone.

Amy pushed the bedclothes aside and reached for a book.

Daddy, read this, mummy started it yesterday." She sat back holding a small paperback in her hand and thrust it towards him. It was "Finn Family Moomintroll".

"Oh" he said delightedly," The Moomins. I used to love these books when I was a small boy. They might be a bit old for Tilly though." He looked across at Amy.

"She always falls asleep." Amy retorted with authority.

Tilly, full of indignation removed her thumb to protest then snuggled back into her position, thought better of it and asked. "Where do Moomins live daddy?"

"In a place called Finland. Up above our country in the North. It's quite far away."

"Does Grandmastralia live there?" Tilly asked.

"Grandmastralia lives miles and miles and miles away doesn't she daddy? Said Amy, searching his eyes for approval.

"Yes, she does, right across the other side of the world." It saddened him to say this. He had always expected his mother to play a major role in the lives of his children but now every meeting took months of planning and then it was only possible to see her for a few weeks.

"I want to see her." Said Tilly sitting up. She placed her small hands on either side of his face and turned him to look at her.

"I wish you could darling but she's too far away." He looked down into her wide blue eyes and marvelled at their clarity. His mother was missing all of this. Even for the few days he had been away he was aware of having missed out. These business trips brought in the money to provide them with a very comfortable life but he hoped, as they grew older they would both be aware that his absences were not absences of affection.

"Tomorrow, I want to see her tomorrow." Her face adopted a look of passion that often preceded a tantrum.

"No, Tilly." said Amy in her `big sister` voice. "We can't go tomorrow, not even in the car." She reached across to pat her arm in a placatory manner.

Tilly's lower lip began to tremble. "I WANT to see Grandmastralia."

Peter saw it was time to change the subject and picked up Tilly's teddy bear "Teddy is waiting for the story. Look how sad he is. Teddy says we can phone Grandmastralia tomorrow. How about that?" Tilly snatched the bear from his hands and held him close in an exaggerated hug.

"Teddy wants a Grandmastalia story, don't you Teddy?" she said in a wheedling voice, her lips pouting as though about to play the flute.

Peter looked across at Amy who shrugged her shoulders pulling them to her ears before allowing them to drop with an accompanying resigned sigh. "Well, just a little one then it's Moomin. That's fair isn't it daddy?" Peter was always surprised by Amy's generosity. She did not allow Tilly to rule the roost but she could very cleverly turn her to accommodate her own wishes. He was not sure he would have been so wily at that age.

"That's fair," added Tilly causing Peter to smile.

"Well alright, just a little one." He said and settled them back into the pillows, his own head resting on the somewhat uncomfortable wooded backboard.

"Once upon a time, Grandmastalia lived in England with uncle Douglas, uncle Hugh, daddy and grandpa Farrington. One day they all decided to go to the seaside in their campervan." He began to tell a familiar story of a certain day in his youth that held affectionate memories. He and Douglas were around seven and ten, Hugh was very small and just about crawling he thought. His parents had left them in the van as they crossed the road to a shop to buy them all ice creams. Douglas had seen a fishing boat arriving back at the shore with a full catch. The seagulls were in full cry circling round and round and the whole thing looked very exciting. They were both desperate to see the catch and, not wishing to leave Hugh alone in the van had lifted him from his restrainer and carried him way down to the beach. He had been immensely heavy and they had shunted him to and fro, their arms juddering under the weight of him, their legs buckling into the pebbles. Eventually they reached their goal and placing Hugh beside their feet had innocently watched the fishermen unload. They were thrilled to be thrown by one of the men a small octopus that had been trapped in their net. They were fascinated by the small, still mobile tentacles of the creature and wishing to examine it closer walked across to a nearby beached fishing boat and laid the poor creature across it's planks. They must have remained there for quite a while, as they had never before seen such a fascinating creature at close quarters. Meanwhile his parents had returned to discover an empty van devoid of sons and spent a frantic time searching for their lost family. By the time they found them Hugh was holding in his hands a small and ugly looking fish that he was proceeding to eat, his mouth covered in tiny sparkling scales as evidence. The girls were amused by this part of the story and shrieked loudly in disgust before asking Peter to repeat the episode once more. They were always relieved to hear Grandmastralia had rescued Hugh from eating all of the fish. Peter was well aware he was using these stories to feed his own nostalgia but he lessened the guilt by occasionally including Edward and his mother's new life into some of his tales. He knew the girls should recognise Edward as part of their family but he still preferred the stories in which he could relive his own past and sense again that feeling of closeness.

As he began to read the next instalment of Moomin he could feel Tilly's body relaxing into sleep. It was enchanting to feel her soft warmth across his chest and Amy beneath his arm. He could not believe he would ever be capable of harming them. He loved Kate and could not envisage loving anybody else as he did her. He often wondered when he looked at his daughters how he would have reacted to his parent's separation had he been their age. It had been difficult to deal with as an adult and part of him would never get over the shock he felt when Douglas had told him. What was it about the chemistry of people that drove them to leave their families making years shared together null and void? A frisson of fear swept over him and he drew Amy closer to his side.

"Don't squash me daddy" she said and pushed herself away.

Peter continued to read aloud as his thoughts wandered through different pathways. He was intermittently drawn back to the text in a slightly bemused manner wondering if he had been reading aloud the contents of the book or voicing his own thoughts. Tilly was now sound asleep and Amy held her head in the manner accompanying full concentration so he gathered he must have been keeping to the text. They were such characters these Moomintrolls and he was enjoying the chance to renew their acquaintance. As a boy he had immersed himself in the series of books. His mother had read them the first two but he had become impatient to discover what would happen next and took over. He missed his mother. He missed the easy access he had when she and his father were together. This year he and Kate were planning to take the girls on a visit. They had not told her yet as Kate was still a little apprehensive about the girls being able to cope with the long flight. They had seen an offer that included several stop-overs and if he could take a sufficiently long holiday they would be able to alleviate the problem by spending a few nights in different countries enroute. They would not tell Tilly and Amy yet until everything was arranged, as they did not want to disappoint them. There would be lots to see and they would love his mother's house particularly the swimming pool. Kate suggested they ask Hugh and Sophie to go with them, at least for some of the time. Hugh was so good with the girls and could help keep them amused. They adored his company and Peter and Kate enjoyed his sense of fun and adventure. He supposed they should all be grateful to his mother for opening up another world for them all. He rather imagined they would not be considering such a trip had she still lived in London. Thousands of families were separated in this way he knew but found it difficult to reconcile this fact to his own family. He felt a slight twinge of guilt at the thought of leaving his father behind and knew it was ridiculous to feel so. Edward was a decent man and made his mother happy. He was due to retire soon and Peter fantasized about them leaving Australia and returning to England; but then he remonstrated with himself for not facing up to reality. They both loved living out there, the climate suited them and they had built up a wide circle of friends. He must accept that this was how things were and would remain so for the foreseeable future.

 The gentle rise and fall of Amy's chest told him she was asleep. Peter slowly eased his arm from her shoulder and brought it round to encircle Tilly. Gently and with caution he swung his legs over the side of the bed and raised himself. Her eyes fluttered open for a while staring into the distance as he laid her on the bed, her mouth sucking furiously at her thumb before coming still. Turning he pulled Amy down into her bed tucking the duvet beneath her chin and stood looking at them both. He was close to tears as he listened to their rhythmic breathing. They were really all that mattered now, Amy, Tilly and Kate. He had so much to be thankful for. They would go and enjoy every minute of his mothers company. Tomorrow the girls would speak to her on the telephone and in a few weeks time when everything was booked he would inform her of their intentions. Life was far too short and unpredictable to do otherwise. Meanwhile he would go downstairs and have that drink he had been promising himself since six o-clock this morning

Hugh made the bed taking care to pull tight the bottom sheet. Inevitably it would become wrinkled tonight. He was unable to lie still, his dreams keeping him active. He awoke every morning breaking their sequence, unable to hold on, the story line fading with the daylight. He had promised Sophie he would clean the flat before her return. She was away with her sister celebrating the end of examinations. Her results were good – an upper second. She worked hard and deserved it. He was thankful he no longer faced examinations of any sort. Too much of a chore. Luckily he could rise in the ranks of his company through effort and initiative. He patted the pillows and threw the duvet into place. He missed Sophie. Tomorrow she would be here in this bed. The thought cheered him. He passed through the main living room carrying an empty cup. The morning was somewhat overcast throwing a grey, white light over everything. Yesterday's papers lay spread across the sofa. He had merely glanced quickly through, skimming headlines, scanning the photographs. He noticed several crumbs upon the rug and hurrying to the kitchen, put down the cup upon the metal draining board and collected the vacuum cleaner from its cupboard. He quite enjoyed domesticity. When he was alone he still allowed a mess to build but sharing with Sophie had changed him. It was amusing to remember how carelessly untidy he was in his teens. It was reassuring not being able to see the floor and to roll around in bedclothes that should have been changed weeks ago. It would never have occurred to him to notice breadcrumbs on the carpet as he did now. There was a kind of therapy in pushing round the Hoover leaving indentations in the rugs and watching the dust pull away from the floor. Everything looked different and expectant once it was complete. He liked this flat. After university he stayed in some pretty awful places, sharing with three or four of his friends at a time. Nobody appeared to respect other people's belongings and arguments often ensued over a missing jar of jam or dirty dishes left in the sink. If Dad had not helped him with the deposit he would still be sharing. Ownership was accompanied by responsibility. This was his and he cared for it.

The flat faced, like that of his father, the river Thames. The walls were off white broken here and there with vibrant abstract paintings. He visited the art schools each summer for the Degree Shows bartering with the students for a final acceptable price - some of their prices being ridiculously over the top. He had also begun to collect glass. One summer in Aldeburgh he saw a beautiful, milky blue bowl, heavy and tactile. The owner of the shop was a glass enthusiast and within thirty minutes had transferred his passion. Since then Hugh was always on the look out for important pieces, hoping to find a real treasure lying unnoticed at some car boot sale. Once word was out about his collection he had to be wary of kindly aunts buying glass artefacts not to his taste. There was a small cupboard kept for such gifts that he retrieved for display when they came to visit. Hugh switched off the cleaner and glanced around. The long, low, sofa was covered in a rich deep, dark brown leather, uncluttered by cushions and an old comfortable long seated armchair, its covers loose and creamy, provided a perfect resting place to view the river. One or two pieces of furniture, the small table and bookshelf, were from Douglas, who allowed him monthly repayments, almost complete. The thought pleased him. Money would then be released and he might, just, be able to afford to change his car. It was time. The hallway expanded to provide a small working area for his computer, printer and fax and he made his way to shuffle some papers into a neat pile. He was tempted to read his e-mail before taking a shower but decided he would wait.

Entering the kitchen he threw the switch on the kettle to make coffee.

As he waited for the kettle to burst forth steam and throw the switch he laid the table for himself. The weather was clearing and he placed the kitchen stool at the far end of the table to give him a better view from the window. A helicopter flew over, surprisingly low though not quite low enough for him to see the pilot. He could hear the whining of a police car, a sound that had become so frequent he almost ceased to hear it In the mornings everything was on the move and he wondered how people found time to commit a crime so early on the day. The river buses carried commuters to the Embankment and would later be filled by tourists eager to learn the history of the buildings they were passing at such a leisurely pace. When his father first told him this flat was for sale he wondered whether he would want to live in the area. The river, of course, was hugely attractive but most of his friends were either in Clapham or Hampstead having deserted the south- eastern parts of London once they were able to leave home. He was worried they would not want to trek into the city to see him. His fears soon evaporated as their visits were frequent and several talked seriously of moving to the area if they could find something suitably priced. It was great, too, having his father just above. He could stand on his balcony and look up sometimes to see him sitting with a glass of wine in hand and usually a book. It was very comforting. In the past he did not like to see him alone even though his father reassured him many times of his growing fondness for this way of life but when he caught him unawares he was sure he could detect a kind of sadness in his soul. As time passed he was relieved to admit, things had dramatically improved. His father's social life was expanding and one day, Hugh supposed, he could meet another woman. The thought frightened him. It would be difficult to accept and selfishly he did not look forward to the day when his father might introduce him to somebody else. He could not picture his father linked to anyone but his mother. The aftermath of her departure had been terrifying and even though his father had told him he had persuaded his mother to go, he could not believe it. Why would his father make such a choice? He could understand if his mother did not loved his father but she did. He knew she did. They could have ridden the Edward intervention and he would have gone abroad and left them alone. He still hung on to the dream that one day they would re-unite. It was because of this belief that he had decided to visit his mother in Australia although he loathed the idea of being with Edward. He told his father he felt he was strong enough to go but he did not inform him of his plan which was to try to evoke so much nostalgia in his mother, she would be so overwhelmed, realise her mistake and return. She had abandoned him at a very crucial time in his life. The ache he carried around had weighed him down, his thoughts like stones falling to the pit of his stomach to lie in cold and uncomfortable heaps. It was time itself that had gradually relieved him of them one by one. When she left he could not study for his exams. How could he revise with conversations he had had with his parents reverberating round and round his head? It had all been so dreadful his father decided he should have extra time out of school and they had gone to America over the Christmas break.

 Hugh cleared his dishes, stacking them into an already full dishwasher and turned it on. Time to get dressed and showered. As he left the kitchen he was drawn to his computer by an urge to make contact with Sophie. There were several e-mails from friends and, yes, she had sent him a message. Since his mother and father's divorce he had been very unsure about forming any relationship with anyone. He had several girlfriends in the intervening years but every time they showed signs of wanting a "relationship" he backed away. He could not endure the pain of being abandoned again. Far better for him to finish with them before they decided to finish with him. At least he would be safe. With Sophie he wanted to allow himself to commit but was aware of gnawing angst every time she went away and held his feelings back. He had not been sufficiently powerful or lovable to keep his mother, it followed therefore he would not keep Sophie. He discussed this with his counsellor at university some time back hoping for guidance. She had helped a lot but he still could not avoid the sensation in his fingertips and the drop in his stomach whenever Sophie mentioned she was going away or, if she were late for one of their meetings, the dreadful fear he felt that she might not come back. Perhaps if they married it might disappear but then, like his father, he could be sitting on a time bomb waiting for the detonator to blow. And what of Douglas? Look what had happened to him! Hugh knew he had fallen totally in love with Polly only to be tossed aside, his usefulness over once she made her point. Again providing proof he had reason to be cautious and should take steps to protect himself. He must continue to build his emotional shield until it was strong enough to guard him from the emotional flack that had caught him on all sides as a young man of seventeen.

Taking his mind back he remembered it was on the return trip home from the wedding he first sensed something terrible had happened. They had piled into a car with his grandmother, Angie and Beth, all six of them bouncing around in the transporter, listening to Grandma going on about the wedding and how wonderful it had been. Angie and Beth, more sensitive to the atmosphere knew something was wrong but discreetly held back their inquisitive instincts. He was convinced, naturally, his parents had discovered Douglas and Polly were having an affair and had been stunned by the news. That was awful enough in his book but when in the early hours of the morning he was still tossing and turning in his bed, unable to expel the vision of Douglas and Polly kissing passionately, he had taken himself downstairs for a drink and found his parents sitting on the sofa, their faces grey with fatigue and distress. He had been gripped by an overpowering wave of fear of what was to come and was convinced some one had died, his mind racing to Kate and Peter and the possibility of a plane crash? Unable to bare the suspense and the powers of his imagination he insisted they reveal to him what was troubling them so. He had previously been planning the correct facial expression to use when they told him of Polly and Douglas but nothing could have prepared him for the moment when they informed him of his mother's infidelity with Edward and he had rushed to the downstairs lavatory and been violently sick. His mother had followed him out wanting to comfort him but he pushed her aside unable to bare the thought of any physical contact. His father had taken him back to bed, given him something to help him sleep and sat with him stroking his head as he had when he was a child.

The next morning, oh God, he did not want to relive that time again, but it was still so clearly imprinted on his memory, that morning, after the wedding he had woken and for a brief second forgotten the news, broken the night before. It was like waking in the aftermath of battle, moaning corpses everywhere, bodies shattered. Nobody capable of making contact, they were all so withdrawn inside themselves. It was agonizing pretending everything was Ok until their guests had gone and then the silence. The three of them sitting in separate rooms staring blankly into space. His mother has approached him finally and he had walked away from her unable to look at her or to be swayed by any persuasive talk. There was nothing to be said. She had betrayed his father and betrayed them all. Eventually they began to talk. The talk became incessant followed by shouting and tears. Their eyes constantly rimmed red by the salt .The atmosphere in the house was heavy with sadness and reproach. He had wanted to stay with friends but felt unable to desert his father. Peter and Kate had rung from Turkey to assure them all of their safe arrival their voices full of excitement and joy. His mother had spoken to them, her face completely dead but her voice produced the correct inflections of pleasure and delight to hide from them any suspicion that all was not well. His father too had managed to be jolly as the phone was passed to him but when they asked to speak to Hugh, he feigned a hangover and withdrew to his bedroom. That bedroom had become his retreat and he had wept many bitter tears for the loss of his family. He had refused to go back to school for a while unable to face the questioning from his friends but after two days life in the house was so unbearably oppressive he was glad to leave each morning to be with his friends. The school was informed and the staff treated him sympathetically even giving their approval for time out over Christmas. His friends had all been so wonderfully supportive and as time went by he joined the ranks of many and was forced to accept his parents were, like theirs, no longer a married couple but legally divorced.

Life had changed. He now had two lives. Pre-wedding and post-wedding. Pre could not help be overshadowed by post. It had taken ten years for the battle scars to heal but on cold days the wounds became red and inflamed refusing to be forgotten. He was able now to speak to his mother affectionately and visit her. He had come to realise he was unable to manage without her love and support. He could not bear to see her so unhappy before she left for Australia and his father worked so hard trying to prevent him from shutting the door on her. He tried to understand why it had happened. Why she had done what she did and whether his own behaviour had helped drive her away. Eventually he had to admit to himself he could not continue life as a hostile son and had arranged to go to Australia to see her.

Hugh clicked to the e-mail from Sophie. She would be on an earlier plane and return tonight. She had missed him so much and couldn't wait to see him. He felt extremely happy and turned up the volume on the radio surrounding himself with music. He would work extra hours today and free himself for Sophie tomorrow. After his shower he would pop upstairs and say hallo to his dad. Maybe they could go out together. They hadn't done so for a week or two. He smiled as he thought of Ralph. He was the best of dads and he loved him dearly. He would always pretend with Edward. It was easier that way. They spent time together and Edward tried hard to make his time in Australia enjoyable. Hugh behaved himself when in his company and even found his jokes amusing at times. He was always happy to see him leave the house for then he could be alone with his mother and talk of England, of Peter and Kate and Douglas. He knew she was hungry for news and he fed her tasty morsels enticing her with his words like sweets. He would bring his father into the conversation, always showing him in a good light relaying to her his success and new life. He wanted to sew the seeds of regret and to present his father as Edward's superior. While his father remained single the door was ajar. His mother for her part always needed confirmation that Hugh was fond of Edward and he would reassure her this was so but when he watched him, secretly, the dreadful thoughts sprang into his mind. Evil thoughts that wished Edward an early death, for then his mother would return. She would be theirs once more and he would be gone. He would never relinquish the dream that one day they would find themselves reunited as a family. This idea sustained him and he vowed that if it were in his power to do so he would make it possible.

Douglas replaced his mobile into his pocket. It scarcely stopped ringing these days. As he walked along the Pimlico Road he paused to glance in the windows of the numerous antique shops. He was interested in the joinery and craftsmanship involved and took note of the techniques. He and Patrick had had a good week. They had completed the last order on time and were now making preparations for their next assignment in New York. There was less "hands on" work now the business had expanded but they always made the bespoke pieces for special clients. Their reputation meant they could charge phenomenal prices which people seemed happy to pay. Two terrific girls staffed their office and the workshop employed a team of very talented people. He and Patrick still found it slightly unbelievable. They had never really envisaged being "bosses". They could thank Miranda for that outcome. She had been employed by a very prestigious company in Boston and possessed a great deal of expertise. On her return to England he was surprised to find her interest in their company growing at the same pace as their own. She had an MBA in business studies and could advise them on practically everything they needed. She was full of enthusiasm and introduced them to several influential colleagues who subsequently placed large orders that set them on the path to success. She was also the instigator in jolting him from his emotional apathy. Her interest in the company brought them together and they were married some time later.

A bus was idling its engine by the kerb; spewing diesel fumes into the air. Douglas increased his speed to avoid it. There was a large Indian family in some dispute, spreading themselves in an amazingly colourful crowd across the pavement. He squeezed past the mother, catching her sari on his jacket button and pulling it towards him. He apologized and as he released himself he could not help noticing her startled eyes. They were an extraordinary colour that drew his attention and held him captive for a few seconds. As he walked away he was reminded of another pair of eyes whose colour had mesmerized him in the past. His steps began to slow as he transferred his thoughts. Polly. He had not seen her for eight years. Sometimes he was aware of a woman on the train or stepping into a taxi, reminding him of her. Each time he caught his breath affected by the prospect of meeting her once more. He had been totally in love with her and she had left him scarred. Looking back he could not believe he and Patrick had returned to Spain to finish her shop fitting. For days he had been petrified by misery and could not move. Every morning he had woken with a deep pain in his chest reminding him of the unwitting role he had played as a scapegoat .He would turn to face the wall unable to face anyone or anything else. Patrick had visited him everyday and eventually convinced him they could win the day by making a terrific job of the assignment and that his only salvation lay in work. He could not let him down and he had finally hauled himself from his bed and carried on in a daze.

The day of the opening was a big event. The press were there together with several fashion journalists from England. Polly had called in to inspect their work before the opening and he, Douglas, had been unable to see her. He had hidden like a cowardly child afraid of his emotions and actions. Patrick had taken over and kept his dealings with her to a minimum. That day they had to present a united front to the press and he was forced to stand besides her breathing in her perfume, their arms brushing as the photographers called to them to stand closer. She had praised their work to the journalists and at one stage pulled him into an interview as they were asking for their details.

She had kept herself engaged after that avoiding his eyes. Patrick had remained loyally at his side introducing him to the clients and guests so that he was unaware of Polly's departure. The following day the newspapers, both in Spain and England, spoke highly of her but the greatest accolades were for Douglas and Patrick's shop design. After that they had never needed to look for work. The accounts came in and their business was featured in glossy magazines. Patrick was right to insist they pulled out all the stops. They were made.

After Polly had placed him in the intolerable position at the wedding, she moved from her house, changed her telephone numbers, refusing to see or speak to him. He was roused to such fury by her betrayal and his inability to find her was probably fortuitous, as he may well have wanted to strike her but then he remembered, somewhat shame faced, he had still wanted her and would have gone to her had she asked. Had cried himself to sleep for the want of her night after night. His dreams were troubled by her appearance. He would meet her in crowds, she seemingly ready to embrace him, but they would become separated by the crowd, unable to speak. He would wake in desperation having failed to obtain her address or whereabouts. A feeling of tremendous loss would remain with him throughout the day. He found himself thinking of ways to trace her, even employing someone to do it for him. He knew what she had done but he was driven by a desire to see her and ask the myriad of questions that plagued him at night. He would re run scenes, there were not that many, in an attempt to recall words she may have said that might have alerted him to her devious plan. The questions she asked concerning his mother always returned and now of course they made sense. He should have probed more into her enquiries and might have discovered her ploy before it was too late. It had taken him completely by surprise to learn of his mother's infidelity. Polly had obviously compiled a dossier on the past to use in evidence. He had unwittingly helped her re-enforce her fears. He still could not understand why his mother needed Edward when she had his father. Their marriage had always seemed so sound but as his mother assured him, although she loved Ralph she could not help loving Edward. Much later when he and his mother had discussed the situation he recognised many of the feelings she had for Edward were identical to those he held for Polly and felt incapable of passing judgement. He was experiencing such a roller coaster ride of emotions that eventually he and his mother agreed to try and accept what had happened and salvage what they could to forge a new relationship. He could see how unhappy she was to be away from them all during the early years. It was a nightmare for him but he was forced to admit Edward had been so supportive and was so obviously in love with her that for her it must have been worth the pain. Surprisingly too his father had developed a life style of his own which he greatly enjoyed. He had changed over the years and was far more self-sufficient. He seemed to have gained an inner strength and determination that had held them all together. Douglas both loved and admired him more now than he had in the past. Back then he had not really given a lot of thought to his parents. They were there for him and he loved them but once he'd left home and started his career they did not figure in his day-to-day activities. Now he often thought of them, particularly his father who had been there for them even though he must have been suffering his own kind of hell. He had refused to put himself first and Douglas would always remember that. Sometimes he wondered if their relationship would have been anywhere near as strong as it was if his parents had remained together. When he thought about his mother he was conscious of the miles between them. He still felt abandoned It could never be the same. When he saw his mother she was Edward's wife and it was difficult. He could no longer drop by to see her and talk. She had chosen Edward and had not fought to save her marriage, as he believed she would. He hated to think Edward had won. He formed a kind of barrier between himself and his mother. It had crumbled slightly as the years passed but he knew that the sense of family and unity they once shared had been lost. The only barrier left between his father and himself was Polly. Douglas could not talk openly about his relationship with her and still could not listen to his father's vitriolic remarks whenever her name came up. He would never be able to reveal everything, not even to Peter for there was one encounter he had with Polly that he guarded secretly and had never shared with anyone. It had happened two years after she disappeared, just as he was beginning to make some kind of recovery. She telephoned him. He was about to leave the house to meet friends when the phone rang. He almost lost his balance at the sound of her voice and found himself trembling and unable to speak as soon as he recognised her

"Douglas, are you there?" she had asked in that so familiar voice.

"Yes" This was all he could muster in response. His mind was racing with possible reasons for her making contact and he braced himself for the unexpected.

"How are you, Douglas?" She made this statement in a very quiet voice pausing to breathe. He was aware of her breath and his heart rate increased to an alarmingly rapid rate as he summoned up a picture of her.

"I'm over here from Cape Town for a few days and wondered if we might meet" She paused demanding he fill the space of silence.

The timbre of her voice had for a brief second, placed him back in the past. He could almost smell her perfume and feel the warmth of her body. He turned his head away from the receiver and steadied his breathing. There was a dangerous lurch in his chest and he forced himself to remember her cruelty and deceit.

"I'm not sure that would be productive" he heard his own pompous reply wondering how it had surfaced from the thoughts and images she provoked.

"Douglas. I know you must hate me terribly but now time has past and we can distance ourselves from what happened between us, I really would like to see you and explain my actions. Please Douglas allow me that." She paused for a moment. "There are things I feel you should know."

Naturally his curiosity was roused and the idea of letting this opportunity pass could not be ignored. They arranged to meet the following day and for the rest of the time he chased reason around in his head, conducted imaginary conversations with her and practiced the tone voice best suited for his greeting

With a heavy feeling of deja vu on his part, Douglas found himself entering her hotel room and his first glimpse of her showed she had not changed. There was still that polished look that expensive clothes could bring. Her hands were deeply tanned and although she wore finger jewellery she did not wear a wedding ring. Her eyes moved across his face until they settled onto his own and he steeled himself against their hypnotic power. They were even more compelling that day and he felt himself fighting to look away. She was thinner but her clothes hung perfectly about her body in the way he always remembered. There was one small discernable difference. Unlike the confident Polly of the past she seemed slightly reticent as though she had not yet gauged the situation and how to play it. Even so Douglas could not dispel the feeling he once felt for her and inwardly remained in awe. His outward expression, he hoped, denied this as he tried to keep his face still and in control. He could not quite believe he was with her and that this meeting was not one of his dreams or a figment of his imagination. His rehearsal forgotten, he allowed her to kiss both cheeks, lead him to a chair, and sit him down.

Polly began to speak and at first he could only listen to the sound of her voice but gradually as he pulled himself back and began to concentrate he realised she was apologizing for all she had done to him. She was re-living their meetings trying to cover her tracks to soften her behaviour with reasoned explanations. She made a positive point of not making apologies for the break up of his parents' marriage, she would not, she said, ever forgive them for their lengthy deception. She explained how destructive it had been over the years to watch Edward move further and further away from her, of her distress as the realisation became more and more positive that she and Edward would never have children, her sense of outrage when she had discovered that his mother and Edward had been seeing each other for many years. Could Douglas appreciate how the discovery had rendered years of her life worthless? When her friend had seen them and informed her of his adultery she did not challenge Edward there and then. With hindsight she should have and not allowed her bitterness take hold. At first she had no idea Judith was the other woman. She had merely received a report that he had spent the night with someone. But when she had him watched and the agency produced photographic evidence she was astounded to discover it was Judith, her friend. The word friend was pronounced with great bitterness and Douglas flinched to hear his mother spoken of in such a vitriolic manner. The hatred she felt for her who, as far as Polly was concerned, had it all and yet wanted more blinded her with rage and ignited her desire to seek revenge in the most painful way she knew how.

Douglas sat through this confessional in silence watching her facial expressions intently. She put forward a strong case for sympathy but what of him? Why had she set out to ensnare him as bait for the final kill? All these questions danced inside his head vying for first place. He had to know what she really felt. He could not bear to ask and have his worst fears confirmed. As he tried to gather his thoughts she began to move toward him until she was close enough to take his hand. The frailty of her fingers moved him and not wishing to lose his resolve he turned away pulling his hand from hers.

"Douglas. Please look at me"

He drew his eyes back and found himself swimming in amber pools now damp with tears. She still had the power to engulf him. He braced himself remembering that day when she had humiliated him before his family and resolved not to weaken. He allowed his eyes to rest in hers and listened to what she had to say.

Polly would not be shaken off and clasped his hand once more. She was there on a mission and it was important to say everything she had planned. "I know you will find this very hard to believe Douglas, but when I left you that day looking so wounded, I wanted to rush back to you, take you in my arms and blot out all that had happened. In the days and weeks that followed I thought of you constantly. I wanted to telephone to tell you of my feelings because I had done what I purposefully set out not to do, Douglas. I had fallen in love with you."

Douglas could scarcely believe what she had said. Instead of joy he felt a rush of anger and cried out "Oh Polly, why couldn't you have shown me in some way? Why did you walk away? If you had known half the agony I went through, unable to speak or see you. We could have talked; we could have worked something out. How do you think I felt having to stand by your side at the opening believing you felt nothing for me and that you'd used me as a pawn in your plan to revenge my mother? I tried so hard to hate you. At times I wanted to destroy all the work in Spain and leave you with nothing but a wreck of shattered pieces. I've lived these past two years shrouded in sadness, my confidence ruined, unable to face another woman and now you're telling me you loved me! Why? Is it that you want to torment me again and use me like some comfort blanket to wrap around your guilty conscience? Would you discard me once your guilt shrivelled away and I'd served your purpose?"

He pulled his hand away from hers and stood towering above her. If she had only taken him into her confidence before the wedding and told him they might have avoided so many of the terrible consequences that followed. She could have confronted Edward and left him. His own father could have been spared for surely, Edward would have left England for Australia alone. Peter and Kate could remain blissfully unaware and poor Hugh left oblivious to the fact. His mother would have got over Edward in time he was sure.

For a moment there was silence and then Polly began to sob, her mouth twisting in contortions as she spoke.

"No, no. I couldn't bear to hurt you again. It was your mother and Edward I wanted to destroy. I foolishly didn't think I would destroy you. You were young and I thought you would get over it. I was driven to carry out my plan and when I saw Kate and Peter making their wedding vows their happiness strengthened my resolve. I was so bitter I could feel nothing but hatred for everybody that day. I hated you all for being so happy, for having each other. Hatred is a terrifying emotion. It takes control and obliterates all other feelings. Nothing could have stopped me doing what I did." Tears had fallen to form a salty line across her cheeks. She wiped her hand beneath her eyes and sniffed. Douglas opened his mouth as though to speak but she held him in check and continued. "When it was all over and we left you there with the wedding party I felt utterly exhausted and empty. The relief I thought I'd feel didn't come and I was left with an enormous sense of misery that outclassed any thing I'd previously felt. It was a dreadful mix of grief and humiliation. I wanted to get away. I needed to be alone and to think." She stopped once more to catch her tears and placed her hands on his sleeve. "You were so young Douglas, I so much older. Did you really believe we could have had a proper relationship? Perhaps it would have been possible. I asked myself that question many times. Oh Douglas I did love you. I didn't know what I was doing. Please believe me?" She looked pleadingly into his eyes.

"What do you want from me?" he demanded. He felt calm and in control. He would not be duped again.

"To make peace with you. To tell you of my feelings. To take away with me your forgiveness." She stood head raised to meet his gaze, her hands together as though before a priest at the altar. "Can you forgive me, Douglas?"

"No. I can't." The answer came from the voice within. There was something in her words that steeled his heart. He could not dispel the notion that she was once more using him for her own means. She had cracked the whip before but now he would. Her face crumpled at his reply and she made no further attempt to persuade him to alter his decision.

Douglas moved her to one side and walked toward the door. He was determined to leave as the victor and was surprised by his own actions. Why couldn't he go to her, take her in his arms and console her? He felt cruel and, ashamedly, a tinge of pleasure as he realised he now could hurt her. As he took hold of the door handle he looked at her for the last time. "I am sorry, Polly" he said slowly "but that's how it is."

After that he had got on with his life. He had happily married and in general life was good. Douglas stood for a while at the door of his office. For the last twenty or so minutes he had been totally lost in thought. Polly had enveloped him as she did from time to time. He did not regret his actions at that last meeting but often, in his private moments he wondered how things might have been had he acted differently and they had had the chance to let their relationship develop. Or he would allow himself to imagine her in her navy shorts and white blouse and relive that day in Spain when his love for her was at its peak. Next year they were to fit out some large premises in Cape Town. Perhaps he would look her up.

ABOUT THE AUTHOR

Janet Fisher was born in London where she has lived for most of her life. She has written plays for BBC television and also writes poetry for which she has received an award. For many years she was the Head of a London Preparatory school. She has travelled widely and is married to the artist John Fisher and has three sons.

Printed in the United Kingdom
by Lightning Source UK Ltd.
126333UK00001B/314/A